Eve

ALSO BY WM. PAUL YOUNG

Cross Roads
The Shack

Eve

WM. PAUL YOUNG

**SIMON &
SCHUSTER**

London · New York · Sydney · Toronto · New Delhi

A CBS COMPANY

First published in the US by Howard Books, an imprint of Simon & Schuster, Inc., 2015
First published in Great Britain by Simon & Schuster UK Ltd, 2015
A CBS COMPANY

1 3 5 7 9 10 8 6 4 2

Simon & Schuster UK Ltd
1st Floor
222 Gray's Inn Road
London WC1X 8HB

www.simonandschuster.co.uk

Simon & Schuster Australia, Sydney
Simon & Schuster India, New Delhi

A CIP catalogue record for this book
is available from the British Library

Trade Paperback ISBN: 978-1-47115-121-7
HB ISBN: 978-1-47115-120-0
B Format ISBN: 978-1-84983-686-9
eBook ISBN: 978-1-84983-687-6

Printed and bound by CPI Group (UK) Ltd, Croydon, CR0 4YY

MIX
Paper from
responsible sources
FSC® C020471

Simon & Schuster UK Ltd are committed to sourcing paper
that is made from wood grown in sustainable forests and supports the Forest
Stewardship Council, the leading international forest certification organisation.
Our books displaying the FSC logo are printed on FSC certified paper.

THIS STORY IS DEDICATED TO MY SISTER,
DEBBIE.
I AM ETERNALLY GRATEFUL THAT I GET TO BE YOUR BROTHER.

Contents

Eve

One

FOUND

Caught in the tidal flows of unspoken morning prayers and simple wonder, John the Collector rested against a tree with his toes burrowed and curled into the coolness beneath the warming sand. Before him, a rippling ocean stretched out until it disappeared, merging into the clear cobalt sky.

The salty fragrance of the sea was overtaken by scents of eucalyptus, myrrh, and hagenia flowers. John smiled. These were always her first embrace! Resisting the urge to jump to his feet, he instead shifted to make room, lowered his head, and took a deep breath. It had been a while.

The tall, fine-boned, ebony-black woman accepted his silent invitation and settled next to him, her hand tousling the gray-black hair at the back of his neck with the tenderness of a mother toward her child. The playful touch sent a prickling peace through his shoulders and down his back, lifting the burden he unconsciously carried.

He could have stayed like this for some time, but there was always purpose to her visits. Even so, he held off his own rising curiosity, preferring the gentle contentment of her company.

Reluctantly, he spoke. "Mother Eve?"

"John?" Without looking, he knew she was grinning. Ancient and powerful, this woman radiated the contagious joy of a child. With one arm she pulled him to her, kissing the top of his head.

"You have been in this place . . . ," she began.

"A hundred years today," he finished. "If that is the reason for your visit, I am grateful."

"It is in part," Eve said. "One hundred years anywhere is cause for celebration."

Pulling himself up, he brushed off the sand before helping Eve to her feet. She gracefully accepted his hand, though it wasn't needed. Coarse white hair formed a woven crown around her face, lined and creased by countless years, a masterpiece of sculpted joy and sorrow. She glowed more like a child than a matriarch, her mahogany eyes lit by expectancy.

His questions threatened to tumble out in all directions, but she stopped them with a raised hand.

"John, one good question is worth a thousand answers," she teased. "Choose it carefully."

It only took a moment to form. "How long?" he asked somberly. "How long must we wait before the end, when our healing will finally be complete?" Reaching out, he took her hand and placed it on his heart.

"Much sooner, John, than when I first asked that same question."

He took in a deep breath and nodded, looking into the amber light that flecked her eyes.

"But I am here about today, John. Today, my child will be born into your world."

John frowned. "Your child? But Mother Eve, are we not each your daughter or your son?"

"Yes, you are," she declared. "But we have long known there would be three in particular who would stand and represent us all. The one to whom was given the promise of the seed, the one whose seed would crush the serpent's head, and the one to whom the seed would be forever united. The Mother, the Daughter, the Bride. The arrival of this girl marks the beginning of the end."

So stunned, he hardly noticed Eve pick up a stone and walk toward the water's edge. John followed, disoriented and overwhelmed. She launched the stone high into the air, and they both watched it zip down into the glassy sea with hardly a splash.

"John," Eve said, "in the ocean of the universe, a single stone and ripple changes it forever."

John let the small incoming waves tickle his feet and tug at the sand beneath them. To be near Eve was always healing and always disconcerting.

A shrill voice sliced the air. "You're dawdling, John."

He turned. A breeze off the water lifted the hair at the back of his head, even as Eve's perfumes caressed his face.

Letty had arrived, and Eve was gone. John sighed.

"The Scavengers have been calling for you for longer than an hour, and since you are the only Collector within a hundred miles . . ."

Turning back to the water, John selected another smooth stone and threw it high into the air so it would drift on its edge and slice into the water's surface with a satisfying sound. Why such a tiny success always pleased him was a mystery.

"What's their hurry?" he muttered, as Letty arrived at his side. He picked up another stone.

She was a bundle of a little old woman, barely three feet tall, with a cane and shawl and mismatched socks folded over mismatched shoes. She looked like an apple that had been left in the hot sun for too long, still round but shriveled up, with piercing black eyes, a crooked nose, and an almost toothless scowl. Her walking stick could have easily passed for a wand of sorts, and it was pointing right at him.

When he saw the intensity on her face, he let the rock fall to the sand.

"Letty?"

Her words were measured. "A large metal container was spotted floating early this morning, hauled ashore, and opened. The Scholars have already ascertained that it drifted here from Earth in real time."

"That's happened before," suggested John.

"We opened it up and found the remains of twelve human beings, all young females except one."

"Jesus," he mumbled, as much a prayer as an exclamation.

"The container seems to have been used to transport people great distances, probably on a large vessel or ship. Since no flotsam drifted with it, we surmise it was purposefully jettisoned, but not before the girls inside were executed. If there is any mercy in such a tragedy . . ." Her voice hesitated as emotion found its way.

John turned and slumped onto the sand, drawing his knees up to his chin. The warmth of the day and gentle breeze now seemed a mockery. Eve's joy had left with her.

He felt Letty's tiny hand rest on his shoulder as he fought his rising rage and grief.

"John, we cannot allow the shadow-sickness to find a place inside our hearts. In this broken cosmos we grieve. We rightly feel fury, but we must not let go of joy's embrace, which is beyond our understanding. To feel all of this means that we are alive."

He nodded. "You said the humans were female, except one?"

"Yes, there was also a middle-aged man. The shared initial view is that he may have been trying to protect the girls. There is a story, I'm sure, but we might have to wait a long time to hear it fully."

"I don't want to see—"

"Don't worry. The bodies have been transported to the Sanctuary of Sorrows and are being prepared for tomorrow's celebration of fire. Right now, you must do what only you can do . . . so the Scavengers can dismantle and the Artists can find ways to memorialize these precious children."

John closed his eyes and turned his face to the sky, wishing his conversation with Eve had not been so unbearably interrupted.

"Go on," Letty encouraged. "The others are waiting."

THE SIZE OF THE container surprised John. At least thirty feet in length, its sheer weight had required a dozen of the Haulers' beasts to drag it out of the water over rolling logs. Deep ruts were clearly visible behind the box on the cove's sandy shore. Tents held tables piled high with its contents: clothing, blankets, and a few stuffed toys. It was colder here, as if the sun itself had turned its warming face away.

From a pocket he took out a small case, opened it, and slipped a ring on his finger. He then turned the edge so that the impress changed. Anything he touched with this ring would bear a date mark and later be taken to his home, the Refuge, where it would be stored for analysis and reference. From his other pocket he took a pair of thin gloves and pulled them on.

The first item that drew his attention was a three-drawer, black, locked file cabinet, which he marked. It was cold to the touch. He waved over a Crafter, a woman with skills for locks and keys, and it took her only a few seconds to open it, leaving John to the contents. It was what he had expected: files of records and information, shipments, and bills of lading, accounting, and various other reports.

The bottom drawer held folders documenting the girls' scant personal information, including a facial photograph of each. Height, weight, age, health. The names were obviously aliases, each an earthly country beginning with sequential letters of the alphabet: Algeria, Bolivia, Canada, and down to Lebanon. He paused for a moment to stare at the images. The faces and eyes in the photos were windows into twelve stories that deserved a proper grieving.

John was about to shut the drawer and move on when a thought crossed his mind. He counted the folders. Twelve, just as Letty had said. But that was wrong. Her number had included the man. He counted again. Twelve photos, all girls, all young. It meant a girl was missing. Perhaps she had escaped or the records were inaccurate, but the discrepancy nagged at the edges of his thinking and wouldn't let him go.

Had Eve been referring to one of these?

On a hunch he walked a few feet over to the container itself. A row of boots for the workers was lined up near the doors, protective footwear that would later be thoroughly cleaned and decontaminated. He picked a pair his size.

An Engineer greeted him, "Hey, John. Terrible tragedy, all this."

He nodded as he laced up his boots. "I want to go inside for just a moment and check something against these records. Anything I should know?"

"No, there are still odds and ends to go through, but we've already removed what's most important."

John nodded sadly, acknowledging the man's kindness.

"Also, we just turned off the refrigeration unit. It's still freezing in there. Probably got damaged and stuck in the cold cycle, which was a blessing I suppose. The bodies were almost frozen. Be careful, it's pretty slick."

The doors opened easily, groaning on their hinges, letting the sunlight spill inward. Internal lighting flickered on, indicating some sort of closed battery system separate from the refrigeration. He realized as he stepped in that he had been holding his breath. When he let it go through gritted teeth, his exhaling vapor drifted up and around him.

The hold was about a third full of larger items—boxes, mats, plastic containers—along with litter and bits and pieces of trash, a hodgepodge he would have to go through at some point. Frozen bloodstains were scattered around the metallic tomb, the walls, the floor. Carefully, he stepped around these, every sound he made reverberating in the stillness.

At the far end he could see the refrigeration fan now silent and unmoving, a thin layer of ice already forming on the blades. A quick survey almost satisfied him that there was no place left that could hide a missing girl.

But an anomaly caught his eye. At the end of the wall near the cooling unit was a welded metallic frame jutting out about a foot and a half. He cautiously made his way back and examined it closely. Under the bottom were hinges, and when he ran his fingers along the top, he found two large clamps. John knew that if he undid them, the entire thing would open down and out. A sleeping area, like a bunk or tabletop perhaps? Maybe for a guard?

He hesitated. Then he blew on his hands and unsnapped the clasps, which released with a hollow *clack*. As he lowered the metal wall, the frosted steel bit into his palms and fingers through the thin gloves. It was heavy and he had to use a shoulder to let it down until chains at either end unraveled their lengths. It stopped a couple feet from the floor, level and sturdy. That is where he found her.

The teenaged girl was broken inside this space. Someone had forced it shut and she had not fit. She could have been peacefully asleep, her limbs at odd angles, her head folded down on her chest, were it not for the cuts and gashes that began to ooze with the release of pressure. One foot was almost severed. As she lay there frozen, he stood staring, stuck in time.

John turned and walked out, too sickened to avoid the blood this time. He needed to fetch those trained to deal with such things.

"I found another girl!" he yelled, setting off a flurry of activity that rushed past him and into the container. Outside, he unlaced the boots and took them off, walked back to the tent where he had marked the cabinet, sat down, and leaned against it.

"God, how is it that You still love us?" he whispered. He paused and glanced in the direction of the container. "Please, grant to her Your peace," he prayed.

Another explosion of activity and shouting brought him to his feet. A Hauler friend burst into the tent and hugged him.

"John! That girl you found! She is still alive! Barely, but alive!" The man beamed and hugged him a second time. "You're a Finder now, John!" the Hauler yelled as he left. "Who would have imagined?"

John dropped his head into his hands, feeling numb. If this was Eve's child, it was a sorrowful and wrenching birth, in blood and water. What good could come of such evil?

Two

BEGINNINGS

Everything exploded inside her. Everything hurt!

Why? Memory failed her.

Images jumbled and tumbled. Flashes of light pierced, penetrated. Harsh sounds—discordant, brash, horrifying!—stirred her panic. Her breathing came quick and loud, roaring in her ears.

Another flash burst into agonizing light, blurred movement, music . . . strings? Black woman morphing into brown-skinned man into red bow tie. Disconnected nonsense. She had to wake up. Tried. Couldn't.

Her head howled like a hurricane at sea . . . sneaker waves drove her down, held her under. A gasp . . . a rush of water . . . she couldn't breathe . . .

When darkness closed in, she welcomed it like a friend.

She woke to another face leaning over hers. A blurry image. A voice? Where was she? *Who* was she? Her eyes clamped down but couldn't block the images. Her lungs ached. The air was heavy.

Liquid. This time the shadows had an edge. They moved inward, swallowing her like a black sack. A shrinking glimmer of white light faded to a dot, then disappeared.

She screamed. *What is happening to me?* No sound came.

Memories or dreams or hallucinations, mixed and mumbling, twisted themselves into carnival-house terrors behind her eyes. She shrank back, tried to hide, to disappear. But where could she go? Her shouts morphed into sobs.

On her forehead—a warm cloth. A comfort. And a pungent scent she couldn't place. It reached inside, spreading down her throat, into her belly, her limbs, her extremities. Relief was irresistible. Sounds were muffled. Stillness settled.

She slept again.

WHEN NEXT SHE WOKE it was to a conversation in the hazy hush of night.

"John." The female voice was sharp and high-pitched. "This young woman is an anomaly. The Healers are trying to deduce her origins, but her genetic code is giving them fits. None of us has ever seen anything like it! It's preposterous!"

A man responded, his voice calm and kind. "It seems that God's playground is the impossible and preposterous."

The girl ordered her eyelids to open. They refused. A weight held them down, exhausting her. *Why can't I move?*

"They'll need additional time to unravel this mystery," the woman said.

"It seems we'll have plenty of time. Her recovery will not be swift." John sighed. "I understand little, Letty, but one thing I know: this girl has become *my* anomaly."

Letty laughed. "Listen to you, all protective and tenderhearted."

She made another effort. *Wake up! Wake up!* Pain claimed the space around her. Her body seemed to tilt. She tensed against the sensation of falling.

"Sometimes I surprise myself." John chuckled. "Why me, do you think? Why has Eve invited my participation?"

"Perhaps because you were a Witness?"

"And what has that got to do with this girl?"

The woman Letty replied by humming a happy melody. The feeling of imbalance abruptly stopped. Her body seemed to right itself. The voices faded out. She floated in a pool of peace.

Daughter. A new voice reached her ears from a distance. *Daughter.*

The fragrance of spice and flowers filled the air. A featherlight touch brushed the back of her hand. Warm. Soft. Stabilizing.

My child.

What child? This time when the girl willed her eyes to open, they did.

A black-skinned woman stood next to her bed. She was young and old, regal and common, tender and strong. Leaning down, she gently kissed the girl's forehead and smiled.

The girl summoned a whisper. *Who are you?* It seemed that only hushed sounds were appropriate, but then she wondered, had she only thought her question?

I am your mother. You are the witness. Come and see! the lady whispered without moving her lips. The woman's long fingers closed around her wrists and lifted her as if she weighed nothing and was not restrained.

My mother? The word *mother* stirred bitter emotions. Confusion set in. She didn't want to go anywhere.

Come, my daughter. Come witness the Creation—the perfection that will heal your broken body and shattered soul!

The girl tugged against the gentle grip, tried to pry away the fingers, but they would not yield. A kiss of air against her cheeks gave her the sensation of shooting upward—and she was now clinging to that hand. The sight of what lay below stole away her breath: the body she had just vacated. Her wrecked, mangled, bandaged body. It was restrained beneath a mass of straps, tubes, and a network of wires, machinery purring in the shadows.

She froze, and for an instant all was still. She held her breath, feeling sick.

How many times can I die? she thought.

No—not death, the mother said. *Life. Come watch. I promise, you won't be disappointed.*

And then the hand released her. Abandoned her.

She shut her eyes tight to lock out the rising panic. Instead of falling, she floated, weightless. A foreign warmth rushed over her, an oily thickness that simultaneously overwhelmed and embraced. But then it slipped into her mouth. The realization she was ingesting this slick sludge swept her to the brink of terror. Again, fluid filled her lungs as she gasped.

But when she didn't suffocate, she relaxed by degrees.

Breathable liquid? Impossible! Insane!

Eyes wide open, seeing nothing, she allowed herself to drift.

She resisted the urge to find an anchor, a mooring to time or place, a tether to memory. She almost felt free.

An underlying peace emerged, a sense that she would not be left alone. Someone knew she was here, if only the ebony-skinned woman who had said she was her mother. Come see, she had said. Watch. But this universe was void, vacant, and formless.

Now she resented the invitation. The bait and switch, the abandonment, was uncomfortably familiar.

She floated for perhaps a nanosecond, or maybe a million years. There was no way to perceive the difference. There was nothing to watch, nothing to see.

Then a detonation. Her whole body flinched. Her neck craned toward the burst of light. It was instant and continuous, overwhelming energy and information spreading outward, rushing toward her, overtaking. It was color. It was song. It was joy and fire, and blood and water. It was voice—singular and many, rising and thrusting, uniting with the void.

Chaos and matter collided, setting off sparks of playfulness and power, creating energy, space, and time. On the periphery, graceful spirit beings applauded the display, their elation bursting from their palms like dazzling water droplets, glimmering beads of perspiration, shimmering jewels. The effect was an overwhelming cacophony as harmony wrapped itself around a central melody.

She felt larger than a galaxy and smaller than a particle. All around her, joyous rapture tore the substance of things apart, then put it back together. A tidal surge of voices rose, engulfing her in an assembly of scents. Sweet incense became a ballad of yearning, a choreographed dance of being and belonging. Around and through it all rippled not One, not Two, but Three Voices—and yet only One. A magnificent laugh of raucous affection.

The Great Dance, a voice affirmed.

The mother's? she wondered.

This is the grand Beginning.

The girl spun in the liquid, searching for the voice. Straining to find the woman, she hesitantly called, "Mother?"

"AH, FINALLY AWAKE. I see, at least for longer than a few seconds. Welcome to the land of the living and the Refuge."

This voice was familiar. *John's*, she supposed. It was firm and altogether ordinary, but compared to what she had just witnessed, this "normal" was a little disappointing.

Great! she thought. *I died again and this is hell and there is a man in it.*

She tried to move her head toward him. She heard him yell, "Don't!"

Too late. Intense pain gripped her neck like a vise. Fog started from the edges of her vision and congregated in the center until she gave in. The last thing she heard as darkening grays descended was that ordinary voice, now exasperated, saying, "And there she goes again . . ."

A BRUSH OF SOMETHING gentle swept across her face. A whisper.

What you saw was the crafting of creation's womb. What you heard was the very first conception. Now we await the coming of the child.

In a twinkling her eyes reopened, and she saw the cosmos still unfolding, alive with joyful abandon, ceaseless commotion.

You mean . . . this is the beginning of the world?

The very first story. This voice was disembodied, around her and within her, everywhere and nowhere.

The girl watched, conflicted. *The big bang?*

A deep belly laugh was the only reply. The sound became a golden rope that joined visible harmonies and melodies, which formed threads of a tapestry woven with precious stones and fire, entwined with faith and hope and love.

The womb of creation was growing and expanding, flexing. It was potent and wild and unfettered, yet orderly and precise.

The girl was enthralled and uncomfortable. Expectant and cynical. Attracted and repelled. She knew this story, and she didn't.

Did she?

It was beautiful and terrifying. In all the magnificent display a tiny blue sphere emerged, spinning fragilely and exposed.

Here is the place where the pregnancy will soon be fulfilled in water, blood, and dust! Here, the child will soon be born. And you will witness it, my daughter. You are the Witness to the Ages of Beginnings.

The words fell hard on her ears. Grating, religious words. They opened a wound in her.

No.

It is for you, my daughter. A gift for you and for every man and woman born under this nascent light.

"No," she spoke aloud. The word went out into the beauty like a poisoned dart. "I'm no witness. And I don't want to be."

The universe blinked out.

• • •

A DIFFERENT MELODY, A simple humming and clicking in the background, snapped her back to her bed. The contrast between these puny noises and the staggering harmonies of Creation's music was beyond disappointing. It was as if an awe-inspiring, roaring waterfall quickly tapered off, becoming an annoying drip into a stagnant pool.

She also felt relieved.

Someone was droning a tune she didn't recognize, a lilting wordless chant. The girl aspirated a weak cough, and the melody abruptly stopped. Sounds of steps approached.

"Going to try again, are we?" It was the same male voice as before. John. This time she could see his face, its details blurred and indistinct, as if she were looking through water from a great depth. A brown-skinned male with a short beard and bushy eyebrows, threads of gray patterned throughout receding hairline. His movements brought on nausea, so she closed her eyes.

Elsewhere in the room, the humming resumed.

He gently wiped the tears that collected beneath a wrapping or bandage that covered most of her face. She flinched at his touch and tried to object. She couldn't move her jaw. It was restrained by some sort of cage that left a distinct metallic taste in her mouth. She struggled to swallow. Again she rode the edge of claustrophobic panic.

"All right then, easy does it." The man's tone, meant to be soothing and reassuring, only stirred her nausea. "I imagine you're extremely confused right now. You must have a million questions.

If you don't, I do. And don't try to talk," he quickly added. "None of that will work yet, but they tell me it will soon.

"If you're able to understand what I am saying," John continued, "please open your eyes and blink once for yes and twice for no."

She blinked once.

"Ah, just to be sure, that was single blink, for yes, yes? Not some random response and unfortunate timing on my part? Again, one blink for yes, and two for no."

A tinge of anger tempted her to pretend to be unconscious. She resented her captivity and his commands. Still, she obeyed.

Blink.

"Excellent." He sounded genuinely pleased. "Good. Wouldn't want to keep babbling just to hear the sound of my own voice. Hmm?"

Momentarily perplexed, she decided to blink twice. Was he asking a question?

"So sorry!" he apologized. "This is our first attempt at an actual conversation, and I must do better. What if I ask 'yes' or 'no' at the end of any real question? Would that help? Yes or no?"

She blinked.

"Good! Then let me start with some basic introductions. My name is John and you are being cared for in my home, which most refer to as the Refuge. And also in the room at this moment is the feisty and diminutive Letty . . ."

"He means short, dearie," came the shrill female voice from somewhere lower than the level of the bed. The unexpected presence of a woman in the room was comforting.

"I'm short and older than him, and he is envious of both," she chortled. "And dearie, in case you are concerned, you are completely gowned and covered, and others of us women have been watching over you. Though you have nothing to fear from John."

Through her distorted vision she saw the man smile toward the voice. "Letty, I could get a stool for you to stand on so she could see you."

"There is no need for that just yet, John. I dropped by to check on your charge and let you know that three strangers have arrived in our community, Scholars from the look of them, and from a very great distance. They want to speak to you and her. That's all." The humming resumed, confirming Letty was its source.

The man returned his attention to the girl. "Do you know your name, yes or no?"

Blink. Blink.

"No? Hmm, then I must assume that you don't know where you're from either, or even *when* you're from. Not a question, simply an observation." She closed her eyes, uninterested. She wanted him to leave. She wanted to sleep.

"Do you have any memory at all of how you came to be here, yes or no?"

Blink. Blink.

For the next quarter hour or so, he asked questions. But the communication was entirely one-sided, and the incessant demands that she answer became frustrating and tiring.

No, she didn't remember where she came from, or her family. She did know she was human and a female, questions she thought peculiar.

Yes, she hurt.

That was true—her head was pounding out the rhythm of her heartbeat—but no, she couldn't wriggle her toes or move her feet, or feel them when he tapped. She could raise her eyebrows and furrow her forehead and blink, but no other movement seemed possible.

Again, she felt panic rise as the throbbing in her head increased its pace, but he immediately explained the reason for her paralysis. Specific healing herbs and medicines had been administered because her initial recovery required complete immobilization. This eased her alarm but raised additional questions, which she could not ask.

As the man talked, he moved about tinkering with or clanging this or that, business that she could only hear and imagine. Finally, he stopped asking questions and began giving her information.

John referred to himself as a Collector. As a Collector, John amassed things delivered by offshore currents onto rock-strewn beaches near his home. She had been in the Refuge recuperating for months.

"Washed up" was how John described her, on the shores of an "island" between worlds, a victim of what he called a tragedy— some event both terrible and destructive. Along with her had come wreckage: a chaos of metal, paper, toys and wood, artifacts, and other detritus of her civilization and time. It had all been boxed and placed in another storage room somewhere nearby. When her strength returned, she could rummage through it.

"I didn't mean to discover you," John said. "After all, I'm a simple Collector, not a Finder."

EVE

Apparently Finders would always be mystically entangled with whatever it was they found. From the way John spoke of it, such a law was authoritative throughout the universe.

The girl didn't like the sound of that. Entangled with a man? Anxiety stirred within her like an agitated wolf.

He carried on for the better part of an hour explaining this, then apologized profusely for another quarter hour because his rant made it seem that her situation, and his as a result, was entirely her fault.

This was mean, she thought, inflicting pain as cruel as her physical injuries.

But it wasn't long before the singsong rhythm of his words along with the quiet background humming caused her to drift. She couldn't keep a grip on what he said, nor did she want to. She gave herself to the current, hoping for inky blackness and freedom from expectations.

Her hope was in vain.

Three

THE LILLY AND THE SNAKE

Approaching the surface of the Earth, the girl floated down onto a small, barren hill. It stood at the edge of a rolling flatland peppered by groves of trees that gathered into forests. Beyond these in the purple distance stood row upon row of larger hills, and behind these, the jagged teeth of a mountain range.

This grandeur she barely noticed, her attention drawn to and then riveted by what was behind her. Turning, she gasped and instinctively took a step backward. A titanic storm of undulating energy and water rose above a plateau. The barrier stretched from side to side and from ground to sky as far and high as her sight allowed. It pulsed like a living thing. Light and heat radiated into every cell of her body.

"It never ceases to mystify and enthrall me," said a voice next to her. Barely able to tear her gaze from the wall, the girl glanced at the tall, fine-boned woman beside her.

"You're the one who calls yourself Mother," she said. "You're not my mother."

The presence of this woman was more substantial and captivating than even the stormy barrier. She stood with noble bearing, more striking and beautiful than the girl had first noticed, with high cheekbones announcing piercing dark-brown eyes flecked with gold, and white hair tightly braided with ends cascading like small rivulets to her shoulders. Her shimmering robes, regal and colorful, flowed as if teased by every thought or gesture.

The woman smiled and leaned forward until their foreheads touched.

"Yes, I am your mother, Lilly," she whispered.

"Lilly?" The name stunned the girl, but she knew instantly it was hers. "My name is Lilly? Oh my God, I remember. My name is Lilly Fields!"

Just as quickly she realized what else the woman had said. "And you're my mother? How can you be my mother? You're . . ."

"Black?" She laughed so cleanly and joyfully that Lilly couldn't help but join her, though still completely perplexed. "Dear one, how beautiful is black, which includes and keeps all color?"

"I still don't know who you are. What's your name?"

"Eve!"

"You're Eve? The Adam-and-Eve Eve?"

"Yes, my child. Eve, the Mother of the Living! Lilly, where do you think we are?"

"I don't know," Lilly stammered. "Lost in some dream or drug hallucination or some kind of catastrophic mental illness?" She hesitated and then blurted, "Am I going crazy?"

Lilly lowered her head and looked toward the ground as if it might help her collect scattered thoughts. Surprised, she realized she also wore a sheer garment of flowing, prismatic light, perfect and pure and protective. Though Lilly instantly felt the familiar threat of being exposed, she was also surprised by a foreign sense of safety. This contradiction could not be true.

"Well, if you really knew me," she mumbled, eyes downcast, "you'd know I don't belong here."

"Dear one," Eve said, "can you ever say you truly know yourself?" Then suddenly the woman's tone changed, her words both declaration and command. "I sense the presence of an accusation. Show yourself to me!"

As she spoke, Lilly heard a rustling in the brush, from which emerged the swaying head of a sinewy asp. If it was aware of Eve, it paid her no notice and instead swiftly rose in front of the girl. Lilly recoiled. It looked her in the eyes, its hood fanning like miniature wings. A tongue split darted in and out, tasting the air. Eve watched, her face blank and arms folded.

"What are you?" it hissed. "I have never seen your kind."

Lilly's breath caught in her chest. She averted her eyes. "Nothing," she whispered. "I'm nothing."

"By your own decree then, you are nothing. But nothing has a voice, so who are you?"

"No one," Lilly said. "I don't belong here." Strangely, with each of her words it seemed the serpent grew in size.

"Curious!" The snake pulled back as if to get a better view. "So tell me, why is nothing and no one here?"

Lilly had no answer for that.

25

It cocked its head to the side and tasted the air again. "You are a strange kind, unknown to me. At most you are an interruption." With that it dropped to the ground and disappeared. Lilly felt agitated and somehow dismissed but remained still. The rustling of leaves shifted nearby, then swiftly moved away.

"What was that?" she asked.

"Sometimes," responded Eve, "a snake is just a snake."

"But it talked to me!"

"Sometimes a snake is something more. If a lie gets too much attention, it can grow. But that doesn't concern me in this moment. What does is that your presence is known to others, some who may not always have your best at heart."

Lilly hugged herself. "You're scaring me a little."

"Don't be afraid," said Eve. "I have seen how this unfolds."

"This"—Lilly held up her arms as if to encompass all they saw—"has happened more than once?"

"No, only once, and this is it," Eve said, as if it made perfect sense. "And you are here to witness."

"Eve?" Lilly instinctively reached for the woman. Their fingers entwined, and Lilly was surprised by the unfamiliar sense that she could openly speak her mind without fear of being judged or punished.

"Yes, my daughter." Eve smiled gently and squeezed Lilly's hand.

"I don't want to be a Witness, whatever that is."

"It is a privilege and an honor."

A knot of shame formed in Lilly's throat. She didn't know why.

"It sounds like another way to be a failure. I'm not into religious stuff, you know."

A question furrowed Eve's brow. "I know nothing of *religious*."

"I mean, I heard the story. I can't remember when I learned it—when I was a kid, I think. God makes the world perfect, God makes man, God makes woman, woman ruins everything..." Lilly hesitated. "Well, I guess *you'd* know."

The gold flecks in Eve's eyes shimmered. "Know what?"

"Um, how everyone has been mad at women ever since. God seems pretty upset too, at least in my experience."

"And what experience is that?"

Again, memory failed her. She looked at her fingers, still locked with Eve's, and suddenly felt like crying for no apparent reason at all.

"Don't leave me, okay?" she asked, her voice barely audible.

"I am never far away." The mischievous sparkle in Eve's eyes became a glistening of tears. "You are my daughter, after all, so I am already in you, and you in me."

The assurance brought a glimmer of peace. Eve looked up and Lilly's gaze followed. "Behold!" Eve said. "The appointed time is here. I will make you this promise: you will not regret being the Witness."

"BACK TO THE MOMENT, are we?" She couldn't see but Lilly knew it was John who spoke, and she felt a prickle of anger to be pulled from sleep.

"I've been watching you dream."

Great. He's a creep.

He chuckled as if he had read her mind but was not offended in the least. Embarrassment flushed her cheeks. "When you dream, your eyes move back and forth under your eyelids, as if whatever you're seeing is really there."

After a brief pause he added, "In truth, whatever you're seeing might really be there. I'm no specialist on dreaming. Not my expertise. I should ask a Scholar. Anyway, you were deeply lost inside . . . whatever it was."

Lost, Lilly thought, was exactly how she felt. Caught between the pain and dull ordinariness of this place and the overwhelming transcendence of her lucid visions. She did not want to be a Witness; neither did she want to be away from Eve. Something in her shifted, and her brilliant dream slipped away like a fading sunset.

Her eyebrows rose in question and he guessed. "Dreaming or Scholars? You want me to tell you about Scholars, yes or no?"

Blinking was aggravating, so the girl focused on her mouth, which had been freed from its cage. What emerged barely resembled a grunt, but John took it for a yes. She meant it as neither.

"I heard that! There you go! Congratulations! Well done." John scooted his chair closer to her bedside.

"Scholars," he said, "are an erudite lot who study this or that and can talk about it in prodigious detail. Very smart and unendingly educated, Scholars! They can explain almost anything, even if it isn't true."

He looked to see if that had made her smile. Detecting nothing, he went on, "Sadly, they spend most of their time speaking only to one another in languages that nobody but their kind can understand. I usually have to find a Translator or Interpreter if I want to engage scholarly profundity. It's all quite tedious. But to be fair, they're not difficult people. And to be very clear, many of my best friends are Scholars."

Catching his breath, he leaned in so she could see his face, and this time she tried to give him what she thought he wanted. It was a weak little wisp of a grin, the first she had achieved on purpose.

To her surprise, his beaming response erased most of her annoyance.

"Again well done," he said encouragingly. "I saw it! A first fleeting smile is a hope of others to follow. Anyway, let me tell you something else about Scholars." He glanced around as if there might be someone close who could overhear, then lowered his voice to a whisper. "Scholars often visit the Refuge. In fact, the three foreigners who have come to see you no doubt will want to put you under a microscope. At some point we will have to indulge them. The trick I have found with Scholars is to give them wine, or something stronger if available. The more they drink, the easier they are to understand."

John chuckled. Lilly had to admit it *was* a bit funny. "Overall, they're a lovable bunch, and I've learned a great, great deal from them. But I rarely admit such a thing in their presence." He looked away thoughtfully. "It's strenuous work, remaining obtuse."

Now John stood up and laughed. Because her choices were limited, she rasped a noise, again managing the semblance of a grin.

"I saw that!" cheered the man. "And might I say, even the whisper of a smile makes you look as radiant as a princess!"

While he probably meant to be encouraging, the remark ignited a reaction that threatened to overwhelm her. What he said or how he said it tripped her headlong into dread.

It started with a slow rising panic, like a sea swell, and was heightened by her inability to move. She concentrated on breathing slowly and deeply. The adrenaline rush of fear gradually subsided. Carefully, she let go the inner grip and inhaled and exhaled through clenched teeth.

As she lay staring upward at the ceiling, tears blurred her vision.

Again the man gently and carefully wiped her eyes and cheeks. Though he meant to be kind, she couldn't stand his touch. And she couldn't pull away. A tremble overtook her body.

"My dear girl." He sighed. "I do wish you could remember your name."

It seemed these tears were her only language now, incoherent liquid words.

"I'll be back soon." He gently patted her arm and left the room.

She dismissed the glimmer of a wish that he might understand. Now she fought against a rising rage. Its grip began to slowly crush her chest. Grateful that he had gone, she closed her eyes.

A hand took hers. A mother's fingers. Warm and soft. Sensation rushed back into extremities and chased away her fury.

"Lilly!" Eve's voice was a breeze whispering low in her ear. "Come back now. Come and see!"

The joy in her tone, the security of her hand, overpowered Lilly's resistance. She looked up, expecting Eve's face, and gasped. Only an arm's length away stood the towering barrier full of lightning flashes and thundering waterfalls. But as she took a step and lifted her hand to touch it, a whisper deep inside her heart said, "Unworthy."

Pulling away, she turned and gazed instead at the horizon, where a fiery sun was slowly sinking. Like a flower girl at a wedding march, the night threw shadows as announcements of a Beloved's approach.

Quietly she asked, "Mother Eve, what is this wall behind me?"

"We are outside Eden's boundary."

"Eden, like the Garden of Eden?" The name surprised a memory that had long lain dormant. "My mom used to walk me down to this corner church when I was little and leave me there to learn stories. I thought Eden got drowned in a flood."

Eve laughed, clear and clean as a mountain spring, but Lilly felt embarrassed. The woman drew the girl in close to her side.

"Lilly, you are not at risk with me. My amusement is because you said something funny. I will never laugh to shame you."

She didn't know how to respond. Finally, when she did, it was a confession. "I feel stupid when I don't know something I should."

Again Eve laughed, but this time Lilly didn't flush. "My dear, how will you ever learn unless you first don't know?"

"I don't know." Then Lilly giggled herself. "Hah, I get it."

Eve pointed. Up, down, side to side, near and far. "Eden has six boundaries, if you include the ground. Eden is a cube. You understand a cube, Lilly?"

"Yes," she muttered. "I did go to school. But listen. I don't mean to be rude, but it's just a fairy tale. All of this. Even you. I'm going crazy, remember?"

"Lilly, you do know that God created everything that exists?"

"Only in these dreams," she began. "In my real life, when I'm

31

not hallucinating, I don't believe any of this. What I believe is that everything came from nothing."

"I did not ask what you believe. I asked you what you know."

"What's the difference?"

"Interesting! Seems these hallucinations might persuade you of things you don't already believe. Experience is a force not easily discounted." Lilly didn't miss the irony of the challenge.

"It's safer to discount everything," she said. "Especially if it seems undeniably real."

Eve fell silent for a time, then turned her attention back to the garden. "Eden is the grand delight, the deepest and the truest. There will come an age when this garden will encompass all creation and all dimensions." The declaration caused something in Lilly to flicker, like a spark stirred to life by a passing eddy of wind.

New movements drew her attention. Gigantic sentinels of flame like multicolored, raging bonfires had stationed themselves precisely around the plateau's perimeter. Within the border established by these pyres, rank upon rank now closed: spirit beings positioning themselves with choreographed exactness. Beyond that boundary, emerging as if from ground and sky and tree, came all manner of soulish beast and hominid and bird. She had a sense that beyond these there gathered multitudes of creeping things: the amphibian and insect, the reptile, the seen and the unseen. And in the ocean, leagues away, all were attentive. The universe had paused from all its effort, from simple chores of motion and daily rigors of survival, to pay rapt and worshipful devotion.

As night descended, a myriad of elegant, flashing lights in wildly mottled colors became distinct and obvious. Waves of countless nimble beings arrayed in spectrum-brilliant shades, gathered in the skies. The assembly grew, as did anticipation. The entire cosmos drew together, here in this place at this appointed time. It was an unhurried but resolute inhalation, initiating labor.

Lilly found herself at the center of the gathering, surrounded by light-beings and an onslaught to the senses. Music wove like threads into a living, scented tapestry. The strings of myrrh and sandalwood, the horns of frankincense and fruits, woodwinds breathing hyacinth, pine, lilac, lavender, and honeysuckle, the rhythmic beats of cinnamon and clove, turmeric and ginger. Even the distant stars joined in with their songs as all creation paused.

Once gathered, they did not wait long, for a doorway majestically opened within the wall of Eden. Intense radiance tumbled out. In an instant Lilly and Eve were standing alone. Everything else bowed, face to the ground in awe-full, joy-filled adoration.

Eve nudged her. "They come." But Lilly could only stare at the approaching blaze. It was a whirlwind of blazing sardius reds with living emerald greens, set in the brilliance of spinning jasper, coalescing until from its center a single personage emerged . . . a human being.

"Who's that man?" she whispered.

"Not just a man. Eternal Man! Who is Everlasting God! Adonai!"

"A man is God?"

But Eve didn't explain.

Eternal Man seemed to dance, dressed in white robes of light. A humble crown of vines encircled His head. Lilly felt entranced; every part of her longed to run to Him and tell Him all her secrets, to be remade, to melt into His magnificence, to find rest from her shame. Here stood trustworthiness. Smiling welcome, He lifted His hands, and the prostrate rose to kneeling.

What happened next surprised her. Eternal Man also knelt upon the ground, and with His hands, like a child in a sandbox, began to gather into one place a pile of reddish-brown dust. He was playing, but His demeanor was intensely focused and brimming with unbridled joy. Then He sat down and gathered the dust in between His legs. A gentle breeze arose, toyed with His hair, and then helped Him collect His treasure. Lilly craned to see. Man and wind were careful and seemed to make certain that not a single mote was lost but all included and essential.

Lilly heard two voices laugh. One came from Eternal Man, another from the Wind. It was a clean laugh, like the giggles of children. Tears too came easily to Eternal Man, joyful tears, and spilled from His eyes onto the dust piled between His thighs by His strong hands.

He began to sing. It was a new song, distinct from the melodies Lilly had heard so far. The song washed over her and dropped her to her knees, filling her with something greater than excitement. For the first time in all of her limited memory, Lilly felt hope.

Hope for what, she couldn't say. Her heart picked up its pace.

From inside out, this mound of dirt now bubbled up bloodred water, gushing from an unseen aquifer. Adonai sang into it and then with tears and laughter plunged His hands into the holy mess with a shout that brought Lilly to her feet. The labor was nearly finished. Then, with a piercing, wrenching scream, Adonai raised above His head a newborn baby.

"A son is born, a son is born!" All creation erupted into jubilant sound, and Lilly rode the crest of birthday's celebration. She yelled to be heard over the crowd: "Mother Eve! Did you see?" It was impossible to find her. But as Lilly turned, a whisper of truth settled on her shoulders: *She* had seen. Although it stirred in her an overwhelming array of longings and emotions, Eve had kept her promise. Lilly had no regrets at all about witnessing this birth.

The crystal-clear and gentle voice of Eternal Man now sang above the cacophony: "This is My heart's delight, the crowning of all creation. I present to you My beloved son, in whom My soul delights. They shall be named Adam!"

They? The baby was not moving.

Lilly's hope faltered. Bewildered and then alarmed, Lilly desperately cried out, "The baby! The baby is not breathing!"

"SHE'S SEIZING!" JOHN'S VOICE yelled as if from a great distance. "Do something!"

Lilly felt her body quaking, muscles firing, contracting and expanding. A flooding sensation of warm and liquid light penetrated her closed eyes. She felt entirely weightless, her spasms buffered by whatever she was floating in.

"Shut it down!" a woman commanded.

But the baby isn't breathing! She screamed the thought before a blinding flash of white. Then her eyes opened to an unmoving expanse. A sky that was not a sky. Blue, flat, unglorious. She was back in her room, lying as still as the lifeless child.

Four

SECRETS

Concern for the baby nagged at her. Like a tongue that returns repeatedly to the emptiness of a recently lost tooth, so did her mind to what she had witnessed. But after two nights without a visitation or dream, Lilly began to doubt herself again. What she saw while floating in the thick, breathable dark must have been a reaction to administered drugs. Random images wandered in her brain: a mash-up of old Sunday school stories and television shows from her hazy past. It was the only plausible theory she could cobble together, and alternatives were too bizarre to consider seriously. But then . . . there was the baby.

Though she could feel her strength returning, Lilly's gaze remained fixed upward. Her chamber was almost cavelike, the curved ceiling shades of seashell and ivory with rippling hues of bone and pearl. A suggestion of periwinkle and powder blue touched the edges of her vision. It was almost like a sky, but one that refused to shift or change. Maybe made of marble, its oddly comforting patterns accentuated by even minor variations of light.

She watched for any movement, some bug or creature flitting on the ceiling, but the room was sterile and her only company was John and Letty. He had given her no reason to fear him, but it still felt safer to be on guard.

Throughout the work of waiting, she listened to John's companionable conversation, absorbing information. Neither handsome nor ugly, he had a pleasant face that lit up and became almost beautiful when he smiled or laughed. She studied that face whenever he leaned over her, looking for something hidden, something suspect, and decided he should not be fully trusted. His skin was a deeply sunbaked brown, his beard short and trimmed, his face framed by black and silver hair. His features made her think he was from the Middle East. He was old. Not old-old . . . but older. Although she resisted the thought, there was something about him she liked.

Her own identity and history remained a mystery to both of them, enshrouded in shadows too thick and bleak to explore. Whatever the details, Lilly felt one thing was certain: men were unpredictable and dangerous.

Though John talked a lot, he also seemed hesitant about divulging too much information. Perhaps he was concerned about overwhelming her or initiating another seizure. It was a delicate dance, a waltz with two lives inextricably connected and yet warily keeping their distance.

Just as her scratchy grunts and incoherent groans had replaced the blinks of yes and no, these too gave way to little whispers that left her mouth as sharp breaths.

"My name is Lilly," she rasped one day as soon as she heard John step into the room. "Lilly Fields. I remember."

"Well, hello, Lilly Fields," exclaimed John. "That is a wonderfully picturesque name. Much better suited to you than Egypt. Not that I have anything against Egypt."

"Egypt?"

"In the container where you were found—where I found you—were files and photos. The closest we could come to ascertaining your identity were documents with a picture that referred to you as Egypt, obviously an alias. You look more like an island girl than a desert one anyway, although according to the Healers you have genetic markers from people in both regions."

"Thanks, I think."

"So I'm curious." John came within view. "What brought your name back to you?"

"A dream," she offered, "or hallucination. Not sure."

"Ah, more dreams. That's good. Anything you want to tell me about them? You seem to have a lot."

Lilly thought for a moment before answering, "No. They're confusing."

How could she tell him what she didn't understand? She felt herself withdrawing. Lilly had no explanations for babies and beginnings or for a wondrous but unfamiliar black woman named Eve who claimed to be her mother, or the certainty that she was just spinning toward the edges of insanity.

That night, when sounds were hushed and lights had dimmed, Lilly had a sense of being outside, looking up into the sweep of stars. Distant lights pulsed into the darkness of her prison and occasionally roamed across the sky in some great, confident dance. Like an aurora the display rose and fell without predictable patterns. The movements blossomed and stirred distinct emotions about what she had seen with Eve—the deep and thickening dark, and then the most beautiful of unfoldings.

She rode the currents between wakefulness and sleep, but each time she edged toward rest's shore, the tiny cry of an infant would wake her anxiety.

She imagined overhearing voices in a late-night conversation. As the pendulum swung between night and day, thin bits of memory began to visit Lilly, but they never stayed.

"Now come and see," a woman said, once more taking both of Lilly's hands in hers.

"Eve?" Lilly snapped awake.

The woman laughed and wrapped Lilly into her embrace. "Dear one," she whispered, "you are alive and I am the Mother of the Living. You must witness with me the child who occupies so much of your thoughts."

Again, Lilly felt as if she was stepping through a black and engulfing drape that separated times and worlds, the dark barrier between the Refuge and Beginnings, and the moment Lilly pierced the divide, Eve again released her hand. They stood side by side, behind them the curtain of light and water.

"The baby?" Lilly asked, taking a step toward the spot where he had been taken from the earth.

A touch on her shoulder gently stopped her. At that same moment Eternal Man, who sat before the boundary, lifted his smiling face. He held the unmoving newborn, wrapped in a swaddling of glorious light, to His chest. He looked directly at Lilly, and she felt His peace wash through and over her. For an instant that single look relieved her of grief and whispered possibilities. Then she looked away and shrugged it off.

The attending Wind and the Energy that tumbled through the wall gathered round the Man. The three formed a single face that leaned to kiss the child, but it was more than the touch of the lips on lips. It was the breathing in of life, and with that breath, the fragile infant became a living soul.

A tiny wail fractured the night, and Lilly gasped, relieved.

"My Adam is born," Eve whispered to Lilly, her hand still resting on the girl's shoulder.

A thunderous cheer arose alongside the baby's life-affirming cry, and the rippling sounds were carried by innumerable spirit messengers out to the edges of the cosmos.

"These know the portals and windows built into the fabric of the worlds," Eve said. "They travel now to bear the news, good tidings of the Father."

Three massive personages approached the gathering, two of them from opposite ends of the wall and one from the darkness beyond.

"Who are they?"

"Cherubim!" Eve stated respectfully. Each of them dwarfed the colossal wall of Eden, but as they approached, their size changed until they were not much taller than the rest. Still, with their approach Lilly felt that she was shrinking. Their feet seemed not to touch the ground, and she sensed the vague movement of massive, unseen wings.

The two from the wall lowered their heads, but the third waited a moment before it also bowed. Its stunning crown radiated twelve gemstones splaying out a rainbow of colors, like a tent pitched above the gathering. To this one Eternal Man spoke.

"Look and see, Anointed Cherub. Here in my arms and nursing at my breast is the highest expression of my creation. These hold dominion over every created thing, the seen and the unseen."

Questions tumbled through her mind, but Lilly was frozen in the moment, helpless in the grasp of exhilaration, drawn to the newborn for reasons she couldn't explain.

The Angel's voice was warm, the tone controlled. "Adonai, this gathering of earth's dust? Does Your breathing into dirt give it new meaning? They may Your image and likeness bear, but they are fragile, weak, and therefore . . . inconsequential. You are the One Who set the terms, Your nature inviolable, so why have You now revealed Yourself in an everlasting weakness? You would place our hope and life in this . . . this helpless bit of living matter?"

Lilly took offense. "All babies are weak," she said through her teeth.

"As we remain," Eve countered gently. Lilly glanced up at her, but Eve didn't explain.

"Surprised?" said Eternal Man to the Cherub. His look of motherly affection and fatherly kindness was pure and right and filled with Love. "It is My nature to surprise. So will you, loved and Anointed Cherub, perform an honor?" He lifted His infant to the Archangel. Lilly noticed the baby's cord still connected him to the earth.

For a moment the mighty being looked puzzled. "Machiara?"

Eternal Man nodded.

Lilly felt Eve's hand grip her shoulder a little tighter. Instead of taking the child, the Anointed Cherub drew from somewhere in its swirling garments a small, razor-sharp dagger and held it up. She gasped. It would take nothing to slit the infant's throat and prove the fragility of this being.

But instead the Archangel severed the infant's cord, and Adonai drew the baby into His chest. The child slept peacefully in the arms of God's good keeping.

"Thank you!"

"I am forever honored," was the astonished Angel's response as it examined the knife. Tiny threads of bloody flesh hung from the razor's edge. "This is the best and highest of Your creating?" The softly spoken question was clear even as the blade was wiped clean against the radiant vestments and returned to the hidden sheath.

"Shining One, there are mysteries hidden from even you." Adonai stood and rocked the baby in His arms, his once-white garment soiled with dirt and blood and water. "This being requires no proof to love. They are bone of my bone, flesh of my flesh, and for them my everlasting Love and affection will never be diminished or darkened. They cannot drift into unworthiness."

Lilly's eyes and throat swelled with tears. She did not know why and felt embarrassed. "Why is He calling the baby boy *they*?" she asked, swiping at her cheeks.

"Watch," Eve said gently. "In time you will see."

Adonai spoke, "Here is My invitation for you: keep your rightful place, remain humbled, bow your head and heart, and let your way be purified by the fires of love and fellowship and service."

"Of course, I bow." The Cherub hesitated, still uncertain. "To You?"

"No, not only to Me," the God-Man said. "But to this little one. They are your kings, they have dominion, and it is for them you give your service and keep your proper place. Your invitation is to serve them wholly and completely."

"With joy, I bow, and vow to serve the Man as I serve You!" declared the celestial being. In spinning light the Anointed Cherub bowed, embraced the child, and kissed Eternal Man upon His cheek.

God now declared, "This is very good! Behold the child! Creation's womb is fully blessed. Let everything, each in its way with voice or breath, now celebrate this coming. The whole of creation is the great Good! With this birth, Day Six is crowned and complete. We rest from all Our labor."

LILLY WOKE WITH TEARS flowing down her cheeks and into her ears. Here in the Refuge, she couldn't wipe them away.

Had she just witnessed the birth of Adam? How was that possible? The newborn baby had stirred up profound longings: to belong, to be held by someone who loved her without reason. It was safer to shut down such disorienting feelings. And Adonai? Why had her first inclination been to run to Him? It was more than that: she wanted to run *into* Him, to be known by Him. Was He God? Was He Man?

The swirl of thoughts was like a sucking whirlpool, dragging her down into darkness. She concentrated on breathing in and out, in and out, in and out.

John approached with a cloth soft as kitten fur and dabbed her tears away. "When you're stronger, up and about, I'll take you to the chamber where I've stored the things that washed ashore with you. It may help."

"What things?" she croaked.

"Odds and ends, the stuff of your time and space and place. Not a single good book, though. Doesn't anyone from your world read anymore?"

"I don't remember being much of a reader," she rasped, and he gave her something warm to drink to ease the rough edges in her throat.

"Sad," he said. "The right book, like the right song or the right love, can change the entire cosmos, for the right person, of course. And then it spills out from there."

"Why can't I remember?"

John reappeared between her and the marble ceiling. "Trauma and tragedy can cause a form of amnesia, but those memories usually return over time. When the council first decided you should be treated here at the Refuge, we had a few frightening challenges. You kept having seizures that threatened to undo everything we were trying to accomplish, so we employed a series of memory inhibitors."

"What?"

"Nothing permanent. We have been easing you off them over the last few days, just a little at a time. You may experience flashbacks. It means you're recovering blocked memories. Not losing your mind."

"Yippee," she muttered.

That made him laugh and returned him to a ramble about children's books and how they create important building blocks for civilization. Something he said—a remark about a book—set her mind spinning without warning.

An onslaught of unanticipated images from her childhood dropped on her, smothering her thoughts like water on a fire.

She was a little girl. A woman was reading to her a story about a prince and snake and fox and rose, while Lilly pirouetted in a tattered dress to a tune inside her head. She spun until the shadows grew around her and then, panicking, she ran.

The assault of images was swift and brutal: terrified, she found safety under musty clothing in a dark closet. Peering through the cracks, she could see the woman lying limp on the floor, a man's form standing above her. Approaching footsteps stopped outside her hiding place. Closing her eyes, she crawled into the only spot she thought safe, deep down inside, as the knob slowly turned.

Again, tears she couldn't stop climbed to the edges of her eyes.

"I sometimes talk too much," John muttered apologetically, dabbing her face again.

"It's okay," she rasped, not wanting him to see her more vulnerable and helpless than she felt.

"Meanwhile, Lilly," he continued, "I have some good news. You've been responding so well that we're making changes to give you back to your own body."

"What?" Lilly responded. "What does that mean?"

"It means, Lilly, that we're going to wean you off the drugs and start you on a physical therapy protocol. We're going to start with sitting up. In time you will walk again, and dance and sing and all those things that every child is born to do."

She winced at the mention of a dance, but how could he have known?

"It will mean arduous work on your part," he continued, "but I personally think there is nothing you can't do. What do you say?"

"I'm beyond ready." She let out a long breath, as if it had been held for months.

"Good! Also, to celebrate, I brought you a small gift that I made."

"A gift?" A wave of nausea again caught her off guard, unexpected and unsettling. Why would the mention of a gift affect her this way?

"You said you didn't remember being much of a reader, but my opinion is that every person is a story and therefore is a storyteller. Trouble is that many fear failure, so they never begin. But you, dear Lilly, are a courageous girl." He paused and then held up a small gift wrapped in floral print and an emerald bow.

"John, you know I can't move, right?"

"Of course! I wrapped it myself, proving that I have the requisite genes to unwrap it."

"Well then?"

He took off the paper, pausing to show each unfolding, until an elegant leather-bound journal appeared. It was hand-embossed with a series of circles and an intricate clasp. In this diary she could scribble daily thoughts and poetry and random musings. In case such things were private, John explained, he showed her how they would secure its contents by impressing her handprint on the cover. He also opened up the inside back, which looked more slate than leather, like the surface of a tablet.

"This is a built-in recorder of another sort, capable of remembering your experiences and emotions. There is nothing you have to do to activate it; it simply works in the background."

Lilly felt gratitude come alongside her wariness. It was a wonderful gift, maybe the nicest she'd ever received. "Thank you, John."

"You're welcome. I hope it becomes a place of safety for you. I also write occasionally. Writing is a refuge in its own way. I hope you find it so."

"Maybe," she said. "John, someplace in your big library, do you have a story about a prince and snake and fox and a rose?"

He thought for a moment. "I do!" he exclaimed. "I know the one you're talking about. I haven't thought of it for years. I will look for it." He smiled. "Shall I read it to you?"

"Yes. You're never too old, too wacky, too wild, to pick up a book and read to a child. Dr. Seuss said that."

The Collector laughed. "Hah! Dr. Seuss? How old did you say you are?"

Lilly felt shame rise up in her face. Defiance inside her instantly recoiled and sarcastically snapped, "Five!"

There was silence and then his face appeared above hers.

"I didn't mean to embarrass or hurt you," he said softly. "I have no idea why or how what I asked would cause you pain. But it did, so I apologize."

She tried to shrug it off. After all, she didn't know why she felt offended.

"It's okay," she offered, her breathing heavier as she worked to control the emotions. "I'm sorry too . . . that I growled at you."

"Then you'll forgive me?"

That little bit of kindness broke apart her resolve. The water-fall of feelings, which she had been holding at bay, came rushing like a torrent. She didn't just cry, she wailed. She sobbed for losses she didn't even remember, for the storehouses of memories and faces that she couldn't access, for pain that only grace and kind-ness can approach, for rising fear, and because she was just a little girl and she didn't know where home was and she felt lost and everything hurt again and she couldn't keep it back.

And this man, this kind man, cried with her. He bowed his head till it touched hers and put his hands on both sides of her face as their tears mingled. She thought it was a sort of baptism. The lost and the found, forever and irretrievably entwined.

Five

The Garden of God

"Come, Lilly," the woman whispered, and for an instant as the girl rose up, the light around her imploded and she thought she was again losing consciousness.

Lilly gasped as her sight returned. "Mother Eve, where are we now?" The colors, sounds, and smells of a grand forest overwhelmed her senses.

"Inside Eden's gate." Eve's strength of presence flowed through Lilly. "It was outside Eden's boundary that you witnessed Adam's birth."

The place was astounding and yet suited her perfectly somehow. The warmth, the humidity, all brought comfort and ease and pleasure. *So this is what normal was always meant to be.* But hard on the heels of that thought came another: *You're anything but normal. You don't belong here.*

"Lilly, would you like to see more?"

When Lilly nodded, Eve grasped her hand. They rose up,

buoyed on the air itself. Her feet felt as if they were on solid ground even as she looked down at the receding earth. The view tipped her sense of balance. Recovering was simple; all she had to do was look up and out, trusting in the invisible solidity beneath her feet. She couldn't resist and tapped her foot. Yes, it felt like something was there. Eve looked at her and grinned.

Above the trees they slowed to a stop, suspended.

"This is the Garden of God," Eve said, "created for all of us to inhabit."

"It's enormous!" Lilly exclaimed. It spread in every direction for hundreds of miles until in the distant horizon the boundary walls rose and disappeared into the sky, each like a geyser of rainbowed water. The nearest border was close and powerfully impressive. The air was clear and crisp and warming, as if perfectly attuned to her.

"You said Eden is a cube, right? As big as it is, I don't think that we would all fit in here."

"Eden expands and contracts as needed. It is not a *place* as you would understand. In the coming age, after all has been finished and allowed, it will grow to include all creation."

"You sound sad," Lilly said.

Eve smiled at her. "Not sad, my daughter. Remembering. It is *here* that righteousness dwells."

"Righteousness?"

"Right relationships, face-to-face and trusting."

"Is that even possible?" Lilly felt embarrassed by her impulsiveness. "I mean, is there such a thing?"

Eve squeezed Lilly's hand. "Yes. And don't be ashamed, Lilly.

52

THE GARDEN OF GOD

Our deep longings remind us we have lost something vital and precious. Such yearnings are the stirring of hope. Of returning."

"Returning where?"

"To this garden."

"But didn't God make you leave?" Lilly asked.

Eve sighed and appeared about to answer when something diverted her attention and she smiled. "Listen," she directed.

Lilly could hear it too. Approaching from a distance, it was a song both beautiful and slightly off-key. It was the clear and joyful voice of a boy making his way through the forest.

"Is that . . . ?"

"Adam? Yes! Look!"

But Lilly glanced at Eve instead and recognized the face of a woman young and in love.

JOHN WAS LEANING OVER her as she opened her eyes.

"Why did you wake me up?" she snapped, groggy and miffed that her dreaming had been interrupted.

"I didn't." His expression revealed his confusion.

"Oh," she mumbled. "Good morning, then."

Under the marble-blue ceiling, John looked around and then back. "Actually, it isn't morning. Late afternoon, maybe?"

"Already?" She turned her neck as if looking for proof.

"Well, look at you!" John exclaimed. "Incredible progress. All that emotional activity this morning seems to have freed up some movement between your spine and head. That's a sign I've been told to watch for!"

She tried it again. The shift in her muscles was barely noticeable.

"Now, you be careful!" he said. "It might be tempting, but this is no time to overdo anything. We will now begin the work of removing the apparatus that has immobilized you."

"What sort of apparatus?"

"Well, I told you that when I found you, you were very broken. In order for the Menders and Healers to work their kindness, we asked the Crafters and Builders to create an *apparatus* that would keep you completely immobile and allow them access and time to repair you."

"So what happened to me? What is wrong with me?"

"Your neck and back were fractured, each in several places, among many other things. We found you in frozen stasis. It's probably what kept you alive." She could tell he was watching his words, perhaps sensitive about divulging too much especially after the cascade of emotions only a few hours earlier.

"Wait." A series of questions were coming into focus. "How long have I been here, like here here? In this room?"

John paused, looking up, calculating. "Approaching a year."

"A year? I've been here almost a year?"

"Yes, almost."

"Where did I come from?"

"We have not ascertained that exactly, but from somewhere on Earth certainly."

"From Earth? You mean this isn't Earth?"

He shook his head earnestly.

"So where is this . . . this island I'm on?"

"It's in an ocean you've probably never heard of. It resides in a wrinkle between worlds, between dimensions. There are many such places."

"John, that's craziness."

"I'm sure it seems that way."

"Has anyone been looking for me? Does anyone . . . care that I'm missing?"

John looked away. "Not that I am aware."

A new kind of fear gripped Lilly's thoughts.

"A year? Really? Is there a way for me to go back . . . home?"

John cleared his throat and shifted in his seat.

"Lilly, all of this must be confusing and frightening," he offered. "I don't begin to understand the depths of what you are feeling, but I am deeply sad with you."

"John, why am I here? I'm nobody." Her throat ached, her eyes closed, and her mind was in disarray. Without any solid memories, she could not tether any of this to something solid or real. All she had were scattered remnants of recollections that came to her in bursts. She had the dreams, but if she told John about them, he might think she was crazy. She wondered why it mattered to her what he thought, but it did.

"Lilly, you are not a nobody," he said firmly. "As for clarity about your coming, that will be revealed in God's timing. You seem tired. Perhaps we might continue this later?"

"No, we aren't done! Don't you dare leave!" she demanded, eyes still closed.

He waited.

"What exactly have your Healers and Menders been doing to me?" She rode the edge of rage.

"They've been reconnecting your spinal cord to your brain and reattaching, um, whatever needed to be, uh, reattached. Things like that."

"What needed reattaching?"

With a sigh, John told Lilly that only one of her feet was original to her body. The good news, as John put it, was that her new left foot was female, a detail that made the truth no less grotesque.

When she had been found, he explained, hardly alive, among the many things broken in her body was her left foot, which had been completely crushed.

She asked from where her new foot had been harvested. The answer was as gruesome as she feared. The metal box in which she was found contained other almost-frozen bodies.

"What?" Lilly felt nauseated. John was talking faster, as if speed would stanch the flood of shock.

"The Healers and Menders immediately deduced that the only option, other than to have the Builders create some sort of prosthetic, was to attempt to match an existing foot from one of the most recently deceased girls. Perhaps it would help to imagine it as a sort of organ transplant?" he suggested, but Lilly preferred not to think about it at all.

"John? What do you think happened to us? To me and to the other girls?"

"I could only guess," he began, then paused. "Lilly, every theory makes me furious and desolate to the core. Whatever was done to you was wrong in every way I can imagine."

Like the last leaf on the autumn tree, Lilly could feel herself being swept away. In order not to fall, she tried to quickly change the subject.

"And when exactly did they do all this . . . reattaching? I don't remember any Healers or Menders. Besides Letty, you're the only one I've seen around here."

"While you slept." John took a breath. "Every day for months they have been working meticulously to put you together!"

When Lilly didn't respond, John continued, "They designed and built this special room for you. Almost every night it's sealed up, airtight. Then it's mostly filled with a breathable liquid. Much of the work requires you be turned over, facedown, but they can't turn you unless you are weightless. In the morning they turn you back over and drain the chamber. You can't see from where you are, but there are all manner of mechanical devices—ladders and things that allow access."

Lilly was silent. For at least a minute she lay there and again resisted slipping into a mental abyss that offered her safety and relief. John came into sight, a look of concern written plainly on his kind features.

"Anything else you'd like to ask, Lilly?"

"I'm done! No more questions." She hesitated. "Wait, one more, for now. Why me?"

That elicited a smile. "Ah, Lilly, why not you?"

While that did offer another way of looking at her situation, it was not what she had asked. "I don't mean why me in a cosmic sort of sense. I mean it more personally. Why would *you* go through all this trouble for *me*? You don't even know me. Why me?"

He thought for a moment before he spoke again. "I believe you have come into my life because God loves me."

"Because God loves *you*?"

Another grin. "Yes, because God loves me, Lilly. The how and why of our connection is a mystery, but it is no small thing! You matter! You are Eve's daughter."

"Eve's daughter?" Was John somehow aware of her visions? "Eve, like Adam and Eve, that Eve? That's just a story. A fairy tale."

"Ah, now the stew is thickening, as they say." He shook his head. "Lilly, fairy tales and myths are born inside imagination's storehouse; just because something is considered to be 'a story' doesn't mean it isn't true."

Once more Lilly resisted the opportunity to open up. However, his words did make her wonder about something.

"So, you think the story of Eden is true? It always seemed unreal, like Santa Claus and the Tooth Fairy."

"I do." John's expression was bemused. "Lilly, would you like me to read you the story from the Scriptures themselves, where it was first recorded in writing? I have it nearby. It would only take a minute to get it."

"If it's not a bother," Lilly said, trying to hide her curiosity.

He ducked out and returned quickly with an old leather-bound book. "My apologies, it's not an original manuscript, but at least it's in the original language, which I can read and translate for you as best as I am able. Better if we had a Scholar. Would you rather wait?"

"I'd rather you read it," she encouraged him. John dragged a stool next to her. He opened the book from the back and then read it backward.

"In the beginning," he began, "Elohim created . . ." John looked up. "Lilly, did you know that in the original and ancient language Elohim, God, is plural, and Ruach, the Spirit of God, or breath, or wind, is feminine?"

Lilly's silent reply was to raise her eyebrows and shrug her shoulders.

"Perhaps, it is better if I simply read it. In the beginning," he began again, "Elohim, God, created the heavens and the earth . . ." and so John read on through the first Creation account.

"So it was all good and God rested?" Lilly asked, lost in her own thoughts and images awakened by the words.

"Yes," John responded. "It was all good, very good." He hesitated as if to say more and then decided against it.

Standing and clearing his throat, he said, "Now, truly, you've had enough excitement for one day. If you like, I'll read more another time, but for now it's past time for you to rest. All things considered, today was a good day. Now blessings on your dreaming." He pushed the necessary buttons to dim the lights in the room, and as if he had drawn a curtain or flipped a switch, her eyelids shut.

Even in her sadness Lilly recognized the increasingly familiar and welcome touch that was lifting her and carrying her to somewhere.

"ADAM HAS GROWN MUCH since you watched his birth," Eve said. It was as if there had been no interruption. Lilly was with Eve listening to an approaching song.

She watched a young man emerge from the forest, slim and tall, ebony-skinned with a deep tinge of dark brown-red, and thick black hair woven and matted with clay. He was striking, even more so as he danced and jumped his way through the trees, singing at the top of his voice. He was clothed in light.

His nakedness made Lilly uncomfortable. She averted her eyes, conflicted over whether to watch. "I see why you like him, but why is he . . . naked?"

"Naked?" Eve smiled back. "He was born naked. Adam has no need of any covering other than God's love. There is no shame in being entirely weak and vulnerable."

"He doesn't *look* weak."

"I don't speak of physical weakness but of his complete dependency on Elohim."

"Okay, that makes no sense," Lilly commented. "And I don't understand a word he's saying."

"You will hear and see whatever it is you are here to witness."

"Can he see us?"

"No. Your presence has not been revealed to him, and you haven't truly even been born yet, so why would he?"

"But what about you?"

Her mother did not answer this question.

They floated along above Adam as he continued to sing and dance through a tall grass meadow, stopping to speak occasionally to things Lilly couldn't see. Ahead of him, a small stream bubbled its way toward the river. Hopping into it with all the glee of a little boy, he suddenly stopped, his attention riveted.

She turned toward the sound of approaching voices singing the same slightly out-of-tune song as Adam's, accompanied by a rising breeze that blew warm and embracing. They were clearly voices he recognized, because he sprinted in their direction, leaping and gyrating to the rhythm.

"This is their time to walk and talk," Eve explained. She anticipated Lilly's question. "God and Adam. Every day near its new beginning they celebrate and laugh and take joy in each other."

Eve paused, listening, it seemed, to a conversation that Lilly couldn't hear. The woman grinned.

"Lilly, why don't you join them? Adonai is inviting you."

"Me? Inviting me?" She felt exhilarated and then terribly shy. A million excuses rushed her, whispering and exposing her unworthiness. "Do I have to?" she asked.

"Of course not. Dear one, this is an invitation, not a demand." The look in Eve's expression was sympathetic and open, accepting of whatever Lilly might decide.

"I can't," Lilly mumbled. "I don't belong here. I wouldn't know what to say. I can't."

Eve hugged her. "The invitation will always be there for you, when you are ready." There was no hint of disapproval in the woman's voice. Lilly felt sad and also relieved.

A flurry of fire and water blown by gusts of wind engulfed Adam in an embrace. The only figure, other than Adam, that Lilly could clearly perceive was Eternal Man. The blood and dirt of Adam's birth had become part of the white light that clothed Him, like an embroidered ornamentation.

Lilly yearned to experience the hug herself. Eve reached out and steadied her.

Adam and God sat down, backs each against a tree near the forest edge. The substantial presence of Fire and Wind danced around them. When Lilly and Eve also sat down on the grass not twenty feet away, Adonai looked right at them, smiled, and nodded in greeting. The rush of acceptance blew through Lilly like a torrent. She did not resist, nor did she want to.

"He sees me," she whispered, barely moving her lips. "Eve, He sees me."

"He always does," Eve quietly stated. "Not only does He see you, He knows you."

"Son," Eternal Man said to Adam, "you are the center of Our affection and the radiance of Our glory."

"And You are my joy! I love You too," Adam said with all the enthusiasm of a child. "I've been exploring." He described creatures he had come across in his adventures. He demonstrated— grunting, growling, whooping—how he had even communicated with them. For all his youthfulness, Adam was smart, grasping ideas easily and with a depth that left Lilly astonished. The ease of their laughter and flow of conversation washed over Lilly like gentle, warm waves.

When Lilly glanced at Eve, she was surprised at the tears rolling down the woman's smiling face. Reaching out, Eve pulled the girl into her side, and without taking her eyes off the gathered community leaned in and whispered, "Thank you, Lilly."

"For what?"

"This is the first time I have ever seen him like this, a boy in love with his Creator. You have given me this priceless gift. You, Lilly."

"I don't—" Lilly began.

"Shhh. Listen now. This is important."

Adam was saying, "Eden is fruitful of its own accord, so is my tending and cultivating important?"

"Yes, important but not necessary," stated God, a twinkle in His eyes.

"Then what about my keeping, my keeping and protecting? Is there . . ." Adam paused as he looked for words to express his question. "Is there something outside the boundaries that I must guard against?"

"You ask thoughtful questions, my son. Besides growing in stature, you are growing in Wisdom, which will help you serve and steer creation into maturity. Take each moment as it comes. Wisdom will guide and teach you. Like the tending, keeping is significant but not necessary. With your restful keeping and your tending, you worship and adore Us."

"I do adore You!" Adam yelled, and scrambled up into the lower branches of the tree.

"As We do you!" Adonai too climbed into the tree until both

were perched on branches looking out into the garden. Adam raised his hands, balancing himself, his laughter as pure as mountain springs.

After a moment to catch his breath, he asked a different question.

"Why can't I fly? I have been watching creatures that soar through the air and I have tried, but I am more like a stone than one of them." With his hands he made the motions of falling straight down.

"There are good powers and forces that hold you to the earth. One day you will explore these and subdue them while still submitting." God smiled. "I have a question for you. Are you free to walk through these?" He knocked on the tree against which they leaned.

"I am free to attempt it. See?" laughed Adam, pointing out a small bruise on his forehead. "I am not so skilled as the Messengers."

"Adam, the life and freedom that is yours, and all who are within you, are bound inside your relationship to Us. As long as we are face-to-face, you will have life and freedom easily and always."

By the perplexed look on Adam's face, Lilly could see that he was wrestling with a new thought. As he did, he grasped the branch beneath him and let himself tumble forward. He hung for a second before dropping lightly to the ground. Adonai was right behind, and Adam turned to Him.

"How could I ever not keep my face fully turned to Yours? My heart and soul and spirit have life only by dwelling in You. How could I . . . ever . . . ?"

God gently reached around His son, embracing him.

"Love takes risks, dear one. You have the freedom to say no to Us, no to Love, to turn your face away."

Adam frowned. "And if I did such a thing, what would happen?"

"In turning you would find within yourself a shadow. This darkening would become more real to you than I am. From then, until you re-turned your face to Mine, this empty nothingness would deceive you about everything, including who We are to you, and who you are to all creation."

"Is there a name for such a shadow, a name for such a turning?" Adam asked, only a few inches from the Oneness he loved.

"It does not deserve a name," whispered Eternal Man, "but it would be called death."

Lilly felt as if a powerful and icy hand had gripped her chest and was slowly crushing it. She forced out words: "I know death. Eve, we have to warn Adam."

Eve took her hand and squeezed. Lilly could feel warmth radiate out, confront, and then advance against the cold. Fury was carved into Eve's creased brow.

Then Lilly heard the Voice, as close to her as thought: "Lilly, trust Me." As quickly as it had arrived, the frigid clasp around her lungs released. She took a deep breath.

"I do not want death," Adam whispered back. "Is death the opposite of life?"

"Life has no opposite, Adam. It has no equal. Life is Good. Life is Our nature."

Adam pondered for a moment before asking, "Is there any of this death within me?"

Eternal Man grinned and gently touched the boy's cheek. "No. Adam, there is no death in you, nor in any who are within you. Only life. Today and always you may eat of the Tree of Life, to breathe in and out My Spirit, face-to-face."

Adam touched the hand that was on his cheek and chuckled. "You know how much I love the trees and the fruit You have created," and then added in mock seriousness, "which I tend and keep, but not for any necessary purpose."

Laughter filled the air, the joy of parents watching their child's first tentative steps and discoveries. As evening descended, the light of God's presence illuminated the area. Creator and created lingered in the fellowship of other-centered love.

Both the women cried silently as they watched this exchange of pure affection. Lilly didn't know why Eve wept, but the girl wanted with every fiber of her being to run into the center of this love—yet the whisper of unworthiness anchored her to the ground and wouldn't let her move, once more taking her voice away and leaving her numb. Such joy was something she could never have.

Finally the young man said, "I only want to know life, to be face-to-face!"

"Adam, you are in the rest of Those Who Know you completely and love you fully. Simple trust is your participation. Hear My word each day and I will tell you the Good. This is neither command nor toil. It is easy and light."

"And what is Your word for me today?" he asked.

"My word is necessity and in this day of rest is this: you may freely eat from any tree in Eden's garden, especially from the Tree of Life that is at the center of the garden. But for now there is the one tree, which I have shown you, whose fruit you may not eat and remain in your freedom. The day you eat of that tree, affirming Good and Evil, you will have already died."

"The Good I know, for You declare it always, but what is evil?"

"Evil is to death as Good is to life. To turn from life, light, and Good, away from love and trust, is to embrace the shadow of death, for life is in the face-to-face and death is in the turning."

"I do not want death or evil!" Adam stated.

"Then take joy in all the freedoms you celebrate in Us," declared God.

Adam climbed up on God's lap as if he were a little boy and nestled into his shoulder and closed his eyes. Eternal Man embraced humanity and sang to him a lullaby.

Lilly drifted off as well, lulled to peace by Adonai's song. In the gentle space between waking and sleeping, she sensed Eve picking her up. The girl lay back in her mother's arms, Eve's warm breath falling like kisses on her shoulder.

Six

INVISIBLES

Lilly woke in the middle of the night with the floral scents of Mother Eve still on her skin. A chill rushed in where Eve's warmth had been, but Lilly felt calm and peaceful. Although it wasn't any time close to morning, she was completely aware. Subtle blue iridescence lit the room, just enough to throw shadows onto the rock ceiling. She glanced around, half expecting to see Eve, and was disappointed.

A conversation of sorts drifted into her chamber, hushed tones and whispers. John was nearby, talking to someone. Lilly almost called out but decided instead to listen. The other voice wasn't speaking exactly, but almost singing. The language, the pitch and rhythm, soothed her.

"I haven't decided yet," John said. "I agree, she needs to be told soon. The Menders and Healers have worked near to exhaustion restoring her, but there is only so much they can do. When it comes to the mind and heart and soul, the best surgeon's knife has its limitations."

The Singer spoke for a time, the timbre of words wafting through Lilly's body and teasing loose deep knots in her muscles. It was irresistible, this voice, and she breathed it in like air, trying to capture the melody. She almost fell asleep again.

"Thank you for saying that," said John. "But may I be so bold as to ask, why hasn't God spoken healing directly to her?"

Again the response came like a song, and again she lay there with her eyes closed, letting the music of the tonal words tumble over her. Inexplicably, in this moment she was not afraid. Within her an assurance grew that whatever was coming it would be all right. It reminded her of what it felt like to be near Adonai.

"I do trust," said John. "I trust both Love and God's purpose. But what you are saying is . . . Well, it's so remarkable! Are you certain that she is a Witness?"

The moment John referred to her as a Witness, vivid memories of her hallucinations returned and took Lilly's breath away. She felt no fear, but rather unexpected warmth and the embrace of hope.

Three worlds had collided within her: The first unknown but for flashbacks. The second filled with hallucinations in which she was Witness to Beginnings. And the last, and in ways the strangest, was this world in which she lay awake, held entranced by someone's unearthly singing.

There was no way to tell which, if any, of the worlds was real.

"Lilly is so young," John was saying, undeniable sorrow in his voice. "And so . . . broken."

The reply was like cascading laughter, notes of humor spilling over each other. Lilly almost laughed out loud herself.

"You're right," John said, chuckling. "I'm old and tired, but I'm not alone. Quite a different figure than the energetic man of my youth, as you well know!"

The thought of John as an exuberant young man made Lilly smile. It made her think of Adam, so sure of God's love and affection. But wait—that was the dream world and this was the true. Or was it the other way around? Or was Earth, her mysterious place of origin—the place she couldn't quite conjure—was *that* real?

John spoke again. "Would you please sing over her? As you did for me when I was the Witness. I sense that she will need the strength of your song this day."

And the Voice did just that. Even if she had wanted to open her eyes, Lilly would have been unable. For the first time in any dream or fragment of memory, she truly rested. Peace came over her like a tidal flow, one harmony rolling over another and then another until she was embraced by song itself. In that solitary moment not one thing in her hurt.

A GREAT COMMOTION OF scuffling feet and voices woke her. Activity swirled around Lilly's bright room but remained outside her vision. Behind the jabbering hubbub were mechanical clicks and clacks and what sounded like ropes being tightened or twisted. Occasionally she heard the ping of a wire and a shriek of satisfaction or frustration.

John appeared above her and smiled. "Today is a momentous day. We've accomplished so much since the day you moved your head on your own—"

"That was only yesterday, wasn't it?" Her voice sounded strange to her own ears.

"Well, listen to you!" John sounded very pleased. "No more hoarse throat. To answer your question, it was more like three days ago."

"I've been asleep that long?"

"Hovering, if you want to be precise."

"Hovering?"

"Um, yes, hovering. Definitely hovering."

"Well, are you going to explain that to me?"

John looked up and thought for a moment before looking back at her. "It is as if we took you to meet death but we wouldn't let you shake its hand."

"You mean I was in a coma?"

"Coma!" he exclaimed. "I don't know that word, but if it explains a procedure in which we intentionally kept you unconscious in order to hasten some specific healing—yes, then, a coma. Does that help?"

She nodded.

John's eyes brightened. "Do that again."

"Do what?" she asked.

"You nodded."

Realizing what she had done, she burst into a grin and did it again. The simple movement sent ripples of cheer through the room.

"We've loosened your head covering and stimulated your muscles," he explained. "You should have a greater range of motion now as well as control of your extremities."

"John," she interrupted, "you make me sound like an experiment. By the way, who is *we*? I can hear them but can't see them."

His eyebrows rose. "You can hear them? That's unusual! Normally their voices are imperceptible to humans. Very strange indeed," he mumbled, rubbing his short beard with his left hand. "Entirely unanticipated. Well"—he lifted both hands and spun around—"she wants to know who is here. Do we tell her?"

The momentary silence was broken by a high-pitched chime that reminded her of a doorbell. "Okay then." And he spun back to face her.

"Let's see. Today we're joined by a rabble of Healers and Menders, and a number of Fixers, Builders, Designers, and Tinkers." He pointed around the room as he named each group. "Various Messengers, who move too quickly even for me to see, a Thinker, a Seer, a Cook, and one Weaver. No Scholars. And no Inventors here today, or Singers, and no Managers, thankfully. There is one Timekeeper and one Curmudgeon." He looked back into her eyes. "And there are always some Invisibles, but you never know who or how many unless they want you to."

She cleared her throat. "I want to see them."

"Well, you can't." He leaned down and whispered with a grin, "They're invisible."

"I wasn't talking about the Invisibles. I want to see the others, the Menders and Healers who have been tending to me, and why are there Fixers and Builders here?"

John glanced around, apparently thinking through his options. "I don't think that's a good idea. When you think Mender or Healer, Lilly, your mind pulls up images of doctors or nurses, and that's not what we have here." He paused and nodded at someone she couldn't see. "The Thinker is in agreement. To see our Menders and Healers could shock you into a relapse."

"You're freaking me out a little. My imagination is probably worse than your reality."

"Uh . . . in this case, I don't think so. You will have to trust my position on this, please." He paused, looked again around the room, and turned back to her. "We're unanimous. Perhaps we'll change our minds at some point, after your strength has more fully returned."

This did not sit well with her, but John quickly added, "But I can do something else for you that will help your perspective. We're ready to move you into the big room and tilt you up so you can see more of this place. Now, when I tell you, I want you to try to move your fingers and toes."

She tried and nothing happened.

"Wait, not before I tell you. It won't begin to work until we are ready on our part. We need to connect only a couple of small things and I will let you know when. Okay?"

She nodded, partly because she was afraid that if she began to speak, all she would do was cry. She felt like a prisoner who heard a pardon was on its way but feared it was just rumor or for someone else.

A few minutes later, John said, "All right! Try now."

Her fingers on both hands moved, as well as her toes on both feet. A muted hurrah seemed to rise in the room. She imagined small high-fives along with whispers of glee and celebration. Lilly even thought she heard the pop of a cork and smelled the fragrance of strawberries. She laughed.

They moved her bed out of the room without a sound. She glided as if on water. As the scene shifted, she saw that what she had thought was a ceiling above her bed was in fact a huge canopy. Behind it was a complex array of miniature ladders and bridges, like the latticework of catwalks high inside an arena. They passed under a massive rock archway and then into a large space, open and wide.

A breeze, the first she could remember in this world, swept across her covered body and played with her face. Scents of sea wind and brine teased her nose. Her ears filled with the crashing of distant surf and haunting cries of gulls and terns. The relaxing effect reminded her of John's visitor.

"John?"

"I'm here." His voice came from her left.

"Who were you talking to the other night?"

"I've spoken to many people while you've slept."

"The one who sang."

With the bed positioned at a precisely chosen spot, again John's face appeared above hers.

"I suspect you heard me talking to Han-el," he said. At the mention of the name, Lilly felt warmth pass through her, energy that stirred her fatigued muscles and bones.

"Han-el?"

He ignored her question.

"Now, we're going to slowly tilt you upward. Your bed, with the touch of a few buttons, can transition into a wheeled chair. We won't do that today, but when you get stronger."

John disappeared from sight.

"Why does he sing instead of talk?"

"Han-el's language is more ancient and advanced than ours." He reappeared on the opposite side of the bed. "Hopefully when we elevate you, your head won't roll off your shoulders."

She furrowed her eyebrows, concerned.

"That was a joke, Lilly." John chuckled. "I couldn't resist, you looking so serious. There is absolutely no possibility that your head will fall off your shoulders."

"Not funny." She tried to feign anger but couldn't help the grin. "Why couldn't I understand what Han-el was singing?"

John vanished again. "All right, here we go, like I told you, this will be very tedious, something in the range of one degree every fifteen minutes. The goal for today is thirty degrees. So, seven hours. Ready?"

"Bring it on!" she said. And nothing happened.

At least it seemed that way.

"John?"

"Over here, just monitoring your progress. All's well."

"What language was Han-el speaking?"

"The same as yours and mine."

"No, he wasn't. I would have understood."

"Didn't you?"

Lilly almost objected, but then she considered this. Though

76

she couldn't repeat the words of Han-el's song, some part of her *had* known the meaning of it, deep down. He had spoken peace over her. Rest. And to John: answers to questions.

Or maybe John was just fishing to see how much she had overheard.

"You're up a degree," John announced. "Well done."

"What's a Witness?" she asked.

"Aren't you full of questions today!" John chuckled.

"I hear you're the answer man."

She heard footsteps and soon saw John alongside her bed. "I don't have all the answers, but a few perhaps. A Witness is someone appointed to a divine purpose—observing God at work, and then reporting what she has seen." He coughed and averted his eyes. "She or he."

Though Lilly intensely wanted to understand what John and Eve meant when they referred to her as a Witness, his apparent discomfort stopped her. *She needs to be told soon, but . . . she is so broken.* The conversation now veered uncomfortably close to Lilly's dreams, to the possibility that her mind was as broken as her body. And also in that moment she realized John's opinion of her was important, something that made her feel uncomfortably vulnerable.

"Is Han-el a Witness?"

John's lips parted in surprise. "Han-el? Oh no. No, Han-el is a dear friend who has seen me through many wonderful seasons. Painful ones too." He rested his hand at the base of his throat, then paused. "Ah. They tell me you're up another degree now."

He continued to encourage her, reporting every fifteen minutes the arrival of the next degree, and slowly she could feel the changes. Lilly's world was incrementally tilting upward. At a point between degrees six and seven, her body objected. The room reeled and then began spinning as nausea rolled over her like a sneaker wave.

"Stop!" John yelled. "Let her adjust."

She focused her mind on Han-el and his song. Like a magnet, the lingering of Han-el's lullaby pulled her back into the vivid scenes she had already witnessed.

The better part of an hour passed before she signaled that her stomach had settled enough for the next elevation. As time and tilt progressed, Lilly realized she was being raised in front of a massive window looking out at a cobalt sky. It was clear for the most part, with an occasional high cloud blowing by, but it reminded her immediately of the places in her dreams.

"John, do you believe in God?" she asked.

There was a thoughtful pause before he spoke. "No," he said.

"I don't either."

He touched her arm. She hadn't realized he was right next to her. "Lilly, words like *God* and *believe* are often meaningless. I don't *believe* in God. I *know* God! Once you know someone, believing is no longer a concern."

Lilly didn't understand. "Is Han-el God?"

John's belly laugh silenced all other sounds in the room. "No, little one. You seem very impressed by my friend, as we all should be. Han-el is one of God's ministering servants." He leaned over and whispered, "Han-el is an Angel."

A horizon appeared at the bottom of her peripheral vision.

Again she experienced disequilibrium and vertigo, and again they stopped the process to wait for her adjustment.

"If you need to vomit, just vomit," offered John. "It might make you feel better."

"I'd rather die."

"It's not like you haven't vomited before." He backed out of view.

"I hate puking!"

"Puking? Hah!" he announced to the room. "Puking. There's a new one." He rolled it off his tongue as if he were a linguist trying to capture a new sound. "*Pyoo-king*. What a great word. All right then, there will be no *pyoo-king* on my watch, is that understood?" He leaned back into her view. "Was I using the word correctly?"

"Yes." She laughed in spite of her lingering nausea.

The horizon where the ocean kissed the sky was fully in view when John announced that the day had been an unqualified success and it was now time to rest. Within minutes all the noise of activity dissipated, replaced by a refreshing quiet.

John left her for a brief time, returning with a bowl of broth that smelled wonderful. Lilly's stomach growled.

"Soon we'll have visitors," John said, sitting next to her. "I've put them off as long as possible, but they're increasingly insistent."

"Why are they coming to see you?" Lilly asked.

"Not me. It's you they want to meet. When you're able to sit upright, I'll allow it. Letty says it has something to do with an ancient prophecy. We'll learn more when the time comes. But for now"—John spooned some soup out of the bowl—"as a reward for all your hard work, I am going to feed you. The Cooks and Healers concocted this just for you. Other than medicinal and herbal liquids, it's the first thing of substance you've eaten. Eating and drinking are keys to your healing."

He raised a spoon to her mouth. "Here. Try it. I already know it's quite tasty." He winked.

It was warm and savory and delightful, and she could feel its fingers of comfort spreading inside, awakening natural abilities that had lain dormant. At first she choked and sputtered. But she grinned as he wiped bits of broth off his face and again raised the spoon to her lips.

They did this, carefully, slowly, and methodically for a few minutes, then he leaned back.

"I know you want more, but that's enough for now. Don't want you puking all over, do we?"

"Not if I have anything to say about it." She took a deep breath, feeling her lungs rise and fall, enjoying the scents of the sea and flowers as the day began to slowly melt into the horizon. Apart from the fact that she was still mostly immobile, she felt better than she had ever remembered. In her waking hours, anyway.

"If I knew God, I'd hope he was like you," she said. John set the bowl aside and stared at her, his eyes welling up. "John, does the God you know have a name?"

She wondered if a name might open a door between her dreams and this reality: Adonai? Elohim? Eternal Man?

John blinked several times. "God has many names. Each is a window into facets of God's character and nature, none sufficient but each helpful. Some are too deep for words, and by that I mean they cannot be formed in sounds. Others are easily identified. Easily spoken."

"You said you think God let you find me because He loves you?"

"I do. On any given day any person might become a Finder; it is one of the truly wonderful risks of life. When you have lived as long as I, you discover that you can never truly walk away from a find. You can try, but it will seek you out until you care for it, or him, or her. The only thing that changes you more than becoming a Finder is when you yourself are found."

"Did someone find you?" she asked, drawn in by his introspection.

"Again, an entirely different story." He sighed and gathered himself to stand. "My cousin. It was my cousin who found me." He laid a steady hand on her brow. "And now you need to sleep, but I will be here when you wake. May your rest be full of sweet dreams, and may only good be in your heart and mind."

LILLY OPENED HER EYES to see Adam put his finger into Eden's liquid boundary. Instantly a wave of the energy and water swept through him, lighting up his body as if with living particles. Every time he touched it, he giggled. Eve too was caught up in his delight. *This is joy*, Lilly thought.

Adam passed through the boundary and left the garden. He crouched low in the grass like a boy playing a game of hide-and-seek. The two followed, catching his excitement. Eve explained to Lilly that Adam had been tracking a specific creature near one of Eden's borders for weeks, but every time he got close, it disappeared into the underbrush or down a hole, just a flash or glint of moving blurs of color. It was built low to the ground and hardly left a trail before vanishing.

Long hours of patience had failed to bring him nearer his quarry, but in the hunt he discovered countless other creatures living in the heights of the forest canopy or crawling inside the dirt.

Disguised in the dark browns and reds of river clay, Adam was sneaking through tall grass canes, moving like a passing breeze, when he was ambushed. An inch from his face was the creature he had been stalking. It so startled him that he fell backward and then began to laugh.

But Lilly was shocked. It was the snake she had met on her first visit to this place. Immediately internal alarms sounded. She glanced at Eve, who also seemed unsettled.

"What do we do?" Lilly whispered.

"It is not our place to interfere," Eve replied, her voice tinged with anger.

Why not? Lilly thought. But she had heard the warning in her mother's words.

This snake was like a living vine, thick as a tree trunk. Two eyes of piercing onyx fixed inside yellow gold were recessed in its swaying head.

"Why do you pursue me?" A split tongue darted out to taste the air.

"You speak?" Adam exclaimed. "And not a rudimentary communication like other beasts'. Your words are clear! They are like the melodies of the Cherubim."

The snake raised its head off the ground, meeting Adam's eyes. Its hood fanned out. Lilly could feel her pulse racing as a combination of fear and rage rose within her. There was something very wrong here and she couldn't find the words to give it voice. Lilly felt Eve take her elbow, as if to hold her back.

"You are a wonder to behold," admired Adam. "In all my explorations I have never before faced another beast like you, none in Eden's garden, so tell me what you are."

It didn't answer immediately, offering only the sway of movement and flash of tongue.

"A wild and wise beast of the field!" it declared. "I am a shining one and my domain is outside Eden's boundaries. And what are you, who boldly speaks to me and is so frail but unafraid?"

"I am Adam, son of God," he declared.

"Adam! Don't talk to that thing!" yelled Lilly, but Adam didn't hear. The snake, however, turned in her direction.

Seven

VISITORS

For a long while Lilly lay quaking as the dread slowly drained. Could the serpent have the ability to pursue her to the Refuge? This fear was irrational, but so was everything else she had witnessed.

Reaching up in the early morning light, she rubbed an itch on her nose. That movement was a first. It broke through her anxiety and brought a smile. And even better, it didn't hurt. Something in her body had changed. Lifting both her hands, she examined them in the early dawning light, moving her fingers in front of her eyes.

A snore erupted from a nearby sofa, startling her. John had spent the night close by, probably in case she needed him. Lilly was finding it difficult to resist her growing appreciation and affection for him.

Voices drifted in from a nearby room.

"I think we have visitors," she indicated.

He woke slowly. It took him several moments to collect himself.

"Visitors? Really? Already?" He mumbled, starting in one direction and then changing course, then halting until Lilly pointed toward the receiving room. He noticed she used her hands and beamed at her.

Taking a deep breath, John asked, "Would you rather meet them in here or out there?"

"Out there," she affirmed. "I haven't been out there yet."

Pushing buttons tilted the bed again, and when Lilly nodded she was ready, he wheeled her toward the room where guests were hosted. It was a grand space, windowed on three sides and sitting high atop an outcropping of cliff wall, offering a magnificent view of the shoreline, the hills beyond, and even the vague purple shadows of distant mountains.

This beautiful morning three Scholars stood waiting for them, teacups in hand, looking out over the sea below. They turned in unison, dressed in similar garb—fairly disheveled, tutorial vestments covered by a fine layer of what appeared to be chalk and road dust. Two were old, older than John perhaps, and while weariness slept in the lines of their faces, their eyes were bright and clear, as were their smiles.

The woman was tall, over six feet, made taller by a hat perched on her crown. She had a thin and angular body, her nose almost like a bird's beak. Overall she looked like a stork, except that the colors of her clothes were all wrong, mostly browns and blacks. The other elder was a stark contrast to her, almost as round as he was tall, which was barely over four feet. He looked about to explode, his breathing labored, as if he had run up the many flights of steps from the bottom of the cliffs where the sand and water met.

The third Scholar appeared significantly younger, though age lines had etched memories into his face. He was taller even than the woman, hair combed and hanging loosely around dark and striking features. Lilly sensed an odd familiarity about him, which was both attractive and disquieting.

"Greetings to you," John said, raising both his hands. Each in turn took his hands and then touched foreheads with him. Lilly guessed this to be the customary greeting.

"I'm John, a Collector. And, I'm happy to add, a Finder, as you are aware." He nodded toward Lilly. "This is Lilly Fields. The Refuge is our home and you're welcome to stay as long as you desire. I apologize for not seeing you sooner. It wasn't the right time." He extended a hand toward their cups. "I see an Attendant has brought you tea. Would you like a biscuit too?"

"We needn't bother you for biscuits yet," said the woman, seating herself on a sofa. "Immensely pleased to finally meet you, John. Your story is renowned."

The rotund Scholar, who had smiled and opened his mouth at the mention of a biscuit, closed it again and kept his smile fixed.

"Where are you from?" John asked.

"Beyond the Thrain," she said.

John's eyes widened. "I didn't know there was anything out there. Well, that explains why I didn't recognize you. Beyond the Thrain, really?"

Nodding, the rest of them settled into chairs. John sat next to

Lilly, and the sudden scrutiny of the group made Lilly uncomfortable. She turned her eyes toward her feet and tried to hide the one that did not match the rest of her body.

"It must have taken you a long time to get here," John said.

"Suffice it to say that we are from a place that is months in the traveling . . . beyond the Thrain." The woman enunciated the last words slowly, her eyes locked on John.

"And as regards a biscuit—" interjected the round man.

The woman raised her hand.

"—I can certainly wait."

"How did you travel so far?" asked John. "I'm trying to imagine such a long journey."

"Riders," she began. "We do not have many Fliers in our parts and I, personally, am a bit acrophobic, at least regarding unprotected heights. The Riders have been well looked after here— thank you! But it has taken us weeks to recover."

Lilly stole a secret glance at their unkempt clothes and wondered if they had no others.

"And *why* have you traveled all this way?"

The female Scholar hesitated, tilting her head in the direction of Lilly without taking her eyes off John. "This is the foundling, I assume?"

"She is."

"Then it is about her that we have come."

Lilly bristled. "I am sitting right here. Don't talk about me like I'm not even here—"

"As if," the woman interrupted.

"What? As if? As if what?" Not only was she confused, she was now annoyed.

"What she means," offered her portly companion, "is that it is probably better to say 'as if' you are not here, than 'like' you are not here."

"Well, excuse me!" Lilly snapped, enunciating the words for effect. "Like, I don't, like, care! As if! And while I am, like, on the subject, as if, doesn't anyone around here have an actual name?" She was now gesticulating with her hands and arms, partly because she could. "This is so aggravating," she continued her rant. "Am I the only one on this island who finds this, like, utterly annoying?"

The conversation flamed out into an awkward silence punctuated by the waves breaking on the shore below.

The woman's eyebrows rose, and the stout man shrank into the back of his chair as if he was trying to disappear. The third Scholar didn't flinch. In fact, the hint of a smile tugged at the corners of his mouth.

"Oh my!" the woman finally exhaled, her face flushed. "That was all rather exciting, and almost worth the trip by itself, I must say!"

John beamed proudly, a distinct twinkle in his eyes. "Did I forget to mention that Lilly is, like . . . an introvert?"

In this space where shocked stares met rising embarrassment, Lilly could hear nothing but the beating of her heart and the ringing of her ears.

The she-Scholar cleared her throat, in a delicate sort of way.

"Lilly," she said softly, "my name is Anita. It is an honor to meet you."

And then, as if the meeting had no chance of going well, a tiny, high-pitched voice called out from beyond the room, "Where is everyone? Have I missed the party? Those stairs are going to be the death of me, I swear."

Lilly recognized Letty's voice. What followed was the patter of tiny feet, then the minuscule woman's arrival. It was the first time Lilly had actually seen the little hummer. Letty was a tiny bundle barely three feet tall, with cane and shawl. To Lilly, she looked like a teeny house sitting on slender mismatched stilts. She was an impossibility of physics and Lilly tried to avoid staring. With the aid of her walking stick, she headed directly toward the Scholars.

"Good day to you, my friends, and to you, dearie." She nodded to Lilly, who was speechless.

"What do you think of all this?" the miniature old thing asked John, pointing her cane toward the Scholars. "It's been ages since we've had a visit from the realms beyond the Thrain."

John threw up his hands. "You knew about lands beyond the Thrain and didn't tell me?"

The little thing just grinned. They all greeted her properly, the Scholars forced to kneel to touch Letty's brow, and then sat again. Letty hefted herself up onto a stool and precariously perched on the edge. Once seated, she began humming quietly. No one but Lilly seemed to take notice.

Lilly nudged John with her elbow and he leaned in to hear. "Why does she hum?" she whispered.

"Curmudgeon," he said quietly, then turned immediately to the others. "Letty, we were just making introductions." He nodded to the smaller man.

"I am Gerald," he said to Lilly. "Vanguard Scholar of Antiquities."

"And my name is Simon," said the youngest, leaning back against his seat and crossing his ankle over one knee. "Vanguard Scholar of Systematics and Philosophy."

Lilly was both strangely attracted to and repelled by the sound of his voice. It reminded her of silky chocolate.

"May I ask your area of study, Anita?" asked John.

"Anita," interjected Gerald, "is a Vanguard Scholar and First Order Counselor."

"First Order!" John exclaimed. "Then I'm doubly honored! Your specialization?"

"Soul psychology with a focus on ENI," she answered, and John reflexively glanced at Lilly.

Even though he looked away quickly, she caught it. "What is ENI?" Lilly asked. Her throat, too long unused before her outburst, felt tight and swollen.

"Epigenetic neural integration," chimed in Letty. "Think of it as putting together a shattered mirror, reconnecting the relational spaces within the backdrop of neural networks in the mind and the relational heart."

"Ah, we used to have one of those on the farm," observed Lilly. No one laughed. "I'm joking," she explained. "It's my way of saying I don't understand anything you just said."

They nodded and laughed politely. Again, Lilly felt awkward.

"Dear one,"—Anita leaned in—"the prophecy told us that your arrival would be through significant tragedy. Even a minor crisis can shatter the human soul. I'm skilled at mending the cracks between pieces. Those were just big words to say I'm a Healer who participates in restoring broken souls."

"You think I'm a broken soul?" Lilly kept a rein on her offense this time.

"Certainly!" Anita was firm and gentle. "Like everyone in this room."

"Even Letty?" Lilly asked, and that broke the tension.

"Especially Letty," John said, and laughed with the others. "From what I have heard, she was seven feet tall before arriving. What you see is the best we could do."

Anita reached across the space and patted the girl on her hand.

The tiny woman smiled and then pointed a long and bony finger directly at Lilly. "Do you understand, little girl, that you are the reason we are all gathered here?"

"Me?" she exclaimed. "Why?"

"Why indeed!" emphasized Letty. The woman crossed her tiny dangling feet. "I do not begin to fathom God's wisdom, but it seems that the destiny of this place and time, and perhaps of the cosmos, has been linked to you and to the choices you make!"

"Oh, I'm sure you've all made a huge mistake," Lilly exclaimed. She noticed a tremble in her fingers. "I don't even know *who* I am exactly, or where I am."

"You're the daughter of Eve, is that not enough?" asked Letty.

Everyone now faced Lilly, seeming to wait breathlessly for her response.

"I suppose so, if by Eve you mean the Mother of the Living."

The elder Scholars sighed in unison and sat back in their chairs. Gerald shook his head. Had she said something wrong?

"Of course," Anita said, and placed a hand on Lilly's knee. "But we were also referring to your distinctive genetic makeup."

Lilly had no idea what she meant. It was Gerald who directed a question at John.

"You haven't told her?"

John took a deep breath and exhaled slowly. "It's never been the right time."

Anita and Gerald both looked surprised. Simon, who had not said another word since introducing himself, seemed oddly distracted, staring out the nearest window as if lost in another place.

"The right time for what?" Lilly asked.

Letty stopped humming to say, "John, my friend, tell her what you know."

"Lilly, the Healers have discovered that your DNA contains markers from every known race on earth."

Anita clapped her hands together and almost seemed to bounce on her cushion.

"What does that mean?" Lilly asked.

John opened his mouth but Anita spoke first, "It means, child, that all humanity is contained in every cell of your body."

"Thus, *the* daughter of Eve," Gerald said.

John wiped his mouth with the back of his hand and glanced at Lilly. "You remember asking me about my friend?" She nodded slowly. He looked at the Scholars. "Since Lilly's arrival I've been visited by a Messenger three times."

This seemed to catch Simon's ear. He turned his attention to John.

"Messengers are always about," stated Anita.

"This Messenger is a Singer!" John said.

"Oh!" she exclaimed. Gerald's eyes got big and Letty just sat there humming and nodding slowly.

"And does"—Gerald cleared his throat—"does this Singer have a name?"

John paused.

Lilly guessed. "It's Han-el."

The others Scholars sat in stunned silence, frozen in the instant. Their movements seemed to slow and almost stop.

"My, my, my!" muttered Anita.

Gerald turned his face and his hands upward in praise.

Simon for a moment looked uncomfortable but recovered quickly. "Not just a Singer but a Guardian!" he murmured.

"A Guardian?" Lilly asked.

Gerald responded. "An Angel, a Messenger who is also a Guardian."

"Angel? You mean one of those little fat baby boy cherubs with tiny wings and bows and arrows? Cupid's cousins, we called them."

"No!" Letty stated strongly. Her little legs stopped swinging. "No! Absolutely not! Cherubim are the terrible ones, and I mean that in a wonderful way. Don't diminish them by ridiculous imagery."

"Cherubim are beings of gathered light," Simon explained, "the sustainers of wonder and worship. Next to the Seraphim, they are the most carefully positioned. As the Seraphim are turned inward, the Cherubim turn outward. As far as we know, and I defer at this point to other Scholars, only two, perhaps three Cherubim are named in all creation. Michael, certainly. Gabriel, perhaps, and"—he paused, a hint of something like a shadow passing across his features—"maybe the greatest is Lucifer, the Anointed Cherub."

Lilly was hardly listening. She understood now what John meant about Scholars being annoying. But her thoughts tumbled over each other. Eden's hallucinations had again linked her to this time and place. She kept her face as impassive as she could.

"John, tell them what Han-el told you," encouraged Letty.

"He announced to me that Lilly is a Witness."

Gerald looked at Anita and patted her hand. "That confirms it. We are not foolish."

"In all my long life, I never thought this day possible," said Anita softly. She stared at Lilly with so much adoration that Lilly had to look away.

"Over a year ago our Scholars, Thinkers, Searchers, and As-tronomers told us the night skies had announced the arrival of a Witness," Gerald said. "Of course it caused great consternation and fierce debate among us, but finally some of us were allowed to embark upon this quest. Nine of us began; only we three are left."

"Only three?" John asked.

"Two turned back early," Anita said. "They were homesick and distressed. Three felt compelled to leave us at the Gregorian Cross-roads in search of another star, and one"—here she paused before sadly speaking—"one of our company, also a Scholar, fell ill."

"Ill how?" John asked.

"Shadow-sick." The term sent a prickle of unease through Lilly. "What's shadow-sick?" she asked.

"You might call it 'heartsick' or 'soul-sick,'" answered Anita. "It happens when humans turn from face-to-face trust and let the darkness of death enter them. Thanks to Adam, we all have inherited shadow-sickness in our mortality. Resisting it is the war in which we are all engaged."

"Is your colleague being guarded, then?" John asked.

Simon fiddled with a ring on his left hand.

"No, she is being companioned inside a community to the north," Anita said. "It is a guarding of sorts—but *for*, not *against*. The purpose is to help her turn once again toward life." She addressed Lilly. "We learned long ago that shadow-sickness feeds on isolation. So we take our stand against it by protecting relationships of intentional love and kindness."

"I'm sorry for all your losses," offered John. "Sorry and saddened."

"As are we," stated Simon softly. "Thank you."

After a moment of silence, Lilly spoke. "So . . . all of this trouble—to meet me? Do you really think I'm the Witness you came to find?" She glanced at John. "I still don't understand what that means."

Anita got up and knelt beside her. "This must be extremely puzzling and confusing. Please, forgive me. Forgive us." And she opened up her arms and, a bit awkwardly, let Lilly lean into her shoulder.

"Yes," Anita continued, "we do believe you are the one we

seek, but I have a few questions of my own before I dare attempt to explain." Anita released Lilly and returned to the sofa. "John, you have told her about the Vault?"

"No."

"I see, and you are certain that she is safe here?"

"Within these walls, yes. It's the Refuge, after all. Nothing has ever found us."

"And Han-el?" interjected Simon, a hint of apprehension in his voice. "Am I correct in assuming that the Singer is this girl's Guardian?"

"No," stated John, hesitating before he continued. "Han-el guards me."

The muscles in Simon's jaw relaxed.

"I see," Anita said. "And your Guardian confirmed she is a Witness. Did he say what she will witness?"

The Scholars shifted to the edges of their seats. If Letty had done the same, she would have toppled off, but she was fully attentive, humming louder than ever.

"She is Witness to Beginnings."

For a second, stunned silence. Then pandemonium. Anita stood straight up and raised her hands into the air and shouted in some language new to Lilly. Gerald danced a little jig in a circle, and Letty, her shoulders heaving, covered her eyes with tiny fingers. Simon had clasped his hands and turned his face upward as if in prayer.

"This calls for food and wine for celebration!" Simon announced.

John laughed and pointed to a door. "Help yourself to the pantry. Whatever I have is yours."

Simon left, followed by the other Scholars.

John sat quietly, looking to Lilly for a response. How could she tell him that he was wrong? That his Angel had misunderstood? Sure, she was witnessing, but she didn't want to. If she had a choice, she'd dream like a normal person. But no, Eve was taking her places she didn't want to go, and now people were getting shadow-sick and messing up their lives to find her. For nothing! Internally she scrambled to justify keeping the dreams to herself. Looking out at the ocean, her mind and heart whirled as separated worlds reeled and intersected. When she turned back toward John, she found him kneeling at her bed, his eyes moist.

"It's a lot to take in. I know," he murmured.

"I don't understand any of this." And of course, the "this" to which she was referring was much more than even he could be aware of. His tenderness made it worse.

"Understanding is not your task. Being Lilly Fields is all that is required of you."

"But if I don't understand, how will I know if I am doing the right thing?" She was almost begging him to stop. "I have nowhere to go. I'm stuck here and don't comprehend why or even how I got here or where this is. I'm supposed to witness Beginnings? *Beginnings?* I don't . . . understand! What do I do?"

John looked as if he was reaching deep into his own heart and past, searching for something that would help her, reach her, and comfort her.

It was Letty who spoke. "Perhaps, Lilly, you might trust. Trust is something that children are naturally good at, until someone lies to them or convinces them that it is dangerous."

"Trust *is* dangerous," she said without thinking.

"It is," John responded, "but not the way you think."

The others returned with plates of cheeses, fruits, crackers, nuts, and of course, biscuits. Soon wine had its intended effect, postures loosening even while intensity did not. Throughout the in-between and back-and-forth of interaction, Letty continued to hum.

During the course of the next hours, John, the Scholars, and one Curmudgeon attempted to answer Lilly's questions.

"Well," stated Gerald at one point in full academic mode, "each age and place has two primary Witnesses: one in Word of record and the other flesh and blood. The latter is more precisely the incarnation of the former, but you can't have one without the other."

"Perhaps it would help," interjected Anita, shaking her head, "to think of it in terms of a photograph, which is the writing, *graphe*, of a moment of light, *photos*. Think of a Witness as both the photographer and the photo."

"Okay," Lilly responded. "I can understand that, sort of . . ."

"There is a third element." Now it was Simon. "A Witness is not only the photographer and the photograph but uniquely an essential living participant *inside* the picture. A Witness is neither outside nor detached, is not objective and is not independent. Your very presence introduces innumerable potentials, and your choices impact history as we now know it. These are then woven in new ways into the unfolding purposes of God."

It sounded complicated and Lilly longed for an escape, for an uninterrupted sleep, but she tried to focus. "Are you saying that without a Witness there is no photograph at all? If someone is not there to see it, it doesn't exist?"

"Close but not exactly," piped in Anita.

Gerald added as if quoting, "God has always been *the* Witness, apart from whom nothing has existed. God is the Grand Observer, always and continually the Picture; the Word in all Their nuance is the Glory and Affection."

"And they are the Grand Interferer," added Anita. "This is why knowing the character of God is essential. Without God being Who They are in essence—Good submitted in knowing Love, One to the Other—then everything would *pffft*." Her fingers twirled up into the air like a balloon that had escaped. "Everything, including us, would vanish into nonbeing."

"Then why does God need me," queried Lilly, "or any human witness?"

"Ah," Gerald replied with a chuckle, "we are back to Beginnings. God has need of nothing, but God will not be God apart from us. To live inside God's life is to explore this mystery of participation."

For Lilly, it was perplexing, but they encouraged her not to get lost in the details. She was a child, after all, they explained, and children know intuitively what they will never learn by education. That didn't help her grasp what they were saying, but it was comforting regardless.

Sometime, as the evening wound down, Letty vanished without saying good-bye. Her humming simply disappeared.

John was about to accompany the three Scholars to their sleeping quarters when Anita held up her hand.

"Wait," she exclaimed. "We have forgotten the gifts we brought for Lilly!"

"We certainly have," said Simon. "But I have left mine in my baggage. I will have to bring it later. Tomorrow perhaps?"

"Gifts?" Lilly was feeling exhausted, but curiosity raised her flagging energy. The prospect of a gift from Simon sent a little shiver of anticipation through her.

The younger Scholar withdrew to the edges of the room while Anita and Gerald each patted pockets, trying to remember where they'd stored their treasures. The woman found hers first and approached Lilly.

"Dear one," Anita began, "When I was praying about coming to meet you—"

"You pray for me?"

"We all do," Gerald said. "Prayer is mostly about talking to God—about life and people and what is before us and who matters to us in that moment. Does that surprise you?"

She nodded.

"Well," began Anita again, "when I was praying about coming to meet you, this token came repeatedly to mind." She opened up her hand and revealed a small, ornate, and finely crafted silver key, hanging from a silver chain.

"It's beautiful!" Lilly exclaimed. "Thank you." Anita placed the delicate piece into the girl's hand.

"This ancient key has a story, a fairy tale of sorts, attached to it. Are you familiar with the tale of the ogre and the princess?"

She shook her head.

"No matter." Anita smiled and they hugged. "Lilly, this is not only a key to be worn, it is a key to unlock something. And no, I don't know what. But you will, when the time is right."

"That is true of my gift as well," chimed in Gerald, holding out a little jewelry box. Lilly opened it to find a single band, a gold ring. "It is a Betrothal ring," he said, and Lilly smiled, unsure what that meant. "This ring has been handed down through my family since the mists of Beginnings. Like Anita, I do not know why it is important that you have it, but there it is."

"Is it the same thing as an engagement ring?"

"No. *Engagement* is much too weak a word. Betrothal is a resolute and firm commitment, a declaration of marriage sometimes years before its consummation. This is a ring the groom will give his bride as promise of a wedding."

"Thank you, Gerald." He leaned forward to touch her forehead, and though she tensed at the intimate gesture, she allowed it.

With that John escorted the Scholars out of the room. Simon, the last to exit, turned, smiled, and bowed slightly.

For a time Lilly sat quietly and tried to grasp the events of the day, but reflecting only seemed to make her more anxious. She hoped that Han-el was real and close, but that also meant the Angel was probably aware of her deceptions, and the possibility shamed her. Even so, the very thought of any Guardian was a comfort.

Unexpectedly, it also raised a different memory: the face of another man whom she couldn't quite place.

Eight

MIRRORED INTENTIONS

Early the next morning, as the whispers of sunrise began interrupting the shades of night's rhythms, Lilly made her first journal entry into the diary John had given her. Invited by its open space, she unloaded parts of her burden and took to writing like an eagle soaring, carried away on invisible drafts into vistas of honesty she had never intentionally explored.

Despite what John says, I don't really think I am a writer. Ha, here I am already making excuses and I'm the only one who will ever read this.

I don't know what I am or what is real. Half the time I think I'm crazy and surrounded by crazy people, and the other half I'm just confused and a mess of angry, overwhelming, horrid emotions.

Sometimes, I just want to scream until I can't. I don't want anyone to care, and then I do and that makes me mad, and then maybe I want to die.

Of all the people I've met here, I like John the most, but I'm really intrigued by this new guy, one of the Three Magi (I think that's what they were called in the Sunday school stories, although I'm not the baby Jesus they were looking for). His name is Simon and he's older than me but closest of anyone to my age. Anita and Gerald gave me a key and a Betrothal ring, but Simon said he would bring me his gift later. I think he just wanted to talk to me alone. I keep wondering about him, like he's dangerous in a good way.

Yesterday was completely nuts. So much happened I don't even know where to start. Eve took me to see Adam—it sounds nuts just to even write that—but anyway, we ran into a talking snake that scared the crap out of me. Then the Magi showed up and I saw Letty for the first time. I still don't know why she is always humming. Then they told me that I'm a Witness to Beginnings. I didn't tell them Eve already told me that.

I've been looking at my arms. Maybe I was a cutter, in the other life. That really scares me too. It might be better if I can't remember, but I can't seem to stop the flashbacks or the hallucinations either.

I watch the waves and the tides. It's like wanting to live and wanting to die, tide coming in and tide going out. Most of the time all I can see is the waves and can't even tell which tide it is. I wonder if Simon is going to come and see me today? Probably not.

At the thought of Simon she pulled back the covers to examine the foot that was not hers. She wondered about the girl to whom it had belonged. It appeared completely functional, though much whiter than her right foot, and freckled.

Women who were dressed as if they belonged to a religious order soon showed up and assisted her with her morning rituals. They were perpetually quiet and kind and smiled a lot, their presence comfortable and welcome. Then John appeared with breakfast, which heralded the beginnings of real food, though it was pasty and bland. He said her bodily systems were still in recovery. When they finished eating, he left her staring out at the ocean, the magnificent view of shoreline and sand below and, beyond the coastal divide, an odd mix of flora both tropical and northern rain forest.

Lilly then went through her regimen of exercises, contracting and relaxing each muscle beginning with her toes and working her way up her body to her nose. This was something she repeated six times each day between waking and sleeping. With a push of a button she could now change her bed to mobile chair, and even though she felt her strength returning, she resisted the temptation to try and step off and stand by herself. Everything, it seemed, was about timing.

Today, John had another surprise. He succeeded in navigating Lilly's mechanical chair up a moderate incline and out a door into an open patio above the rooms where she had been healing. For the first time she could feel the air and sun's embrace without any sense of separation. The space was small and sat like a crow's nest atop a mast and offered a stunning panoramic view. He left her to attend to other matters.

A strong rail was all that stood between solid footing and a couple of thousand feet of open space. She opted not to approach it in her chair. Even from her position a sense of vertigo overwhelmed and exhilarated her.

Face upturned, she reveled in the late afternoon sun. A playful wind tugged at her hair, which she had let loose from all ties or bands. In spite of the ever-present sadness, she was almost happy, when suddenly her reverie was broken by the sense of being watched. She flinched. It felt as if a hand of ice had touched hers. Not ten feet away, looking out as she was, stood Simon, positioned strategically between her and the exit ramp.

Tall, slimly built, he was dressed carefully but almost too heavily for the day's warmth. His white buttoned shirt topped by a scarlet bow tie enhanced his features and dark hazel eyes. Oddly, while the wind swirled around her, it seemed reluctant to approach him. Simon spoke without turning, his voice surprisingly gentle.

"I am sorry if I startled you," he stated. "Don't be afraid!"

She let herself draw in a deep breath, relieved without a reason. "You did! I didn't even hear you, at all, and it . . . surprised me, that's all."

"I am like that. Quiet, that is. I don't draw a lot of attention, at least not directly. Where's the Collector?" he asked, turning with a smile toward her. "I assumed he would be with you, your ever-present guardian."

"I don't know," she said.

"It is just as well," the Scholar declared. "I wanted an opportunity to talk to you alone, if that would be all right?"

Lilly almost let her internal smile play on her lips but resisted. This man was a stranger and she needed her guard in place. But there was an aura of the dangerous and delicious about this one, and it felt good to be sought out.

"That's up to you," she offered. "We could call for John to join us."

It was a game, and she knew it and suspected that he did as well. He smiled and looked away, out in another direction and then back before speaking.

"Lilith . . ."

"Lilly," she interrupted. "My name is Lilly."

"Of course." He pursed his lips. "Regardless, you have been chosen as the Witness to Beginnings, and that is unimaginably significant. I am deeply honored to have met you, no matter what any of the others have said."

"What others? What have they said?" The flattery she'd enjoyed vanished, replaced instantly by insecurity.

Simon appeared to be embarrassed and quickly apologized. "I didn't mean at all to cast aspersions. I'm sure they mean well."

"Who?" she demanded.

"The others, the older ones."

"What did they say?"

"Well, for example, that you are just a child, which is not at all how I see you. However, they are accurate in pointing out that you are young and lack experience. But that is not the point I was attempting to make. I actually agree with them that you have not yet grasped your singular importance and the significant choices that lie ahead of you. It is my humble opinion that you are going to need some very real and present guidance."

"From you, I suppose?" Lilly was irritated at everyone, her general frustrations now finding a focus. Simon didn't answer.

"Why am I so *singularly important?*" she finally asked.

"Because you have the power to change history!"

The staggering potency of his declaration was almost too much to consider, but his demeanor was as intense as his statement.

"H-How?" she stammered.

"Lilith, you are the chosen Witness to Beginnings. Focus on what you were told last night. As the Witness, not only are you the photographer, you are also in the picture as an active participant and your choices can change everything, everyone's history."

Lilly was in such a whirlwind that she didn't bother to correct him again about her name. What he was saying finally made some sense. There was a purpose to her being here, being the Witness. What if he was correct? By affecting history, could she also change her own? If one altered Beginnings, would one not also change the Endings?

As quickly as the wave of possibilities lifted her, she dropped, the immensity of what she imagined too much.

"I thought I couldn't interfere," she said, then clapped a hand over her mouth.

"Not interfere, participate," Simon said. He didn't react to her outburst. "I can help. And God will give you wisdom. Why would God put you in this situation, if only to abandon you to failure? You can do this, Lilith. I believe in you."

That was the little encouragement Lilly hadn't realized she

needed, and taking a deep breath, she relaxed into her chair. He took a step toward her but maintained a distance she considered safe.

"So, what do I do now?"

Simon took another step closer. "We must get you to the Vault. It seems to be the key. My advice, for now, is trust your own instincts. You have been chosen because of who you are. The right choices will arise from your knowing who you are."

"Simon, my past is all a fog most of the time. I have flashbacks, but they're almost always terrifying." Even as she said it, Lilly realized that she was already allowing this man into places where no one else had been invited. "How do I find out who I am?"

"That, young woman, is why I brought you *my* gift." And with a flourish, Simon withdrew from somewhere in his coat an elaborately framed mirror with an artistically crafted handle.

"It's beautiful." Taking it, Lilly laid it on her lap. "Where did you get this?"

Simon hesitated, a fleeting look of grief momentarily darkening his eyes. "It belonged to my wife."

"Your wife?" Lilly felt a rush of compassion for this man and was also repelled by the thought of such a gift. She tried to hand it back. "I can't take this."

"But you must!" insisted Simon. "My wife . . . my wife is in a much better place. If she were here and knew who you were, she would want you to have it. Please. This is no ordinary mirror. This mirror reveals the truth, if you know its secret. Legend says that its power of reflection comes from the very first pond into which Adam gazed and saw his own face. Please take it."

Lilly hesitated, realizing that she hadn't seen her own face since arriving at the Refuge. Even in the archives of her memory there wasn't a face she was certain was her own. Lilly glanced at Simon, who nodded, encouragingly, so she lifted the mirror and peered into it.

Nothing. It was only a moving cloud of gray, shifting as if blown by the wind around her. She looked up at Simon, confused.

He smiled, playful and gentle. "I told you it had a secret." Reaching out, he put his hand on hers and turned it upward. His touch was cold, but in a way that was bracing against her sun-heated skin. It felt good and she didn't pull away.

"See this brilliant red stone?" he asked, and she inspected it more closely. "The one here where the handle meets the frame. When you put your right thumb on that stone and raise it to your face, this mirror will reveal the truth of who you are."

She moved her thumb over the stone.

"Before you do that, I must warn you." His voice was firm, his manner focused. He placed his hand strategically over hers. "This is not a painless process. You will see the truth, which can be very difficult and troubling. But you'll only fulfill your destiny if you commit wholeheartedly to believing what you see."

At that moment a shadow passed across them and Simon snatched the mirror from her hand and thrust it inside his coat. A massive eagle flew by, not a hundred yards away.

"Simon, what's wrong? It's just an eagle. Biggest eagle I have ever seen, but just an eagle."

"It is a thief!" he said. "They look to steal reflections for their nests. Those creatures make me nervous."

They watched the wind rider disappear into the distance before Simon slipped his gift back to her, his eyes still fixed on the sky.

"You must be on guard and keep it hidden. It is for you and you alone, a gift commensurate with your unparalleled importance."

He turned and again smiled, his intensity replaced by cordiality. From another pocket he pulled a cloth bag. "Here. When you place the mirror in this hood, both will be camouflaged by whatever they touch." As he lowered the gift into the cloth, both vanished, not entirely but almost. Against the sky it looked like a barely shimmering but warped window. He placed the bag on her lap and it absorbed the colors of her blanket, blending in completely. The only indication of its presence was its weight.

Lilly reached out and squeezed his hand. She felt conflicted, both repelled and attracted to this Scholar's words. The ease that she took for granted with John was absent, but in its place arose an entirely different spectrum of emotions. How was it that she could feel both scared and intrigued, hopeful and tentative? Simon brought up all these feelings and more.

"Simon," she began, "thank you. There are some things I need to tell you . . ."

Lilly intended to confess to this man everything she had hidden from the others, but as she opened her mouth to speak, the sound of whistling could be heard approaching from below. She turned toward the doorway to see John arrive, shielding his eyes as he left the darkness of the building.

Lilly glanced back at Simon and did a double take. He was

gone, evaporated or disappeared as completely as the mirror. Quickly she folded her gift inside her covers. The rush and flush of deception rose in her face. She hoped the sun would hide it.

"There you are!" exclaimed John. "I can tell by the pink on your cheeks that you have enjoyed your time up here. But I've come to collect you." He looked around, curiosity on his face. "Did I hear you talking to someone?"

Already feeling trapped inside growing duplicity, she expanded the lie slightly.

"Perhaps you heard me talking to the Invisibles?" she offered, waving her hand at the emptiness around her, and he laughed.

It wasn't an actual lie, she justified it to herself, *only a suggestion*. If John chose to accept it, that was his problem.

"Perhaps. Are you ready to leave your perch? The Scholars may join us for supper, and you should rest a bit first."

As they slowly descended, Lilly kept her hands folded on the mirror that lay hidden beneath. It felt ominous and intriguing, like a gift that lay unopened. It would have to wait.

"John, I have a favor to ask."

"Of course," he responded.

"I've been resting all afternoon. Do we have time, before the meal, to read me the remainder of Eden's story?"

"I certainly do." John was quiet for a moment. "Why the sudden interest?"

"I've been thinking that it might help me understand why I'm here and what I'm supposed to do. Up till now all the Adam and Eve stuff has been on the same shelf in my mind as fairy tales and make-believe, so I would like to hear it again, from the Scriptures. I guess I want to be prepared."

"Hmm." Once he'd parked Lilly in the receiving room, John excused himself, returned quickly with the large book, pulled up a comfortable chair, and opened it once again at the back.

"Let's see, where did we leave off?" He looked up at her and she nodded to start.

"This is the account of the heavens and the earth on the day . . . ," he began. As he read he would occasionally look up. Lilly was always intent and focused, listening and absorbing. A few times during the reading she asked him to repeat a line or phrase but other than that asked for no additional explanations.

He concluded with, "So God drove the man out and at the east of the Garden of Eden, God stationed two Cherubim and the flaming sword, turning in every direction and keeping the way back to the Tree of Life."

"Wow," Lilly stated, heaviness in her voice. "I don't think I ever heard the actual story before. It's beautiful and incredibly sad."

"Do you want to talk about it?" asked John, setting the book on the nearby table.

"Not now. I just want to let it sit for a while. Would you, please, take me to my room?"

He nodded, stood, and wheeled her out and down to her room. "I'll come get you when the others arrive. It won't be long."

"One more question?" she asked.

"Of course." He smiled. "It wouldn't be normal without one final question."

"Were you a Witness too?"

He looked surprised. "Lilly, I have no idea how you knew that."

"Someone said it a long time ago, while I was still flat on my back. I didn't mean to eavesdrop."

"That's all right. And, yes, it is true."

"What did you witness? Beginnings?"

"New Beginnings, I suppose you could say. I witnessed Eternal Man come as the second Adam."

"The *second* Adam?" she blurted, but then she held up her hand and shook her head. "Tell me later. Did you know what to do?"

"Do you know this makes five last questions so far?" He laughed, gently and easily, but then answered. "Yes, I knew I was a Witness, and that I would have to learn to trust. Everything else came as it came and I responded, some say not very well. But even after all these years I wouldn't do it differently."

"John, did you change the world?"

"I did, Lilly. I changed the world," he stated, with a smile. "It's what Witnesses do." Then he quietly closed the door.

Unfolding her covers, she sat looking into the mirror, the surface the same swirling cloud of gray. The promise that lay on her lap was an enticing invitation to truth, but it seemed dangerous too. Did she even want to know the truth about who she was?

She rolled her chair over to a dresser and opened the top drawer, placing the mirror next to her other gifts: Gerald's ring, Anita's key, and John's journal. Whatever truths her reflection held for her, they would have to wait a little longer.

•   •   •

AS PROMISED, JOHN SOON knocked and wheeled her down to the waiting meal. The seasonings of grilled meats and fresh vegetables teased her nose, but on Lilly's plate was a boring concoction of bland grains, herbs, and medicines. She didn't question any of it, her mind caught in things that seemed much more relevant.

Lilly sensed the prickle of his presence before he stepped into the room. Simon entered dressed the same as in the afternoon, still wearing his brilliant red bow tie.

"I've seen a similar tie only one other time," John stated. "Belonged to a character named the Caretaker."

Lilly laughed. "You have a friend named the Caretaker?"

"I suppose that in a twisted sort of way his relationship to me would be that of a friend, but I confess"—he grinned—"he is one friend that I have been avoiding, for quite a long, long while."

"A friend with a flair for fashion," suggested Simon, and both the men laughed.

"I have never understood that accessory," returned John. "Overstated. Not in your case, Simon. On you it seems fitting."

Possibly because of her heightened senses, Lilly believed every conversation had a subtext, an underlying intent and meaning that no one was directly addressing. Trying to deduce the layers was tiring, and soon she gave up.

Over dinner Lilly would occasionally glance in Simon's direction, but he never acknowledged her. He acted as if nothing had transpired between them. This made her doubt herself somehow. Had she imagined their chemistry?

As the meal ended, Lilly excused herself and John helped her to her room. A moment after he left, a night Nurse entered and assisted her with nighttime routines. As requested, she was left in a sitting position. She could make adjustments when ready.

Moving the chair to the dresser, she opened the top drawer and touched each gift in turn, her hand pausing on what appeared to be empty space, where she had laid the hidden mirror. Finally she picked up her journal and pen and began again.

I am more confused than ever about pretty much everything. Simon came to see me, alone, up in the Castle Patio (my name for it), at the very top of the Refuge. We almost got caught by John. Simon makes me feel alive, but I also feel bad about keeping more secrets, especially from John. When I start to think about it, I mean really think about it, it feels all wrong . . . so I try not to think about it. Lame!

Anyway, Simon gave me a magical gift, a mirror that will always tell me the truth about who I really am. It has a secret too but I haven't tried it yet. I'm scared and there really hasn't been the opportunity. What else . . . John and Simon talked about a friend of John's named the Caretaker, like I need more mystery people in my life. Actually, John seemed a little uneasy about the Caretaker, so "friend" might be overstated, to use a John word.

It feels like a big adventure is just beginning, but with Simon's help, I think I can do whatever I'm supposed to. I'm glad that Anita and Gerald and John will be with me, and I hope Han-el is real. It's all messed up, keeping secrets about what I saw, Eternal Man and Eve and Adam and Creation. I really miss Eve. Maybe she can give me some answers. Then, maybe I'm just crazy.

Lilly closed the clasp, her left thumbprint sealing it shut. Odd, it had not occurred to her before that the journal and mirror were activated in opposite ways. Her left thumb locked the journal's secrets; her right unlocked the mirror's.

A vague scent of incense and sage began to fill the room, as if a combination of herbs were smoldering close by. She dismissed the idea as exhaustion and placed the book and stylus into the drawer.

But her perceptions were changing; the room shifting. She felt giddy and unbalanced and then, as if strangely through the mists, she thought she heard the sound of Letty's humming at a distance.

Lilly was about to close the dresser when it attacked. From somewhere in the dark recesses of the drawer emerged the snake, striking directly at her face. Instinctively she shrieked. Her arm rose in time to catch the first blow, the serpent's fangs sinking deep into her arm above her wrist. She screamed again, flailing as the creature continued to slither out. It was massively long and began to wrap its coils around her, pulling her from the chair and onto the floor.

Rearing back, its hood fanned out, it poised again to strike when a brilliant, blinding light flashed through the room. The door burst open and shouts of voices followed. Lilly was paralyzed, unable to move or see, only her hearing unimpaired.

John was yelling directions and Lilly could make out other voices, including the Scholars and Letty.

"This is not a seizure." Worry was heavy in John's voice. "This is something else. Don't move her until she has been examined by a Healer."

She could sense him close as he whispered gently, "Lilly, can you hear me? Are you able to open your eyes?"

Frozen, she could not respond, could not feel his touch, but his presence filled her with relief.

"By the tears, I believe you can hear me, Lilly," John reported, his voice husky with emotion. "We have you, you are safe, and there is nothing you need to do right now."

"What happened?" Anita said from somewhere near.

He paused. "No one knows yet. Letty blasted through here like a whirlwind yelling something about the Refuge being compromised and then disappeared in a flash of light. We heard screaming and found Lilly lying on the floor frozen like a stone, but nothing else in the room seems disturbed."

"We're ready to move her to her bed," an unfamiliar voice said. "We need to raise her core body temperature, quickly."

Lilly felt nothing except a sense of being weightlessly euphoric. Whatever it was that owned her in this moment had some benefits. But slowly and unexpectedly, one feeling did return, as two holes of fire bored into her wrist where the serpent had buried its fangs. *Why haven't they noticed?*

"Simon, the top drawer of that dresser is open. Would you please tell me what's in it?" Frustration was evident in John's tone.

A moment later, Simon said, "There's nothing in this drawer except for what looks like a personal journal. It appears to be locked."

"That's all?"

"Nothing else."

Where were the other gifts? The ring, the key, and the mirror? Lilly could now hear the hammer of her heartbeat accelerating, the pulse extending from the bite and flowing into her body, drowning out the conversations. Panic replaced all sense of blissful floating. She tried to scream but couldn't.

"She's crashing," someone yelled. "Letty?"

And then another flash of blinding light and all went dark.

Nine

SHADOWS OF TURNING

Lilly, still frozen and immobile as stone, slowly opened her eyes. She stood in a glade facing away from the undulating walls of Eden. Before her, Adam's attention was on the serpent, but the snake was looking at Lilly as if not a heartbeat's moment had passed. The burning pain in her wrist continued to pulse, but the weight of Eve's hand on her arm seemed to lessen its intensity.

"We have to stop this," Lilly whispered through gritted teeth. "Something terrible is going to happen." The serpent's tongue flickered out and tasted the air as if searching. Lilly stepped back and deeper into the assurance of Eve's presence.

"No," Eve responded firmly. "It is not time."

The beast gave the young man its full attention once more.

"Since you are the son of God," it spoke respectfully, lowering its head in homage, "I will humbly and forever serve you."

Adam sat back on the ground, and with a rush of emotion Lilly could feel what he was experiencing. He was intrigued.

121

"How is it that you speak?" Adam asked, curious.

"All creation speaks," it answered. "Perhaps as you mature, I may impart such knowledge to you. Knowledge that will open up your eyes to see and ears to hear."

"Have you not been inside Eden?" Adam gestured toward the pulsating wall of energy. "There is knowledge there. I have a Tree of Knowledge."

"You have a Tree of Knowledge? That is good. With knowledge comes dominion," answered the serpent. "Like you, I was created outside Eden's wall—"

"Like me?" Adam laughed, and so too did Lilly, not understanding why. "I thought you didn't know who I am, and yet you know I was birthed outside Eden's boundary?"

"All creation was formed outside Eden's walls. Your breath and life may come from God, and my wisdom from creation, but we both were made from the same dust. Then you were placed within the garden."

"But not you. Is there death in you?" he asked the creature.

"There is no life or death in me, young Adam. I may be subtler and craftier than all other field beasts, but I too am a part of God's very Good creation."

"It lies," growled Lilly.

"It does not," whispered Eve. "Not until Adam lies."

Lilly could feel and see that Adam was entranced. Here was a creature of the field with whom he could converse. He was both mystified and elated.

"Why have you never been through Eden's gates?" he asked.

"Your domain is Eden. My habitation is the rest of creation," it stated.

Adam thought for a moment. "Adonai told me that I will expand Eden to include all creation."

"That is why I work: to prepare a way and place for you and your dominion."

Lilly knew that Adam thought this was fascinating and wonderful, to have an advocate already within creation.

"Are there more of your kind?" Adam wondered.

"There are many of my *kind* outside Eden. Are there more of yours?"

There had been no accusation in the serpent's question, but Lilly could feel it catch Adam by surprise. He appeared baffled and thoughtfully stared at the ground while the creature waited for his answer.

"No, there is no other of my kind," Adam finally admitted, a hint of sadness in his voice. "But tonight I will speak to Adonai to extend an invitation to you."

"If Eden is your domain, is it not your right to offer invitation without counsel? Why not clothe your childish weakness with your own authority? Perhaps this is a test of your maturing, to encourage you to act within your own right as son of God, since you *alone* are son of God?"

A frown crossed Adam's face. He stood and walked toward the snake until only inches separated them.

"I am created and born of Adonai's eternal being!" Adam sounded like he was trying to convince himself. "I live by the very Breath of God."

"God is not alone."

"*I am not alone!*" Adam shouted, but even as he did, Lilly knew that the question had taken root in his mind. "I have never been alone. I trust in Adonai's Love and Word. I am the son of Their delight."

Lilly was transfixed but could also feel Eve's agitation increasing, the grip on her arm tightening. Finally, the woman drew Lilly close and spoke directly into her ear.

"Now it is time. One of us needs to find Adonai, and tell Them this is happening."

"But don't They already know? Aren't They already here?"

"Yes, but we are also here and our participation matters. Go to Adonai, Lilly."

Something small had changed between them, like an unexpected note in a familiar song. "Don't you trust me, here alone with Adam?" Lilly asked.

"I trust Adonai." Lilly felt a stab of disappointment. She couldn't argue with Eve's response, but she felt as if she had been pushed away.

"I'm staying with Adam," Lilly decided. Immediately, her injured arm began to throb but she ignored it.

Adam meanwhile had fallen silent, feeling for the first time a hint of a new emotion, loneliness. Lilly knew it well and shared his pain, her heart breaking as she watched him turn to walk away, his head downcast.

"Before you go," the serpent called, "I have a gift."

Adam turned. From the nearby undergrowth the serpent pulled

a sack of twisted vines and woven reeds and tossed it at the young man's feet.

"What is this?" Adam withdrew an object and lifted it into the light.

"Pull it from its covering like a field creature from its hole. It is called a blade, and this one has a name: Machiara."

Lilly recognized it and shrank back. It was the same knife that the Anointed Cherub had used to sever Adam's cord and free him from the earth. As Adam drew it from its sheath, it flashed in the afternoon sun, causing him to squint and lose his grip. The blade sliced across his palm as it tumbled to the ground.

"What!" Adam yelped, watching the blood trickle down his hand. He glared at the snake. "What kind of gift is this? A gift to cause me pain?"

"A gift to bring you life. Machiara has been used but once."

"For what?" asked Adam.

"To separate the son of God from creation's hold."

Adam faltered. "But *I* am the son of God."

The serpent bowed its head toward Adam's face. "You bled then as well. Your life is in your blood, young son of God."

"In my blood? Then this blade might kill me." Rubbing his hand into the clay caked on his body, Adam stopped the flow from his cut. "Or do you mean to say that living blood can destroy death? That this blade has the power of both life and death?"

"Only the son of God can say such things. You have dominion. You will determine its purpose." Its tongue flicked out to touch the human's cheek. "Unless you are unworthy."

Lilly felt she was being swallowed inside Adam's thoughts, utterly alone and desperate to prove her own worthiness. She wished Eve would return.

"Me?"

"Yes." The snake moved away. "Once you were one with us, but Machiara separated you. Now it seems you are alone and in between, not God and not creation. Go eat of your Tree of Knowledge and return when you are worthy."

Again the young man faltered. "I cannot."

The serpent was silent. Adam returned the knife to its sheath and without another word, turned and walked toward Eden. Lilly also turned and watched him go.

"What are you and why are you here?" The snake was right behind her, and Lilly closed her eyes, too terrified to face it. The fire of its bite began to spread up her arm. The pounding in her head accelerated. But woven into the dread she felt was a subtle sweetness, an underlying haunting melody that called to her like the stirring of deep waters. Lilly was about to give herself to it when two familiar hands grasped hers. Startled, she looked up and into the eyes of Eve.

"Shhh. Lilly, listen. The snake cannot see you clearly but in some strange way knows you are here," the woman stated quietly. "Come. Follow me!" And by the hand Eve led Lilly away from the serpent and back toward Eden.

When they were at a distance, the girl finally exhaled. "Is it gone?"

"Yes!"

Lilly stopped and pulled away. "Mother Eve, where were you? You left me with that thing. And where is Adonai?"

Eve looked puzzled. "Lilly, we were present with you the entire time. Could you not see us?"

"No. I thought I was alone. I felt abandoned and completely on my own." Lilly lowered her head again and began to cry. "I was so scared and felt terribly lonely. It was awful."

"Lilly, you were not only feeling your own sorrows but Adam's. Dear one, you are also his daughter." Eve now sighed deeply and hugged the girl close. Her voice was hoarse with emotion. "Lilly, you felt the despair of Adam's turning; he has made the choice to believe he is alone. You are indeed your father's daughter."

"What happens now?" Lilly wondered as she regained control, a sense of emptiness lingering in her words.

"Tonight you will witness the first Great Sadness."

Eve was right. That evening there was none of the usual play or banter between Adam and God. Something had changed in the rhythm of their relationship, and Lilly could feel Adam withdrawing into turbulent thoughts. Although he and Adonai walked silently hand in hand as they moved into the dark, it seemed that Elohim was absent. Even when the breeze played with Adam's hair, he now thought it probably was only wind. The questions that had capsized his soul had become suspicions, and these slid into the center of an unspoken conclusion: he was alone.

Adam said nothing to Adonai of his visit with the serpent, and Lilly knew why. Unspoken secrets burned inside them both. Yes, she was her father's daughter.

"Would You love me . . . ," Adam finally began after a long silence, "if there was darkness within me?"

"My love for you will never be conditioned by anything, not

127

darkness or whatever may be found in you," replied Adonai, squeezing Adam's hand. "I know the truth of who you are."

"Would You turn away, if I would turn away?"

"No, my son. We will never leave you nor forsake you."

It was a comfort to hear it, and enough for this day. No further words were spoken as Lilly witnessed Eternal Man hold His son and weep while Adam slept.

"It has begun," said God, "the Sadness of the Turning," and God agreed as They comforted Each the Other.

"This is the first Not Good," lamented Adonai, "that Adam would choose to believe he is alone and live outside the only love that holds him day by day. We will fashion from him another power, another face-to-face, before his turning is complete."

"In the morning when he wakes," the Wind of God whispered, "we will begin the naming."

A sense of hopelessness threatened to destroy the fabric of Lilly's soul. "Are we forever lost?" she whispered to her mother.

From the night behind Eve, arms reached around them both. Lilly knew without turning that it was Adonai, and in His embrace her desolation retreated. He stood inside her darkness and pushed it back.

"Lilly, you are forever found," He whispered. "Forever found."

THE PALPABLE SENSE OF being held continued, even as Lilly woke to her familiar room in the Refuge. By the light she knew it was predawn, but she'd lost track of days. John was fast asleep in a chair next to her bed, and she smiled to see his hand resting on hers. For a time, she lay in the stillness, silent, letting the waves of emotions and their residue wash gently over her soul.

When she finally moved her hand, John woke. "Welcome back," he rasped. "You do make my life exciting, Lilly. How do you feel?"

"Okay. Maybe a little warm."

"You've been running a low-grade fever. We can't seem to figure out why." He stood and smoothed his rumpled shirt. "Lilly, do you remember what happened last night?"

"Yeah, I was bitten by a snake!"

John looked stunned. "A snake? Here? Where did it bite you?"

Lilly held up her right arm so he could see the two enflamed fang punctures. He looked closely, then raised the lights and looked again, then lowered her wrist to the bed.

"I believe you, but I don't see anything."

"What do you mean? It's right here." She pointed to the red spot that was growing larger. He touched the area and she flinched. When he glanced at her, his face was ashen.

"Not good!" he declared. "Letty told us the Refuge was breached, but we didn't know by what and we certainly don't know how." He turned toward the door, then stopped. "I need to inform the others. You're not safe here, and I won't risk another attack. We need to move you to the Vault, today."

"The Vault?"

"It is the safest place on this island. Where was the serpent when it bit you?"

Lilly pointed to the dresser. "The top drawer."

"Was there anything else in there?"

"The gifts the Scholars gave me. And my diary."

"Your book is still there but the rest are gone." He ran a hand over his beard. "This gets stranger and stranger."

John's uncharacteristic hesitancy was upsetting. Though still recumbent, Lilly felt increasingly faint. When he noticed her distress, he immediately shifted his expression from concerned to confident.

"Don't worry." He took her hand and squeezed. "The Scholars and I won't let anything hurt you again. You're too precious to us. Do you believe me?"

Did she? She closed her eyes, overwhelmed by doubt, the serpent whispering in her memory. *Perhaps you are unworthy.*

She managed to nod once.

Almost as quickly as John left, the Nurses quietly entered, assisting Lilly with her morning rituals. They took care not to touch her wrist, though when she asked if they could see her injury, they too shook their heads.

Once again alone, she rolled her chair to the dresser and opened it slowly, prepared to slam it shut.

As John had said, the only thing visible was her journal, which Lilly removed and placed on top. She felt along the bottom of the drawer. The mirror was still there! It blended invisibly into the wood. Placing it on her lap, she rolled her chair with its back against her door. This would give her extra time should she need it.

Pulling it from its hood, she could feel the mirror pulse to the rhythm of her heartbeat. *Am I worthy of being loved? Or do I deserve to die?*

Its surface was still a swirling gray. Hesitantly she placed her right thumb on the red stone.

"Ow!" She yanked her hand back. The mirror had pierced her thumb deep enough to draw blood, which the jewel now absorbed. As it did, the swirling surface changed, but her reflection was not what she had hoped.

It was partially the silhouette of a young woman's face, her own. Its jagged edges resembled chipped porcelain. But most of her face was covered by a mask of putrid lace, drooping like a rotting bridal veil, too sheer to hide her grotesque ugliness. The girl staring back at her was decaying and disgusting, damaged beyond any possibility of repair. Her vague smile twisted in seductive innuendo, one eye full of fiery hate, the other screaming shame.

Repulsed, Lilly dropped the mirror onto her lap. The surface returned to cloudy gray as she retched. Could this be the truth of her being? Was she at the core an evil monster?

Again she picked it up and placed her thumb on the stone. Again it drew blood, but this time she didn't care. She scrutinized the surface as it changed, but if anything it was even worse: a screaming accusation declaring she was worthless, nothing but damaged goods, irreparable and infected, a tease, a whore, a fake. Her mask had been removed to reveal the disease that was beneath. She felt horrified, utterly undone, and worst, exposed. Lilly screamed and screamed into her pillow until she again regained some semblance of control.

Jamming the mirror into its cover, she threw it back into the dresser, waiting until the sack disappeared before slamming it shut.

Lilly washed her face, then rolled her chair into the receiving room, grateful it was empty. For a moment she sat looking down through the window, the bright and cheerful world turned into mockery by the storms within. The urge to throw herself out was compelling. Would Adonai catch her if she fell? Would he even notice? The only reason anyone had ever showed care for her was because they needed something or she had completely fooled them. If they knew the truth . . .

But John had showed her how this window worked. It was covered not by glass but by flexible filaments, which like a balloon, resisted with increased pressure. It offered no way out. However, the Castle Patio had no such barriers and for a moment Lilly imagined throwing herself over its railing.

But John told her something else and with the simple touch of a button, she reversed the window to a full-length mirror. Lilly examined her reflection carefully. She had to look more intently, but this one also revealed the same truth as Simon's gift. Her eyes were too far apart, her nose too wide, her skin too blemished, her frame too skinny, and on and on. She mentally cataloged each flaw. Here was evidence of what had already been revealed. She was worthy of nothing but self-loathing.

Hearing a sound behind her, she quickly transformed the mirror back into a window.

It was Simon.

"I came to see if you were all right." His calm voice held enough concern to invite her into conversation.

"I looked in the mirror, Simon," she blurted. "I hate what I saw."

"I am sorry." Walking over to her, he put his hand on her shoulder. Lilly pulled away, disgusted by herself. "I tried to warn you that what you would see might be painful."

"It was way beyond painful. It was horrid and disgusting," Lilly muttered. "I am a monster."

"Lilith," he began, drawing up a nearby chair to sit next to her. "What you saw is the truth of your being and why God has chosen you to be the Witness. It is because of who you are that you are uniquely qualified for God's purpose."

"Uniquely damaged," she retorted, to which he offered no response. "Am I supposed to be grateful, or honored, because I am the perfect piece of crap that God can use? Frankly, I think I am done with being used, by God or anyone."

Simon was quiet for a moment. "Then take control of your own destiny. Make your own choices. Change history. If for no one else, do it for yourself. I believe you are the one we have been waiting for, the one who can change Beginnings."

"How can I change Beginnings? I barely have control over my own body." Lilly was infuriated and despairing. The day had barely dawned and she already felt exhausted. Her arm was burning almost to her elbow.

"As the Witness, you can change Beginnings. You must stop Adam!"

"Stop Adam?" she snapped. "From what?"

"Through one man, Adam, sin entered the world." He sounded as if he was quoting something she should have known. "You must stop Adam from turning."

"Stop Adam from turning?" She shook her head. "It's too late."

"What?" Simon looked shocked. "Too late?"

"There you are!" Anita entered the receiving room from the direction of Lilly's room. Simon quickly removed his hand and stood. "Lilly, I was looking for you, but it seems you are already in good hands."

"Seems everyone finds me eventually." Lilly was relieved by the diversion but couldn't muster a smile.

"Clever girl." Anita chuckled. "John told us we need to proceed quickly to the Vault, and I wanted to make sure you are able. Simon, John has asked if you would also go with us."

"Of course. I would be honored." He paused. "If that is all right with you, young woman?"

She nodded without looking at him.

"We would welcome the company." Anita turned to the girl. "Lilly, let's get you some food. How do you feel? John told me about the attack."

"Not the best, but I'm ready to get out of that snake's range."

"Understandably! Those creatures have always disturbed me." With that Anita wheeled Lilly toward the kitchen, leaving Simon looking out the window.

"I'VE EATEN ENOUGH," LILLY declared, pushing herself back from the table. The Scholars too had eaten their fill and wiped their chins, satisfied. John was lost in thought, his food untouched.

"You worried about something?" Lilly asked him as the others cleared the table.

134

"*Worried* is probably not the right word. Concerned. A little anxious, as if there is something tugging at the corners of my thoughts but I can't quite pull it from the shadows. I have never been one who liked hidden things."

"Should I be worried?" she asked.

"Not at all." He smiled. "I doubt this is about you, at least not directly. I think it has more to do with my own choices regarding trust."

"Trust? You?" she punched his arm lightly, wishing he would snap out of his mood and cheer her up. "Do you trust me, Finder?"

"Completely!" The simple declaration surprised her and slipped past her inner guard.

"Why?" she asked.

John looked into her eyes. "Because of who you are."

Her efforts at lightheartedness vanished. "I'm a piece of trash that washed up on your beach."

"No." John looked her in the eyes. "I'm not talking about who you think you are, but who you *truly* are."

I know who I am, she thought. Would John trust her if he knew the secrets she was keeping? She felt caught in the crossfire between hidden things and her sense of integrity.

It was Gerald who unwittingly interrupted her from blurting out secrets. "So we're off to the Vault, not the Library?" He sounded a bit disappointed.

"The Library will have to wait for another time," said John.

"Where exactly is this Vault?" asked Lilly.

"Down in the depths of the Refuge, beneath the ocean's

surface," replied John. "It will take only a couple of hours to descend, but once there, we'll stay. It has sleeping rooms and all the amenities we need."

"How long are we going to be there?"

"As long as it takes. At least a few days would be my guess," responded John. "Until we are certain the Refuge is safe. The Vault is where you'll experience and record what you witness." Then he chuckled. "Once you get there, you might want to move in permanently. It's that sort of place."

"Let's do it," agreed Anita, and the other Scholars nodded.

They dispersed to their rooms to gather a few things, putting them into travel sacks. Lilly didn't have much, some clothing and toiletries, her diary and stylus, and of course, the mirror. She wondered if her key and Betrothal ring might have been shuffled to the corners but didn't have the courage to run her hand into the shadows. John said they were gone, and she felt their loss more acutely than expected, as if the fault were hers. Maybe it was.

She took a moment to write a quick entry in her journal.

I don't even want to write about what I saw in Simon's mirror. I can't. John, Anita, Gerald, Simon, and I are about to go down to the mysterious Vault. From what John told me, Letty showed up last night and saved me from the snake. I feel safer when she's around, even as grumpy as she can be at times. My arm really hurts where I got bit, but it seems I am the only one who can see it. We're in a hurry to get to the Vault because John believes me. Maybe that's not true either.

I'm scared about the Vault, maybe because I haven't told

anyone my secrets, not even Simon. What will happen when they find out I've already been Witnessing? Will I mess up the process? Why can't I tell? John says he trusts me, and I don't think he's lying. But I'm good at fooling people. That's what liars do. Gotta go.

Ten

THE DESCENT

John led the way down multiple ramps, the hallways narrowing, the blue iridescence brighter, the crash of sea on sand eventually above them, sometimes distant and occasionally disappearing. Simon volunteered to push Lilly's chair, and she enjoyed his close proximity.

As they descended, Lilly peppered the others with a barrage of questions. The Scholars seemed to love this. Unlike John, who seemed to hold ideas lightly with open hands, the Scholars had a certainty in their perspectives about most things. And when they didn't, they seemed eager to find one.

"We are now into the storage levels," John announced as they passed a webbing of halls. "This is where we keep the things that wash up on the shore, including yours, Lilly. You arrived on the eleventh day of the first month, and because we thought from the records that you were most likely fifteen years old, the number of your chamber is one-eleven-fifteen. Simple to remember. We

139

took an impression of your hand so only you or a Collector could open it."

It was a vast labyrinth of passageways and catacombs. Lilly didn't want to think about the mass of rock and ocean above her, which only increased as they descended. The passageway filled with echoes of their footfalls, and distant thunderous booms of surf on land still occasionally reverberated. Air flowed clear and clean, but that didn't lessen the sense of oppression hovering over Lilly.

"Tell me again what the Ages of Beginnings are?"

Gerald answered. "The term refers to events surrounding the Creation, primarily first things and first times. The roots of everything that exists today and—"

"Wait. Was there a *before* the Beginning?"

"Of course! If there was not a *before* the Beginning, there could never have been a Beginning."

"I suppose that makes sense," she said. "I just always thought the world exploded out of nothing."

"Not even nonsense could explode from nothing. Nothing can't create something, or anything." Gerald raised his eyebrows. "*No thing* would be no energy, no time, no space, no information. Nothing. Since you are Witness of Beginnings—"

"It's all too big for me." She sighed. "I don't understand and I feel foolish."

Anita laughed. "It is too big, for all of us. It seems that even the foolishness of God builds extraordinary purpose into the ordinary. Miraculous and mysterious."

"In my case, *ordinary* would be an improvement," Lilly muttered.

"Truth be told, dear one," Anita responded, "no human is ordinary."

By the next break and rest, Lilly had formed another question.

"So, the something that created the world—that was God?"

"Yes," answered John. "Creation was crafted inside God. Specifically, inside a Someone, Adonai."

Her mind made a connection and it escaped her mouth before she could stop it. "You mean Eternal Man, right?"

Four shocked expressions turned toward her. "Uh, I must have heard that or read about it somewhere. I think we should go."

Anita gave her a quick hug before they all headed down another set of ramps. Leaning in, she whispered, chuckling, "My dear, that was a surprise. Eternal Man, indeed! What else are you not telling us?"

Ignoring the comment, Lilly asked another question. "So God created Adam in Adonai. Does that mean that man was made inside Eternal Man?"

"Created and birthed," offered Anita. "To say God *gave birth* would probably be more appropriate."

"So you knew Adam was a baby?" she asked.

"Knew? Of course Adam was a baby, why would he be otherwise?"

"I thought God created him, you know, a full-grown man."

Her companions laughed.

"Mythology is responsible for many odd ideas," mumbled Gerald. "Did your Storytellers think that Adam was created as a young man with no capacity, a brute ready to be programmed?"

It sounded silly to her now and she quickly asked another question. "If he was just a baby, what did They feed him?"

"What you feed any baby," responded Anita. "Adonai nursed him, of course! If God could birth a baby, you think They couldn't feed him? The very reality of nursing an infant had to originate in God's being, don't you think?"

"I suppose so, but that would mean that Adonai has . . ."

"Breasts?" John finished her sentence. "Of course They have breasts, and full of milk according to the Scriptures. Mother's milk."

John underestimated the time it would take to descend with Lilly's chair. Nearly three hours had passed before they arrived at a dead end, a wall of stone smooth as glass.

They all abruptly stopped except John, who didn't hesitate. He walked straight into the wall and vanished.

"It's an illusion." His voice came from the other side. "Just act like it isn't there. If you hesitate, it will hurt."

"A little warning would have been nice," retorted Lilly.

"I forgot. Old habits of solitude."

Lilly found it difficult to ignore her perceptions. The roadblock looked impervious in spite of her seeing John walk right through it. When she reached out and touched it, it was firm and solid under her fingertips. She rapped on it, and the sound echoed down the corridor.

"That won't help," John called. "Hold on." He reappeared right in front of her. "You'll have to ignore it. We're creatures of 'seeing is believing,' but after you've done it a time or two, it's as easy as falling."

She hesitated.

"Here, watch me," offered Simon, who walked through the wall as if it were mist. The others followed him.

"Tell you what," encouraged John, taking a kerchief from a pocket. "Let me tie this around your eyes, spin you about, and then at some point get you through the wall."

It sounded like a good plan, but the thought of being blindfolded troubled her.

"Can I just cover my eyes with my hands?"

He returned the hankie to his pocket.

"Perfect," he said. "As long as you keep your eyes shut tight. Even peeking a little might result in a bloody nose."

"I promise." She kept her word.

"Ready? Okay, now I'm spinning you round and round this way, and then round and round that way . . . and then I am going to push you a little ways back in this direction . . ."

Lilly felt a whoosh of wind skim her arms, and mist that wasn't wet kissed her cheeks. She squealed as she opened her eyes to a hallway of mirrors—infinite reflections of herself and the others.

"That was kind of fun!" she yelped.

"I know!" he declared like a joyful child.

"Though you tricked me," she accused, laughing.

"No tricks," he said. "You can always trust me to do exactly what I say I'll do." He grinned at her.

A floor-to-ceiling mirror behind them marked the wall through which they had entered. More mirrors lined the entryway, and a large but cozy living space opened up before them. One side of the room was flanked by the ocean. Lights penetrated at least a hundred feet of water, enhancing corals, sea plants, and fish of every size, shape, and color. The membrane on this window space surely separated them from tons of pressure.

Lilly had no way of telling how deep they were beneath the surface, except that she could barely see shards of light reaching down from above.

"This is the Vault?" she asked. It was nothing she had expected.

"Not quite! These are the living quarters. The Vault is right down that hall at the other end of this suite." John pointed. From where they stood they could see a massive door looming at the far end of a wide hall. "I'll show you in the morning. For now, choose a room for sleeping. We'll eat and rest today."

There were about a dozen interconnected rooms here—sleeping, bathing, and sitting rooms, as well as a kitchen and a pantry.

Lilly noticed Gerald and Anita choosing their room together. As they disappeared, she grabbed John's arm.

"Are they an item?"

"An item?" His perplexed frown was followed by a huge smile. "I suppose, if being married for many, many years qualifies as an item?"

"I had no idea. I thought that they were just friends and work-mates. Married?"

"Lilly," he said kindly, "from what I understand, married persons can actually be good friends, and some can even work together."

"Have you ever been married?" Lilly asked.

"Me? No. I've befriended many women, all extraordinary and a few beastly, but marriage is not for me."

"Beastly?" Lilly grinned.

He grunted, rolling his eyes. "One in particular, the most

manipulative human being I ever met. Quite attractive, though, in a garish sort of way." He let the distant memory take him for a moment. "But that, dear Lilly, is another story for another time. Go find a room that suits you. The *item* will be returning soon, and you can ask them all your questions about the mysteries of marriage."

As she turned to wheel herself away, John stopped her. "How's that arm?" he asked.

"It's better," she lied.

He nodded and they parted ways to settle into their rooms.

Lilly dropped her little knapsack in one with a bed and canopy. She hid the mirror in the dresser before returning to the central area. The three Scholars were waiting, and soon John joined them.

After checking the status of Lilly's fever, which had neither risen nor fallen, John grunted and exchanged an inscrutable glance with Anita.

"Now, we eat," he said, leading them into an alcove where food and drink were spread on a table with five settings. It was a feast of fruits and vegetables, crackers and cheese, and many sauces and dips, some chewy while others smooth as cream. Water, juices, tea, and coffee were plentiful.

Lilly was pleased to have an appetite, and doubly happy when John indicated she should sample whatever she liked. She chose a plump bunch of red grapes.

Knowing that Gerald and Anita were married somehow deepened Lilly's appreciation for the integrity of their friendship. She watched these two at ease in each other's presence, respectful of their differences. One and then the other would defer, as if they had learned to navigate a secret language.

145

As John explained to Simon and Gerald about the room's antiquities, Lilly nudged Anita.

"Married, huh?"

"Of course, dearie," she responded, "I thought you knew. It wasn't meant to be a secret, but I can see it made for a good surprise. I do love him, this Gerald person."

"What is . . . love? I don't think I know what that is." Her question slipped out easily.

Anita touched her arm in a motherly way. "It's both mysterious and simple. Gerald's good is more important to me than mine, and mine is more important to him than his. We each own this conviction individually, not expecting it to be reciprocated. Healthy love looks different from one second to the next because it's built on respect for self and for the other. A lot of work, though, getting to know someone."

"How do you know what that is—the good for the other?" Lilly asked.

"Ah,"—Anita patted her arm—"that is a profound question, dear one, a deep mystery of all relationships. Only God Who is Good can reveal what the good is, and often He does that only in the moment such revelation is needed. Part of the great dance."

"As I said," muttered Lilly, under her breath, "I don't understand what love is."

"That's what your head is saying," Anita said gently, touching the girl's cheek. "But I am convinced that you already know, somewhere inside you."

• • •

Turns out we won't go into the mysterious Vault until tomorrow. I'm supposed to "record" the stuff I witness but I don't know how that works. It's all messed up, keeping secrets about what I saw, Eternal Man and Eve and Adam and the Creation. I lied outright to John today. What if it's true that I have lost my mind? In some ways that would be easier. I would have an excuse.

Simon told me I had to stop Adam from turning, and I told him it was too late and he looked really shocked. I did tell him that I looked in the mirror, but I didn't tell him what I saw. Still don't want to talk about it, or write about it. I'm trying to figure out how accepting what the mirror showed me as the truth of my being will help me change history. Change history . . . right . . .

Lilly looked up at the glorious ocean wall that filled one side of her bedroom, watching the water dance with the anemones on the coral. The peaceful scene seemed to taunt her. She added a final note to the diary.

Adonai said that I am forever found. When I think of how Anita and Gerald love each other, I think maybe that love is what it means to be found. All I know is that since I saw Adam turn and looked into the mirror, I feel forever lost.

• • •

SOMEWHERE IN THE STOREHOUSE of the soul everything is kept, and while access to remembering may be restricted, history continues to find a way to make itself known.

In the space that night between sleep and wakefulness, Lilly's past rudely emerged. These memory spasms were vicious and violent, lightning strikes that destroyed her connections to reality, to love, to wholeness: A book being read to a young girl by a woman—her mother? The smash of a fist across the girl's face, blood blinding as she reeled, dark shadow men stalking her, prowling with razor-sharp fingernails and foul breath, a pressure on her chest that squeezed until it paralyzed, brief bursts of trains and warehouses and screams, crouching in the dark on a dirty floor, hoping to go unnoticed. She screamed without a voice, and then watched helplessly: a little girl dragged into a room, and the door slammed shut. Safety dissolved into a tiny circle of darkness inside her heart, her only refuge from the terrors.

Her eyes opened to Anita, sitting next to the bed, holding Lilly's hand, eyes closed and lips barely moving as if in silent prayer.

Lilly squeezed her hand. "Hi," she rasped.

Anita squeezed back, opening her eyes with a tired smile. "Hi, little one. Go back to sleep. I'll be right here."

A rush of fatigue rolled over her and Lilly let it sweep her gently away.

She floated on Anita's upturned hands into another dream that was not a dream. Now Eve was sitting beside her, but Lilly's blanket didn't register her weight.

"I'm so glad you're here," Lilly exclaimed, and turned her head into the woman's shoulder.

"I am too," Eve acknowledged.

"Mother Eve, what am I going to do? I hate not telling them, and I don't know why I don't. I get close, like I'm at the edge of a cliff, and just before I jump, I get terrified and hide."

Eve was quiet before answering softly. "Lilly, hiding behind secrets is like walking across a frozen lake as it melts beneath your feet. Each step is filled with fear."

"I don't know how else to try and get across."

"Keeping secrets is a dangerous endeavor. You must learn to think like a child. Children don't keep secrets until someone convinces them that the keeping is safer than the telling. It almost never is."

"But I'm not a child!" Lilly could not stop her own internal reaction.

Eve hugged her. "Lilly, we are all children. But once persuaded that secrets will keep us safe, we slowly fade into our hiding places and forget who we are. It is no wonder that the shadow-sickness grows in isolation."

"So am I going crazy?" Lilly asked, exasperated. "Am I talking to myself in a padded cell somewhere? Are you the result of medications or mental illness? What happened to me? Which world is real? And everyone talks to me like I'm important and I matter, but I can't meet their expectations!" She knew she was venting and didn't expect a response. It was a relief to talk out loud about things she was avoiding, and she was grateful that Eve let her talk without expressing impatience or discomfort.

"I have seen this all before," Eve finally said, "but not with you."

"Seen what exactly? A girl with someone's else's foot?" Lilly lifted the hem of her skirt to look at it again. "Or someone stuck between worlds with creatures she couldn't imagine? Or a Witness to the very first moments of creation . . . ?"

Eve chuckled. "No, many of these are a first for me too. I was referring to having seen the destiny of the entire creation, of man and beast and spirit—even the very being of God—entrusted to another girl, about your age."

"Really?" Lilly was genuinely surprised. "So I'm not the only one? I'm not alone?"

"You have never been alone, dear one."

Lilly looked down at her hands, lying open on her lap, and let her hair fall down around her face. "That's not what I was asking, but . . ." When she spoke, barely above a whisper, her voice broke. "Then why didn't—why didn't God protect me?"

And there it hung, the question.

Eve let it hang there, suspended and ominous, the question uttered by a billion other voices. It rose from grave sites and empty chairs, from mosque and church, from offices, prison cells, and alleys. Tattered faith and battered hearts lay broken in its wake. It demanded justice and begged for miracles that never came.

Eve touched Lilly's shoulder and the girl again felt warmth spread out inside her. "I have no answer in this moment that would satisfy you, Lilly. No words that would knit together what is wounded in your soul and in your body."

Lilly closed her eyes but refused to cry, instead allowing the tingling comfort to climb into her tired body and calm the rising fever. Despite hearing no answers, she felt safe in this mother's presence. Minutes passed before she spoke.

"I feel like I'm climbing a mountain that has no top. I'm barely holding on to the rock wall. I'm scared, and everyone expects me to make it. If I don't, it's like all that's wrong in the world is going to be my fault." Lilly leaned her face into the woman's neck and whispered, holding back emotions. "What if I can't do this and I let go? Or what if I jump, will God still catch me?"

"He will, but to you it will feel as though you hit the ground."

Again they were quiet for a time.

"Mother Eve, do you know how this turns out for me?"

"No, neither of us has been here before. But I am not afraid."

"Did it turn out okay for that other girl? The one my age?"

"Yes! It did. Lilly, her participation changed everything."

Everything. It was a big enough hope for the rest of the night. Lilly slept at peace, no vivid dreams or hallucinations, no questions worrying her mind.

But much later, with no way to tell the hours that passed or even the time of day, she snapped awake, alarmed by something crawling up her arm.

Eleven

THE VAULT

Lilly almost snatched her hand away before realizing it was a furry little forest marsupial sniffing at it, barely visible whiskers tickling her arm. Carefully, so as not to scare it, she reached her other hand across to stroke its back, but as she gently touched it, the animal screeched and bolted into the underbrush.

That was weird, she thought. The inflamed fang marks pulsed above her wrist. Could this creature have sensed the poison that was slowly spreading in her body? It was stranger still that any animal was aware of her at all, her presence here usually intangible and masked.

It only took a moment to get her bearings; she was somewhere inside Eden, but alone: no Eve, and no sense of any Invisibles. Lilly walked toward a rock outcropping, overlooking a broad and busy plain. Adam stood pointing down, surrounded by Fire and Wind and next to Eternal Man.

What are they doing? Lilly wondered. She stopped, close enough to hear. Adam, sensing her presence, turned and looked straight through her, as if trying by concentration to give substance to an apparition. He was unsuccessful.

"This is the closing of the final day of naming," Adam stated sadly, as if to her, "and I have yet to find a face-to-face other."

Spinning away, the young man raised his fists and screamed fury into the sky, one word. It reverberated and echoed back as time and place and beast stood still.

"Alone!"

Lilly felt it penetrate her to the core, shredding her with hopelessness, the resolute declaration of the lost.

Adonai reached out to touch His son, and Adam flinched, his head bowed, hands covering his eyes, embarrassed by his weakness. Lilly tried to move, to take a step toward him, but it was as though her feet were mired in unyielding clay. And then she heard what she thought was Adam's voice say something completely unexpected.

"Lilith? Lilith?"

"Lilly? Lilly!" It was Anita, shaking her arm. Jolted out of her vision, she found herself staring into the older woman's expression of focused concern.

"Anita?" Lilly looked around and quickly tried to mask her absolute confusion. They were all at breakfast and looking at her, some with silverware frozen halfway to their mouths and she with no idea how she got there, no memory of the morning, of waking, or of anything except terrors in the night and Adam's naming.

"I'm sorry," she stammered, scrambling for an excuse. "I was lost in something John read to me the other day." They seemed to accept this explanation, and everyone relaxed.

"Lost!" Anita exclaimed. "I think lost is an understatement. More like gone. Dear one, you had us worried for a moment! Whatever were you thinking about? It must have been important."

The woman's relief gave Lilly the moment she needed to collect her thoughts. "John read to me the story of Beginnings and I was thinking . . . who is Lilith?"

"Lilith?" blurted Simon, almost choking on his food. She thought she saw him barely shake his head, as if in warning. The others looked equally shocked.

"You didn't hear that name from anything I read to you!" avowed John.

Lilly faltered. "Then what's the deal with her?"

"Sheer rubbish, my dear girl," stated Gerald, almost sternly. "Mythology at its most insidious. Utter nonsense. Where did you ever hear of Lilith?"

"I'm not sure?" Lilly replied. "Maybe in a dream?"

"Maybe in a nightmare!" Gerald was as animated as Lilly had ever seen him. "Or a snakebite."

"Gerald, calm yourself." Anita reached and patted his arm. "I think you may be upsetting the poor girl. Obviously, she doesn't know who Lilith is."

"My apologies, dear girl," Gerald sputtered. "No intentions whatsoever to upset you or fault you for bringing that . . . thing . . . up in conversation. Please forgive me for my fervor."

155

"Of course, Gerald," Lilly stated. "What is it about this Lilith that has you so riled up?"

"There is a myth," resumed Gerald, calming himself but focused, "about Lilith. According to the tale, which I take no stock in whatsoever, she was the first wife of Adam."

"Adam had more than one wife?" Now Lilly was surprised.

"No, of course not," emphasized Gerald. "It is a myth. Eve was Adam's only wife."

"So in this story, was Lilith good?"

"In most of the versions, she was anything but good. An aberration of nature, part serpent and part woman, a terrifying moon goddess that haunted the night." Gerald had his hands raised like claws to emphasize his point.

Again, Lilly saw the hint of warning in Simon's look along with another slight shake of his head. She abruptly changed the subject.

"So what about the part where Adam named the animals? Why was that important?"

Simon was the first to respond. "Excellent question. Naming is of great significance. God brought the beasts of sky and field to Adam to ascertain their essential nature. In naming them, Adam established his dominion."

"True," inserted Gerald, "but Adam was in a desperate search for a counterpart, an 'other' to relate to him face-to-face. Someone or something to assure him that he was not alone—though he never was."

"What Gerald is trying to say, Lilly," Anita said, "is that if one is seeking a face-to-face relationship, naming is a futile exercise.

Dominion cannot carry you there. There was no counterpart in all creation for Adam, and God patiently let him prove it. His counterpart was—"

"Within him!" Lilly connected the dots. "Eve is his counterpart and she has been inside him since Creation."

"Exactly!" declared Anita. "And Adam is inside God; God Who has never been alone. Face-to-face-to-face-to-face . . ." And she swirled her butter knife in circles in the air to emphasize her point.

"Naming is still rightful dominion," stated Simon, and from there the conversation turned scholarly and Lilly disengaged, again wondering how she had gotten from her bedroom to breakfast and bewildered by the hornet's nest she had stirred up with the mention of Lilith.

John, who had been serving and clearing the table, announced that the Vault was waiting, if they were ready. Although Lilly's temperature was still elevated, which continued to concern John, she played it off as nothing. The reality was that every time she moved her arm, jolts of pain like tiny electric shocks exploded in her wrist and elbow. She could tell the venom was spreading toward her shoulder. But it seemed easier to downplay her pain than take the chance that the opportunity to do her part, whatever that might be, would again be postponed.

Having convinced them all was well, Lilly soon faced the goal of their adventures, which waited only feet away. The entry door was substantial and looked impenetrable, without a visible knob. Symbols were carved deeply into its surface, as if etched by ancient artists, each precise and detailed.

"What do you see, Lilly?" asked John, wheeling her almost close enough to touch. "Can you describe it to us?"

It was a strange request, but when Lilly looked at the others, they too were waiting expectantly.

"Well, look for yourself." She traced it with her hands in the air. "Here is a perfect circle stretching from side to side, so deep that it looks as if what's inside is hung suspended rather than an actual part of the door. Even this close I can't tell it's not. The circle is divided from side to side and top to bottom into four sections by these wooden beams. Each of the four spaces holds an intricate carving, some kind of symbol or image." Lilly recognized two of them instantly but started with the others.

"This one in the bottom left quarter is a pyramid mountain with the staring eye."

"You are able to see the One Mountain?" Anita sounded astonished.

"Uh, yeah." Lilly hesitated as if she had done something wrong. "I mean, look, it's right here."

"No, dear girl, you don't understand. None of us see the same thing when we look at this wood. You are the only one who sees what you do."

"Is that bad?" she asked, confused. "To see this mountain?"

"It is neither bad nor good," said Gerald. "It is what it is, but that you can see the One Mountain is so unlikely as to stagger the mind. What else?"

Lilly looked more closely. How could they not see the mountain? She reached out to touch the eye, but Anita grabbed her hand and yanked it away.

"Don't!" she commanded, and Lilly turned to her, perturbed.

"You're freaking me out! What's going on? I was just checking to see if it was real or my imagination," she fumed.

"If you had touched it," Anita stated firmly, slowly releasing Lilly's hand, "it would have pulled you in. Where it might take you none of us knows, nor would we know how to get you back."

"Really?" She examined it more closely, leaning in for a better look. "It just looks like a door with fancy artwork."

"It is a portal," offered John. "While each of the quadrants is unique to the person looking, we all see the circle and the cross. If you touch any of the four spaces, each will take you to a different destination."

"Wow, so you can't see this?"

Their silence was her answer.

"So in the lower right, down here," continued Lilly, making sure her fingers didn't get too close to the carved surface, "there is a figure eight on its side . . ."

"Infinity," blurted Gerald, then he grinned apologetically. "It is the symbol for infinity, in case you didn't know."

Something about the symbol drew Lilly's attention. "At the center where the two ovals of infinity meet is a snake's head, and it's swallowing its own tail . . . forever?" Involuntarily, she shuddered.

"Go on," Anita instructed, her tone serious and focused.

"Up here"—Lilly pointed toward the upper left—"is Adam . . ." She caught herself. "I mean, a carving of a man who possibly represents Adam. He is on his knees looking down at the dirt that he is scooping up in his hands. He's naked, like the woman in the upper right, who might represent Eve? She is turned toward the man, and her hands are outstretched, empty palms raised as if holding something precious." As best she could, Lilly took the same posture in order to show them what she meant.

"Astounding!" exclaimed Gerald.

"If there had been any doubt about you being the Witness to Beginnings," Anita said, "it has been completely erased."

"Because I can see a door?"

"Because of what you are able to see *on* the door," emphasized Simon.

"So now what?" asked Lilly.

"We enter," uttered John, a weight of importance in his tone. "This is the entrance to the Vault. Shall we proceed?"

"How?" asked Lilly.

He smiled, lifted his hand, and placed it on the very center of the portal. Without a sound it swung open, slowly and majestically.

"Sometimes"—John grinned—"you only need to touch the center of the cross, where everything comes together."

The area they stepped into could have been featured in a magazine of high culture and taste, as a richly appointed courtroom or opulent hotel. Its crafted woods and array of objects placed strategically by superb artistic decorators created an exotic impression.

"Wow!" Lilly exclaimed. "Not what I expected. I was thinking more like a big safe or something."

"There's a small larder and additional resting areas that way." John took on the role of tour guide showing off a prized property.

"And four special rooms over here, each with its own specific purpose. I'll show you."

He ushered them into what looked like an observatory. "The Map Room!" he announced. "These aren't walls exactly, but space in motion: countless stars and galaxies, constellations, giants and dwarfs, and tiny asteroids and comets drifting around and so forth."

Each of the two long walls offered an overwhelming view into completely different places in the cosmos. It felt like everything was moving and Lilly had to concentrate to keep from toppling out of her chair.

"Takes a moment," John reassured her, "like the first time at sea on a sailing ship. There is a rhythm to it, and once you move with and not against it, it will settle down."

"I've only heard stories of these places," disclosed Gerald. Anita, outlined by a flare of some sort, was simply shaking her head in amazement.

"Oh, look, Gerald! Pods!" she squealed, pointing to a row of seven emerald orbs, each about the size that would fit comfortably in a palm.

"Don't touch, please!" said John. "That's a warning, not a command," he added, as if he had surprised himself.

"Moving along, why don't we make our way down there to the far wall?" Whether they got there by walking or gliding, she wasn't certain. Simon pushed Lilly until they were in front of what looked more like a typical map. It was the layout of an enormous complex, and it took a moment for Lilly to realize what it represented.

"This is a map of the Refuge!" she exclaimed. The Refuge was huge, much bigger and more sprawling than she would have guessed, almost like a city. She could make out the upper rooms where she had recovered from the tragedy, and it even showed the ramp and staircase to the Castle Patio where Simon had given her the mirror.

But what amazed her most was the subterranean expanse. The levels stretched out under nearby hills and valleys, and maybe even to the boundaries of the purple mountains.

While the view of star systems had been too big to comprehend, this map gave her a new perspective of the Refuge's scale. She felt small and astonished.

John showed them their location in the Vault, barely below the surface of the ocean. Then he touched the screen with his thumb and index finger, and the map expanded.

Now John moved to the adjacent wall, where a row of ten small triangles outlined in crimson red was mounted on the wall. Lilly realized that she had seen similar triangular, empty spots in the walls of the Refuge. She had thought they were lighting or temperature controls.

"With these"—he indicated the triangles—"we can instantly travel anywhere in the Refuge."

"Really?" Lilly exclaimed about the same time Anita let out an "Oh, my!"

"I have never heard of this," Simon muttered. "How does it work?"

"If you touch one of these travel pieces to a triangle on the map, you'll be transported there. The piece will return to the Map

Room within ten minutes. If you desire to return with it, you have to find a return receptacle for your triangle wherever you are before the ten minutes are up."

"Would I be able to travel?" Lilly asked. "With my chair?"

"Yes. Anything you are touching will travel with you, including your clothing, which for some of us is God's kindness." At that everyone laughed. "But each person must carry his or her own travel piece."

John pointed back toward the hall. "Those orbs, the pods as Anita referred to them, are like triangles, except that you can travel between worlds and other such places. It's not for the faint of heart . . . or those who don't know exactly where they're going."

No one seemed inclined to challenge him.

"The three other rooms are simpler," he said, leading them to the nearest door. "Especially the Chamber of Witness and the Records Room. But the Study is its own wonder." He opened the door with a proud flourish. "Here is where you Scholars can study, explore, or research if and when Lilly has need of your expertise, or just for fun."

The Study was tastefully appointed and had desks and chairs and couches and anything else that might be needed to do scholarly work. There was an array of books, quills and pens, parchments and journals waiting to be filled, and trays of teas, coffees, and cookies, and fruits and nuts. It was beautiful but nothing out of the ordinary.

"So let me tell you the wonder of this place," announced John. "Whenever an Artist or Scholar such as you three enters the

Study, everything you have ever considered, written, or explored, even those things you don't remember, arrives with you. It gathers and waits for you in the drawers and cabinets and walk-in closets along that wall."

All three Scholars stood stunned, their mouths open.

"This is beyond imaginable," Gerald finally managed, running his hand along a shelf of thick tomes.

Anita had tears in her eyes. She put her fingers to her lips. "My dear," she said to her husband, "our life's work is here. Now. In this room—not a moment of thought or consideration lost!"

"This is a treasure beyond profound," Simon said.

The Scholars were filled with thanksgiving, and Lilly smiled to hear each whispering their gratitude to God.

Simon picked up a silver pen and tested the weight of it in his hand.

"Before I lose you to this place, let's quickly visit the other two rooms," John said, taking over for Simon in pushing Lilly's chair. "Follow me, please."

The Chamber of Witness was a small green room with a very comfortable-looking flat sofa in the center. Four overstuffed chairs of various sizes and shapes occupied each of the corners. "It's simple, really. You stretch out, get comfy, and . . . witness . . . whatever you are here to witness. Not certain why green, but it seems to be a shade that aids the process, color of life and all."

Lilly wondered why anyone needed a special room in which to witness, but thought it best to ask a different question. "Will everything I witness in here also be recorded here?"

"No. That's done over there, in the Records Room." And John

led them out the door and through another archway. Along the hallway was another door, which he ignored.

Lilly couldn't help herself. As John pushed her past, she reached out and tried to turn the knob. It was locked.

"You don't want to know," said John, without slowing or turning around.

"Really? I thought I wanted to know," she mumbled.

"Lilly, mystery creates a space where trust can thrive. Everything in its time, and timing is God's playground. Trust me, being surprised by everything is so much better than needing to control everything."

Lilly wasn't sure if that was true but didn't respond as they entered the Records Room. It was bright and almost tropical in pale blues, purples, and whites. Looking down, she half expected there to be sand between her mismatched toes. The thought made her smile.

Like the Chamber of Witness, the Records Room was quite modest. A square table stood in the center, one chair on each side. Each of the four seats looked like a mix of work chair and step stool, with high and interlaced backs. The table surface appeared to be alive, shifting dramatically between sandy browns and watery blacks.

Along one wall, trays protruded from slots less than an inch wide. Each of these held a very thin black tablet.

"This is where you will record all that you witness, Lilly," explained John.

The others shrugged, which Lilly took to mean they didn't understand it either.

"I told you I'm not a good writer," Lilly said. "And my spelling is atrocious, and what if I forget the stuff I witness?" She already felt like a failure.

"Not to worry." John smiled, indicating the room with an up-turned hand. "Look around. No writing instruments."

"I thought this is where I record what I see?"

"What you witness, Lilly."

"So how does this work?"

Walking over to the slots, he scanned the tablets until he found the one he was looking for. After pulling it out and opening it, he laid it on the strange table. The tablet vanished into the surface much like Simon's mirror. John pushed her chair in front of it, and she looked closer.

"Can you see it?" he asked.

"Barely," she answered. "The very faint reddish edge?"

"That's right."

"Whatever this table is, it keeps shifting, but that thing re-mains still."

"When you are ready, you put both your palms down in the center of that outline. The device will do the rest, capturing and storing whatever you experience."

Simon cleared his throat. "Do you think we Scholars might be let loose to explore the Study?"

John nodded and the three left. But Anita returned a moment later and took both of Lilly's hands in hers. Lilly tried not to flinch as pain shot through her arm.

"Dear one, you and I need to talk, perhaps not now, but soon. You need to let me in, okay?"

Lilly took a deep breath and looked up into the woman's bright and beautiful green eyes. "Okay. You're right. I think it's probably time."

The woman clasped Lilly's face and lifted her chin. "Remember, Lilly, you are here because of who you are. Now, let me practice my hugs, and then I will join the others. We will be ready for whatever you might need."

They hugged and Anita left. A moment later, Lilly heard her fuss with the knob on the locked door—on purpose and as loudly as possible. Anita's little statement of solidarity made her grin.

John also heard it and unsuccessfully tried to look disapproving.

"Should I do it now?" Lilly asked.

"I don't think anything will happen. You have to actually witness something in the Chamber of Witness in order to record it here."

For an instant Lilly hesitated, thinking about her dreams and hallucinations. But just as quickly she dismissed them.

Lilly placed her hands on the table's surface inside the red outline. For a brief moment everything seemed to slow down. Then it slowed again, almost to a stop. She saw John lifting up his hands, shock plastered on his face. And for a moment she could hear his drawn out and slowing shout of "*Wa-a-a-i-i-i-t!*"

Then everything went black.

Twelve

Six Days

Lilly floated, weightless. At first she fought the familiar oily thickness that overwhelmed and embraced her at the same time, especially as it slipped into her mouth. As before, breathing this slick sludge swept her to the brink of terror. Fluid filled her lungs.

But she adapted quicker, knowing she would not suffocate. Eyes open, seeing nothing, she relaxed into the drift. Soon, an underlying peace emerged. Lilly knew where she was and remembered what she had done. In the Records Room with John, she had placed her hands on the table.

THE FIRST DAY

The spewing detonation was instantaneous and continuous, not only overwhelming light expressing force and information with all its shades and hues but also expanding sound and universal song. First a brilliant but not blinding inspiration, then exhalation of ecstasy and wonder, unhindered and held within consuming fire, a rush of wind and water: the culmination of Almighty Voice thrusting into other-centered union.

Behemoth of matter squared off against leviathan of chaos, sending sparks of play and power outward, creating space, energy, and time. These were attended to and applauded by graceful spirit beings whose inhibited elation scattered like far-flung beads of perspiration, scintillating jewels, spun out and up and in. It was an overpowering, discordant riot, an overwhelming cacophony as harmony wrapped itself around a central melody.

It was all happening again. Lilly was reliving Creation's first explosion, and the crafting of the womb in which God would form Man. But now she knew why she was here: to witness the Ages within Beginnings. There was no going back and no way to stop, so she rested into it, to feel, experience, and know it, allowing the cosmic surge to pick her up and carry her on its crest.

Lilly wasn't there to understand or measure or set limits but to hear and see and feel in the simplicity of bearing witness. How could she comprehend light, energy, spirit beings, and layered wrinkles formed between force and matter? How could she wrap her mind around the mysteries of quantum strings and quarks and multiple dimensions? She couldn't, and it didn't matter. But what Lilly knew beyond all doubt was that the focus of communal Love was settled on one tiny, secluded, precisely constructed planet tucked inside the rim of a spiral galaxy.

Lilly moved closer as the potter's wheel spun out the clay into a rippling space. A violent stranger with a fiery tail gouged out a cavernous wound. The moon broke off but couldn't run away, held in place by the grasp of spinning earth's gravitational affection.

Now the Witness stood upon the shell of the new world, a formless empty wasteland enshrouded in a canopy of dust—star wreckage and gases. Lilly couldn't see but heard and felt the slow-pulsating wings of the hovering Spirit, and the shouts of attending Angels who proclaimed Her name with every beat: *Ruach! Ruach! Ruach!* The Spirit blew away debris to let light from the nearest star penetrate the surface's chaotic turmoil.

Evening turned to morning, and it was Good.

THE SECOND DAY

The fiery Joy of God pushed apart the churning matter, an opening invitation for atmospheric gatherings as sunbirthed warmth and swirling dust-laden moisture played upon Lilly's upturned face and outstretched hands. The first day's penetrating light had probed the liquid deep, awakening new songs within its swirling depths. Lilly watched transfixed as a finely tuned and synchronized living dance responded to the melody, biomass and diversity rejoicing in a harmony of purpose, as evening turned to morning, and it was Good.

THE THIRD DAY

Earth trembled. Its crust buckled. Volcanoes raged in tectonic praise with hands of silicate reaching skyward. The land emerged and, cooling, clothed itself in vegetation's cover. With isotopic, photosynthetic, eukaryotic flourish, the Artist splashed across the earth's broad canvas a stunning layered landscape.

The Spirit frolicked like a child, abandoned to the Father's Love. Within the very being of Eternal Man, She finger-painted uninhibited design. Inspiration, inhalation, exhalation, exaltation! Evening turned to morning, and it was Good.

THE FOURTH DAY

Lilly could see out to the starry host. The moon lit up the night, surrounded by countless attending stars. Daylight scrubbed away the thick clouds of shadow dust, transforming Earth's skies from translucent to transparent. The lights that God had blasted into being now hung visible and waiting. The stage was set by the Playwright, and with the audience expectant, evening turned to morning, and it was Good.

THE FIFTH DAY

The sea swarmed, stirring up all that once was fragile. Out of this soup swam fins and gills and squirting things, and colossal sharp-toothed killers in search of their next meal. Then the land gave itself to the creeping and the crawling, a vast army that prepared the soil and air. They joined their Creator in constructing the world as evening turned to morning, and it was Good.

THE SIXTH DAY

The *nephesh*, soulish creatures, along with an array of other living things, emerged from oceans and from lands, the panoply of crafted kinds diverse in form and feature. Lilly was awestruck by their simple beauty and design in tooth and nail, in claw and bone and feather.

Another shout of elation thundered through the universe like a million instruments within a single room. "The appointed time is now! Come gather!"

As evening ascended, the entire cosmos drew near, dancing lights and nimble beings, hastening toward the Holy Voice.

Lilly stood once more on the hill looking over a vast and circular plateau. Behind it, Eden's boundary rose like praise from the earth into the sky.

"Astounding!" came a singsong voice above her. Lilly glanced and jumped back a step. At eye level was the top of a sandaled foot. She looked up—way up—into a gigantic smile. He or she was resting on one knee, an elbow across the other.

"Do not be afraid." Then the being disintegrated like exploding fireflies, only to materialize again in a shape about her height.

"Size is relative," it declared in melodic tones. "Are you the Witness?"

Lilly felt confused. "Where's Eve?"

"Eve? That word has no meaning for me."

"Eve! You know, the Mother of the Living."

The being laughed as if a sweet melody tumbled from its lips. "That is a wonderful new name for God!"

Lilly looked around again to ascertain where she was, then returned her attention to the smiling being. "Really? You don't know Eve? Who are you?"

"My name," it sang, "is Han-el, and I am at your service."

"Han-el?" Lilly exclaimed. "John's Guardian?"

Another burst of laughter. "I am certainly not a Guardian. I am a simple Messenger and Singer." It paused. "John?"

Lilly lifted her hand to indicate that she needed a moment to process. Han-el reached out and touched her fingers, sending a familiar tingling surge throughout her body, everywhere except into the arm that had been infected.

She stepped back from the Messenger.

"How is it that you don't know Eve or John, but you know that I'm a Witness?"

"Adonai announced that a Witness would be here. I, Han-el, have the honor of attending you."

"Adonai announced?" None of this was what she had expected.

"He said your presence is a treasured anomaly and ambiguity, and He is especially fond of you!"

"He did?" Lilly could again feel the war within, the conflict of attraction and repulsion. "An anomaly? Then you know I don't belong here."

"And yet here you are!" Han-el sang.

Tentatively, Lilly reached out her hand to touch the being, but it went right through it. "You aren't real."

Han-el laughed again. "If my existence depended on your perceiving or touching me, then so too would love and hope and faith and joy and a vast array of other Invisibles. I am a spirit being. Perhaps *you* are the one who is not real?"

Lilly carefully crossed her arms and could feel her heart's anxious thumping. Why was this different than when she was with Eve? If this was what the Vault was recording, did it mean she could still stop Adam? Was that why Eve had come to her before the actual witnessing? *This has happened only once . . .*

And then she knew. It hit her like a lightning bolt that left her doubt dismantled. She had been summoned here to witness the highest point of God's Creation. Eve was absent because she would be formed inside Man, and Lilly was here to witness their birth.

"I am real enough," she said. "My name is Lilly, and I am the Witness."

"The time is now!" cried Thunder Song, and the announcement transported Lilly to the center of the gathering. She was surrounded by light-beings and an onslaught to the senses. Music came from everywhere with wondrous scents and shifting light, forming a fluid tapestry. The strings of myrrh and sandalwood rose on ocean breezes. The horns of frankincense and fruits joined the songs of distant stars. Woodwinds exhaled hyacinth, pine, lilac, lavender, and honeysuckle in time with the rhythmic beats of spice—cinnamon and clove, turmeric and ginger.

Once gathered, creation did not wait long. A doorway majestically opened in Eden's wall, and radiance tumbled out.

"They come." Lilly heard Han-el close by but could only stare at the approaching blaze. It was a whirlwind of fierce reds and animated greens, set in the brilliance of spinning jasper, coalescing until from its center a single personage emerged . . . a human being.

"Eternal Man," she whispered. "Everlasting God! Adonai!"

Lilly was entranced; every part of her longed to run to Him and tell Him all her secrets, to be remade, to melt into his magnificence, to find rest from her shame. Here stood trustworthiness. Smiling welcome, He lifted hands, and the prostrate rose to kneeling.

Eternal Man knelt on the ground and with His hands, like a playing child, gathered a pile of reddish-brown dust. Intensely focused and brimming with unbridled delight, He sat, gathering it between His legs.

Laughter and tears flowed unrestrained.

And then a song.

"The Song of Songs," Han-el whispered to her. "The song of Life and all the Living, of word and bread and truth and hope, of giving and forgiving."

From inside this mound of dirt now bubbled up the wine of water, like the force of hope swelling in Lilly's heart. With concentrated intensity He plunged His hands into the holy mess with a grunt that brought Lilly to her feet. The labor was nearly finished. Then, with a piercing shout, Adonai raised above His head a newborn baby.

"A son is born, a son is born!" All creation erupted into jubilant sound, and Lilly rode the crest of birthday's celebration.

The crystal clear and gentle voice of Eternal Man now erupted above the cacophony of gladness: "This is My heart's delight, the crowning of creation. I present to you My beloved son, in whom My soul delights. They shall be named Adam!"

The scene changed quickly as Lilly watched the kiss and breath of God transform a child into a living soul. She witnessed the Cherub cut the cord, declare allegiance, and bow with other celestial beings in service to the delicate infant.

"Wonder of wonders!" Eternal Man declared, lifting the

sleeping baby in his hands. "Behold the child! Creation's womb is fully blessed. Let everything, each in their way, celebrate. With this birth Day Six is crowned, and now We rest from labor."

Evening turned to morning, and it was Very Good!

LILLY JERKED HER HANDS off the table as if shocked. The movement sent searing pain rippling up her injured arm and into her throat. For a second she couldn't catch her breath or figure out where she was.

"She's back! She's back!" yelled John, and Lilly heard the sound of running feet as Simon, Gerald, and Anita rushed into the room looking both worried and relieved. Lilly sat back, weighed down with a new and heavy exhaustion. John too looked overwhelmed but grateful, his eyes red as though he had been weeping. Lilly noticed that the others were all dressed differently than she remembered.

"How long have I been gone?" she asked, willing the ache in her limbs to recede.

"Roughly?" stated Gerald, calculating in his head, "Our time? The better part of five and a half . . . days!"

"Five and a half days?" she exclaimed. The news only made her more tired. "I have been gone five and a half days since I put my hands on this table?"

"Roughly," asserted Simon.

Anita nodded. "Probably closer to six full days."

"We were quite concerned about whether you were going to return or not," Simon interjected.

"It's true," John said. "We considered pulling your hands from the table by force, but the risk . . ." He shook his head, relieved. "It's good to see you back."

She looked down at her hands, then clasped them together to hide how much worse her arm felt than when she'd first been bitten. "I can't believe all I saw happened in six days."

"Our time," emphasized Gerald. "What you witnessed, especially the Days of Creation, likely took billions of years."

"I witnessed this before." Lilly spoke it softly so as not to be heard, a confession that barely met the requirements.

John nodded. Of course, they had plenty of time to figure out the truth.

"I am so sorry," she began. "I thought they were hallucinations, that I was losing my mind, so I didn't say anything. I didn't know what was real." She thought for a moment before sadly adding, "And I'm still not sure."

"Not to fret, dearie," Anita said quickly. "Trust is a difficult road for some of us. I understand. It was Gerald who first suggested you might have already witnessed, and yet in spite of that likelihood . . . we panicked!"

"I'll have you know," said Gerald with a little chuckle, "panicking doesn't help, although it does occupy large amounts of time."

A note of resignation tainted John's voice. "The important thing is that you're back, so let's get you some food and water. You probably need a toilet too, am I right?"

She barely smiled. "You aren't disappointed in me?"

The question was an invitation, a risk, and everyone knew it.

"Disappointed? No. Grieved? Yes. Do you trust me enough to let me be sad without thinking less of yourself?"

He was asking her something important. Shame and self-loathing were her oldest acquaintances. They relentlessly interpreted words of grace, kindness, or confrontation as proof of her unworthiness. Even the word *disappointment* could shove her into an abyss. John was asking her to resist, to believe that his affection and care were the higher truth.

To do that meant she would have to care for him too.

"Okay," she responded, though she still felt the stab inside as if she were betraying a precious agreement. "That helps. I'll try. Thank you."

After using the bathroom, where she finally was able to master the hurt in her arm, Lilly rolled out drying her hands. "So I was gone almost six full days and billions of years without needing to pee? How does that work?"

Gerald answered as the group walked toward the dining area. "When you touch the table, time and perception slow down. In fact, they almost stop. Your heartbeat, for example, decelerates to about one beat every minute. If my calculations were accurate, in six days your heart beat only 8,640 times, approximately. That seems a lot, but actually it's not. Suppose your regular heart rate is sixty times per minute, which for you I think is fairly conservative, but it makes the arithmetic easier. It means that your body felt only the passing of a couple of hours."

"Oh! So *that's* why it sounded like John was yelling 'Wa-a-a-i-i-i-t!' " They all laughed.

The table was set and aromatic food placed in front of her,

vegetables and grilled green beans and a stew. Before they ate, they all held hands, which was customary and usual, but tonight she decided to join in the simple prayer: "My thankful heart today is my best offering." They were kind not to draw particular attention to her participation, but she thought she saw John smile ever so slightly, and it pleased her.

The food was delicious, though weakness prevented Lilly from eating as much as she probably needed.

They had almost finished when John spoke. "Lilly, we watched most of what you recorded. We could see it on the table. One or the other of us was with you every moment, all four most of the time. We didn't want to leave, not only because of our concern for you, but"—he paused, looked down, and gripped the table as a wave of emotion washed over him—"because . . ." His voice cracked, and his red eyes glistened. "Because . . . it was too wonderful for words."

Her own feelings matched his. She reached over and took his hand. "I'm glad you saw it. I could never describe it in any way that would do it justice."

The silence that followed became awkward. Gerald reached out and squeezed her infected arm. Lilly steeled herself against the pain. But John was looking right at her, and a question passed through his eyes.

Quickly she announced that she was exhausted and wanted to sleep. "I'm sure the rest of you do too," she said.

As John wheeled her toward her room, she asked. "Does this mean I'm finished? I recorded everything from the explosion of Creation to the coming of Man, so am I done?"

"I don't know. Are you?"

The simple words stung her. They challenged her integrity. She could see that he was trying to rebuild the bridge of trust, which she had broken.

Lilly shrugged. "I don't know either."

John sighed. "Then I suppose there is only one way to be certain, and that is for you to lie down in the Chamber of Witness and see what happens."

"All right." She was too weary to think about what that might mean. "Oh, one more thing?"

"I suspected as much." He smiled a tired smile. "You are the girl of one-last-questions."

She briefly returned the grin. "Can't help myself. My mind never stops moving. I was wondering, if I hadn't come here, to the Refuge, would I have ever known about . . . you know, about God and Adam and Beginnings?"

"You are treading on another mystery," he replied. "When it comes to plans and purposes, God is not a Draftsman but an Artist, and God will not be God apart from us. You are here, and that changes everything. If you were not here, that too would change everything. For me, a little selfishly, I am grateful you are here."

"Me too," she admitted. "Most of the time."

I did it again. I told the truth because I got caught. I don't think that really counts. And I didn't tell all the truth, only the part I had to. I've hurt John. I can see it on his face. And now, because I didn't tell all the truth, I feel even more stuck. How many times can I burn down a bridge before people will stop rebuilding it? I hate that it even matters. It makes me feel weak and unprotected. Maybe that's what lying is—a way to cover myself.

The recording didn't even get everything I've witnessed so far. What does that mean? I don't want to be recording for ages and ages. Just the thought of that makes me more exhausted than I already feel.

I want to stop Adam. I want to look into the mirror. I want to talk to Simon. I want to die, or leave, or find a way back home. Well, I don't think that's true . . . the home part. From the little I can remember, that was never a place I wanted to be. I hate to admit it, but this weird freaky Refuge feels more like home—or what home should be, anyway.

Today I witnessed Creation, again. It was the same but different. I met Han-el, who didn't know me or John or Eve. My arm hurts so bad. I lied to John about it. I think he knows. I'm becoming more convinced the mirror is right, that the truth of my being is that once you get to the core of Lilly, all you will find is a worthless piece of crap.

But maybe Simon is right too, that I am Lilith and there's one thing I can do before I die: take charge of my otherwise useless life and change history. I just have to figure out how.

Thirteen

THE BIRTH OF EVE

In the solitude of Lilly's room within the Vault, a familiar hand slipped into hers, and she felt a huge surge of relief. She had not seen Eve since God expressed so much sadness over Adam's turning. There was something deeply comforting about this mother's presence, as if it helped to chase away her doubt, urgency, expectations, and demands. Except for brief moments with the others, with Eve was the only time Lilly felt as if she belonged.

"Can I ask . . . ?" whispered Lilly, hesitant to break the spell of holy quiet.

"Of course." Eve's smile was so distracting that Lilly almost lost her question.

"Why didn't you go with me the last time? Usually we're together."

"Dear one, I am not a Witness. Today the road we have been traveling together splits, and we each must walk a different path. I will wait for you in the distance."

"So we aren't going together again?"

"I am already there. The next time you witness, our paths will merge in new ways. No matter what happens, remember this: I have always loved you, and you have always been worthy of my love."

When Eve spoke the words, Lilly almost believed them. So strange, how a statement of affection could morph into a sharp stick that poked the soul and stirred the muck at its bottom.

The woman bent and kissed Lilly's forehead, then sat for a few minutes stroking her hair. "Even though you will recognize me, I won't remember you. But Adonai never forgets. He is especially fond of you."

"Don't go." Lilly leaned into the woman. "I don't think I can take being left again." The confession fractured her voice. "Mother Eve, I'm not sure who I am."

"Ask Adonai and trust what He tells you. True love always tells the truth, even if we can't hear it. Lilly, you are my daughter and we will never be far apart. You are in me, and in the mystery of God, we are all in you—you, Lilly Fields. You will never be alone."

Lilly didn't dispute what Eve was saying, but deep wounds in her resisted. Unexpectedly Eve began to sing, a sweet, soft melody that picked up Lilly and gently placed her into Another's arms. She fell into the sleep of peace, where dreams and nightmares were not allowed.

• • •

THE NEXT MORNING LILLY'S body felt worse and she immediately gave up on her usual regimen. Pain pulsed entirely through her right arm with every movement, and she practiced compensating with her left until her movements looked almost natural.

By the time she wheeled herself alongside the couch in the Chamber of Witness, where John and Simon awaited her, she was sweating.

John put his hand to her head. "Your temperature has risen. I don't think you should be doing this today."

"Do you feel up to this?" Simon asked. "It is up to you."

"This is why I'm here, isn't it?" she said. "So let's just get it over with."

Moving her took a little work, but as Lilly let herself relax, she was unexpectedly enfolded in a superb sense of comfort. Whatever this device was, it was good at what it did.

The next instant Lilly found herself standing on a wooded, rocky hill looking down onto a sweeping plain bustling with activity. She was alone, surrounded by massive trees, and her body didn't hurt. In fact, nothing hurt. When she reached out to lean against a tree, it reacted to her touch with melodic laughter.

Startled, Lilly jumped away. She had leaned against Han-el.

"Now you're a tree?" She giggled but was glad for the Angel's visible presence.

"No, but perhaps I appear as you expect," Han-el sang. "And you are in a forest."

Lilly laughed aloud. Pleasure caught her by surprise. It came easily, as if she'd taken her first deep breath in days. Looking at her hands and arms, she found no sign of the serpent's strike, nor its spreading poisons. Lifting the hem of her dress, she squealed in delight. Both feet were hers. Had she been so caught up in the grandeur of the Beginnings that she hadn't noticed?

Lilly took a step and then twirled like a little girl, her face tilted toward the sun. Golden threads of light streaked through the canopy and tenderly kissed her cheeks. She closed her eyes.

"Han-el, what am I here to witness?"

"Look there."

Opening her eyes, she saw Han-el point to a rock ledge about a hundred yards away. It projected ten feet above a broad plain that teemed with movement. Lilly blinked, and that quickly she and the Angel were standing at the center of the activity. Adam was nearby, surrounded by Fire and Wind and Adonai. He pointed at a rotund hippopotamus and after a thoughtful moment announced, "River horse."

"I know what Adam's doing," she realized, suddenly perturbed.

"Yes, this is the final day of naming," said Han-el. "Since Adam's turning, God has opened up this way for him to re-turn to Them, to trust."

"He has already turned?" Lilly was stunned. Again, it was too late. "Han-el, how is naming animals an invitation back to trust?"

"Look and understand. Adam no longer sees what you are able to see. In turning his face away, he believes he is alone. That lie has already twisted his vision. For Adam there is no Person in Wind and Fire. There is only Adonai, and even Adonai is fading."

"But Adam was tricked! By the serpent! It told Adam he was alone."

"No. Adam empowered the snake and now it speaks on his behalf."

Adam sank to the ground at Adonai's feet and dropped his head into his hands. "I am all alone," he uttered, as if it were the last word he might ever speak.

"The naming is complete!" declared Han-el in tones of minor keys. "The naming did not give Adam what he hoped."

Adonai reached out to touch Adam's crown. His hand rested there. What happened next was like a kaleidoscope turning.

Lilly witnessed Adonai place Adam into a deep and loving sleep atop a feather bed of celestial wings. A canopy of woven reeds sheltered him as he lay still, attending Angels ready. Time lapsed. Days slipped into months. Adam's belly grew, expanding with a pregnancy. And then time came to a stop.

In nine months God fashioned the feminine side of Adam's humanity, the female who slept within, into a breathtaking being of corresponding power but weak and fragile as the source from which she was withdrawn.

Creation held its collective breath. Adonai opened up his son, and the she was taken out of the he, one separating into two. No longer would either ever be the all, and yet Adonai promised that by Love's knowing, the two could one day choose to celebrate as one. The wide expanse of God's one nature was now expressed in two, the female and the male, both by nature designed to live face-to-face with Father, Son, and Spirit.

The infant girl's cry pierced and penetrated Eden's night, and from there Messengers again carried celebration's news into the vast reaches of creation.

Lilly watched as God closed Adam's flesh. Then He stooped and kissed the man, waking him from sleep's depths. Adam rose and touched his side, which was already healing. Then Eternal Man held out the baby girl clothed in love and light and wonder. When Adam took her in his arms, he threw back his head and laughed in jubilation.

"At long last! This is my kind, my bone, and my flesh. She shall be named Isha, a weakness, because she has been drawn out of Ish, my strength."

Lilly began to clap and dance, delighted. She flung her hands outward and twirled and shouted with the rest of creation. But when she noticed that Han-el's and Adonai's expressions were similar looks of somber resignation, she slowed and then stopped.

"Han-el? Why aren't you happy?"

"I am ecstatic. She is Love's response to Adam's choice of turning. I perceive that in her participation God will craft redemption and reconciliation, but I also see in Adonai's face that there will be a cost. That saddens me."

"Her coming doesn't save him from his turning?"

"It promises to." The Singer left it at that.

"What will happen to Adam?"

"In turning to her now, he has stepped away from the precipice, but only for a time. She is Adonai's invitation to embrace frailty and softness, to be whole and unashamed, to return fully from his turning. But this power of face-to-face will never be enough."

Lilly shook her head, realizing. "Isha. He didn't call her Eve. He named her, like he did the beasts and birds, didn't he?"

"Yes!" Han-el's voice had become a lament. "Even now he

could not stop himself from bending away from God toward power and dominion. He named her 'weak and fragile'—the truth about his own being, of which he is ashamed. So he will try to separate himself from truth and choose aloneness as his strength, as if he could be like God apart from God."

Lilly tentatively held out her hand to the Angel, not knowing if Han-el would accept her comfort. Reaching out, the Singer took her arm, with a grip soft and powerful. The Angel's strength and sorrow flowed into her.

"I'm sorry," she said, referring to Adam.

"I am too." And Lilly somehow felt that Han-el was referring to her as well.

"But here," the Singer added, "the story has only begun. Look!"

Again time spun and accelerated: Isha too nursed at God's breasts and took her first tottering steps into Adam's arms. She walked in woods and fields, a girl clothed inside Fire and Wind, holding hands with Eternal Man. Soon Lilly could see hints of Eve's regal bearing emerging. Eden's girl grew quick in her understanding and blossomed inside the laughter and adventures of relationship. As she matured, so did the depths of her love and affection for Adam, and his for her: the flirtatious glances, the grins without a reason. The joy they took in each other had no limit.

But when conversations with Adonai turned from the wonders of creation to those of procreation, Lilly looked away, feeling a shame she could not define. But these two were unaware, anticipating the pleasure and beauty of this design. They laughed and teased, knowing that when the right time was appointed, their union in Love would be wondrously enjoined.

The girl became a woman, tenacious and quick of wit, swift and strong. She sometimes explored the garden on her own, but when she danced, it was to the music of God's boundless affection, which always brought her back into Adam's open arms.

But Adam began to drift. Lilly noticed the shadow cast by his withdrawal before Eve did. It appeared incrementally: a sentence left unfinished, a smile a little out of tune, a gentleness withheld. Dread rose in Lilly's heart.

"I don't want to see this part," she said to Han-el.

The Angel's voice was tender. "I understand, Lilly. Are you asking to return to the place from where you have come?"

"Yes!" And that was all it took.

"OKAY!" LILLY ROSE UP straight, surprising John, who had just sat down next to her. Her reckless movement startled her too, especially as her pain reasserted itself. She groaned and closed her eyes, willing the hurt to the margins. Slowly, she refocused on John. "I have questions!"

"Questions?" he exclaimed. "You were gone less than two minutes."

"That's all?" The heat of fever returned to her cheeks. "Well, according to Gerald, two minutes could be two million years. I don't understand why I witnessed what I did just now!"

"Uh . . ." John scratched an itch at his hairline. "I don't know what you saw."

"You chose to be a Witness," commented Simon, and Lilly

twisted to find him in the room. She had forgotten he was there. "But you can't choose what you will see."

"I didn't choose to be a Witness. Apparently I don't get to choose anything. Who chooses what I see?"

"The Wisdom of God decides," Simon stated.

"And who chooses what gets recorded?"

The men looked at her blankly.

"I don't understand the question," John said. "Everything is recorded."

"Oh brother." She sighed and shifted, uncomfortable in the limitations of her body while the memory of dancing was so fresh. "You aren't going to understand until you see for yourself. C'mon, let's get this recorded so I can ask my questions."

They wheeled her straight to the Records Room, stopping only to invite Anita and Gerald to come along.

When Lilly touched the table, the transfer began, and everyone observed her experience. When the process was complete, she lifted her hands and turned to the four. Gerald was standing with his hands over his mouth, Anita was shaking her head, and John and Simon looked as stunned as the other two.

"What?" the girl demanded.

Gerald was first to speak. "I have studied the texts for years and did not understand the depths of what happened. Not that I do now," he was quick to add. "I feel as if I have been looking at the mountain of Scriptures from the bottom of a valley, and now I'm actually standing on the mountaintop."

"What we have witnessed," replied Anita in a solemn tone, "was the beginning of Adam's turning."

"No! That's my point!" Lilly was confused and exasperated. A new pain radiated along the full length of her spine and launched a headache. "The naming is the *result* of Adam's turning, not the beginning of it. I witnessed the first stages, but for some reason the recording skipped over that part—the part when Adam talks to a snake that gives him a knife? And then what? The universe explodes?"

By the expressions on the others' faces, Lilly realized she had again inadvertently exposed herself, but in the moment she was more perturbed than self-conscious.

"Wait!" John said. It was as loud as Lilly had ever heard him speak, except when she was seizing. That flash of memory made her bite her lower lip to avoid smiling. It felt somehow good to hear John be loud!

Everyone was silent while John collected his thoughts.

"Lilly, maybe you should tell us about this conversation between Adam and the snake? And about the knife?"

She told the story as completely as she could remember, including Eve's presence and Adonai's sadness. As Lilly talked, grief replaced curiosity on every face but one; Simon looked agitated and began to pace.

When she finished, the silence went on for several minutes. Then Gerald spoke, "The moment of the turning has never been recorded." He shook his head.

John rose and went to a cluttered shelf near the slots that housed the recording tablets. He began to rummage.

"Lilly, you must understand," said Anita. "Every evil the universe has endured, every betrayal and loss, every wrong that has been committed in the name of good or evil, all the suffering of creation—it originated in Adam's turning. Before this there was nothing that was not good. Nothing. To the contrary, everything was very good."

"Han-el said something like that," Lilly offered. "But I don't get it. Where did Adam go wrong? I keep thinking it's the snake's fault."

"No," responded Anita. "The serpent did not originate the darkness of the turning. It was Adam."

"I don't understand." Lilly wheeled her chair back and forth, which helped her think. "Why is everything about turning? It's not like Adam lied or killed somebody."

"Sadly, it will lead to that, and very soon," said John. He lifted a sticklike device off the shelf. "Maybe this will help." He twisted it near its base and instantly it produced a blinding light, powerful and focused. Lilly had to shield her eyes.

"This light, while dazzling, will not hurt you," he assured her. "Please, trust me. Would you look directly into it, then let me ask a question?"

She did. At first she squinted; then her eyes adjusted and the beam became entirely soothing. In fact her headache, which had spread across the back of her skull, now receded.

"So," continued John, "as you are fully facing this light, how much darkness do you see?"

"I don't see any," she responded. "There's no darkness at all."

"Exactly. So, another question. How would any darkness or shadow of any kind occur?"

"Something could block it?"

"True, but what if there was nothing and no one who could block it?"

It only took a second before she knew the answer. "I would have to turn away. That is the only way that a shadow would be possible."

"Precisely," John affirmed. "God is light, and in Them there is no darkness at all. None! And God, who is light, embraces the whole created universe. By turning away from God, Adam cast a shadow, his own shadow. Adam has dominion and drags the serpent and creation into his own shadow."

John twisted off the light.

Gerald stepped forward. "Lilly, I hope this might help too." He wiped his hands on his shirt as if cleaning them, and then awkwardly reached as if to take her face in his hands.

"May I?"

Her first reaction was to pull away, but she agreed, not wanting to hurt his feelings. His palms were smooth and warm.

"When you and I are like this, completely face-to-face, what is one thing that would never occur to you?"

Again, it took a moment before Lilly understood. "It would not occur to me that I was alone."

"Exactly!" Gerald released her and stepped back. "Adam was completely surrounded by the love of God, face-to-face-to-face, as Anita said. No matter where he turned, he was face-to-face with Love, so he turned to the one place unthinkable . . ."

Lilly finished his thought. "He closed his eyes and turned away from face-to-face and into himself, and when he did that, he believed he was alone!"

John restated the thought for clarity. "When you are really face-to-face, you know you're not alone."

The realization was staggering. "So, why didn't Adam turn back? Re-turn?"

Anita answered. "Once Adam believed that his turning was the good, darkness became his reality. Control replaced trust, imagination took the place of word, and power the place of relationship and love. His own darkness redefined his understanding of everything, including God. He quickly forgot that he had even turned. He is still the son of God, the epitome of creation with authority and dominion, but now asserts this as independent power. Sadly, all of us, as Adam's children, continue to live in the shadow of death, each of us determining on our own what is good and evil."

"All because of turning!" Gerald said. "Without trust in the word or character of God, death is our contribution. That is the legacy we continue to perpetuate, unleashing principalities and powers to serve the beasts of politics and religion. We replace our desire for union, which originates in God, with self-satisfying lusts for conquest. We sanctify money as if it were life's blood; we turn art into propaganda and weapons into instruments of worship. For the good of the many, we would sacrifice the one, over and over and over, the ends justifying means, all for the good, of course—as we each determine it."

Silence met his words, not only because the outburst seemed out of character. Gerald's intensity and passion carried weight, and everyone respected it. Finally, Lilly broke the quiet.

"But we're Eve's children too, aren't we? And she wasn't even there when Adam turned."

"She was there, inside Adam," said Simon, "but not yet awake. One purpose for taking her from within him was the gracious mercy of God inviting Adam to re-turn. She was withdrawn to call him back to his humanity. If only Adam had been stopped!"

Tension gripped the base of Lilly's neck once more. She tried to massage it out, but her arm and hand ached from the venom spreading through her veins.

"I think you should rest," announced Gerald. "I need to lie down for a while myself. This grieving is too much at times, and I am feeling overwhelmed."

"Adam must have broken God's heart," Lilly said, thinking out loud. The others nodded.

"I know what it's like to see the one you love turn away," Simon said, then left the room.

Anita comforted her with a motherly kiss atop her head. Lilly soon lay in her bed, heartache's tears flowing like a river onto her pillow. She felt that she had witnessed the saddest day of history, and although she shed tears for Adam, and for God, and even for herself, she especially wept for Eve.

Fourteen

STORED LOSSES

A hand covered Lilly's mouth and a heavy weight held her down. Her eyes snapped open and she flailed her good arm, barely able to breathe in the space between the fingers.

"Shhh!" a voice commanded, and panic overwhelmed her before she recognized who it was. Simon. Slowly she stopped resisting, and he released her.

"Simon," she whispered harshly. Her heart continued to race. "You totally scared me. What are you doing here?"

"We have to talk." Pleading desperation filled his eyes. She nodded and converted her bed into a chair.

"What's going on?" she asked, still gasping from the fear.

"Lilith, you can't trust them."

"Who? Can't trust who?"

"The others: John, Anita, Gerald." Simon held up his hands. "Do not misunderstand me. They truly think they are your friends,

197

and in some misguided sense they are, but they do not understand your significance or what you are here to do."

"Which is . . ."

"To change history. Prevent the disaster that we are all now stuck inside."

"So, who is on my side in this? Only you?"

"Yes, me. And in a strange way, so is the serpent."

"The serpent?" The claim was so unexpected that Lilly would have stood up if she could have. "That *thing* bit me. How could that snake possibly be anything but my enemy?"

"It is your ally. Think about it." Now Simon was focused. "Remember what the others said. The turning did not originate in the serpent. It is not the serpent's fault. Because of Adam, death resulted and that must be atoned for. Only a sacrifice of life will vanquish the shadow-sickness of death."

It seemed as if he was about to be carried away on a tirade, but Simon caught himself and took a breath. "I am so sorry," he apologized. "This means a great deal to me."

"The snake bit me!" Lilly said. "It hurts, and the venom is spreading."

"Exactly! The bite was to empower you. Haven't you figured that out?"

Lilly flushed. "So explain it to me."

"I do not think you, as a Witness, can change anything, but as Lilith—you are more than a Witness. What if that mythology is meant to open a possibility to change history? You have already been inside the story in ways that have not been recorded, right?"

"Yes. Like when I saw Adam's conversation with the snake."

"Yes!" His face now shone with excitement. "Tell me, did the knife the serpent gave Adam, did it have a name—Machiara?"

"Yes!" she exclaimed. "How did you know?"

"Praise be to God!" exclaimed Simon in as quiet and controlled a manner as he could. "I knew it. It is all starting to make sense."

Lilly was baffled. "I'm glad to see this is making sense to somebody."

"Machiara is not any knife, it is *the* short sword of sacrifice used throughout the ages to sacrifice animals to God and atone for Adam's turning. A worthy sacrifice is pleasing to God. What did Adam do with it?"

"I don't know." Lilly tried to recall. "I think he took it with him back into Eden."

"Good!" Simon looked away, deep in thought for a moment. "You didn't stop Adam's turning, but it doesn't mean that you can't still change history."

His remark entered Lilly like an accusation, a confirmation of her incompetence. "How am I supposed to do that?"

"I think the serpent's sting empowers you to be substantial inside your visions, to be even more 'real' than when you witness. I think you have to be 'real' in order to change things. It's still not clear to me exactly how."

"Not helpful." Lilly sighed.

"There is something that we can do. The mirror is the key. What it revealed to you is essential, a declaration of the truth of your being, and you have to embrace that."

"No! Simon, I can't." Now it was Lilly who was begging. "If you saw what I did, you wouldn't even want to be in the same room with me. I am a horrid, disgusting, evil person, everything worth-less and wicked."

"But don't you see? That is why you were chosen to be here. Lilith, I hesitate to say it, but God needs the worst in order to ac-complish the best."

Simon could not have said anything more hurtful, but even as her first inclination was to hit him as hard as she could, she felt the breath rush from her lungs. Abhorrent as it was, what he said resonated within; she knew he was telling her something true. It made sense and in a twisted way stirred a sense of purpose in her.

Simon reached and touched her shoulder. She didn't pull away. Without looking up, she uttered, "What do I do?"

"You embrace the truth of your being and your destiny! We need to get you to your belongings in storage. I believe seeing what is in there will help you put together some of the pieces that have kept you from accepting your critical part in all of this."

"But how? It's a long way . . . Oh wait, are you thinking of using the Map Room?"

"Exactly. We can get to storage and back in ten minutes. Isn't that what John said? Aren't you curious about what is in there?"

"I am, but I'm not sure I want to know."

"You have to. Trust requires risk. You have to know who you really are in order to be at peace and participate in God's pur-poses."

"I don't think I could ever be at peace with what I've seen in flashbacks or in mirrors." She fought the idea of remembering what her mind had tried to forget. This unknown terrified her.

"What have you got to lose, Lilith? You have nothing to lose."

He was right. She had nothing to lose, not really. These relationships with John, Anita, Gerald, Letty, and even Simon were just imaginary. At best, they liked a person who did not even exist.

She nodded and Simon silently wheeled her down the hall and into the Vault. The place seemed desolate; the others were probably still resting. Soon she was parked in front of the Refuge map. It was easy to find where they were and pinpoint the target location. Simon handed her a triangle and pointed to another on the map.

"Just touch a corner of this to that spot right here. I will be right behind. Whenever you are ready."

Lilly didn't hesitate. A wave of light and mist swept through her, for an instant clouding her vision in swirling gray, and when it cleared she was sitting in her chair in a stone hallway.

A moment later Simon appeared next to her. "That was unusual! Let me get my bearings."

He instructed her to place her triangle in the receptacle that was in the wall next to her. This would send her back in ten minutes. Simon excused himself to find another slot and returned a minute later.

"Thanks be to God, there was another one close. Now let's find your belongings. The number?"

"One-eleven-fifteen. The day John found me and my age."

It took almost five minutes to find the right unit. It reminded Lilly of the back of a moving truck with its large flip lock. This one slid sideways instead of up. The plaque on the wall to one side was inscribed with the numbers 11115 and the faint outline of a palm.

She looked at Simon, who tilted his head in the direction of the imprint. "I can't open it," he said.

Lilly tentatively raised her left hand and pressed it into the wall. Faintly, they heard some sort of locking mechanism unwind, then stop. Simon pointed to the handle as if unwilling to touch it.

"I can't do this," she stammered. "I'm afraid."

"If you do not, no one can." Simon was resolute. "If you choose not to find out who you are, we are all stuck in the mess Adam caused . . . and probably lost forever."

Lilly leaned her head against the metal door and moaned. It felt as if an unbearable weight was on her shoulders. "Why does everything depend on me?"

Simon did not reply.

The longer she waited, the more conflicted she became, so as much as it pained her, with both hands she pulled the locking lever sideways. It opened easily, and as it did, the room lit up.

It was not what she saw that triggered the rush of memories but what she smelled. Years of layered nicotine permanently woven into threadbare carpet, entwined with the pungent mix of stale and moldy food and cheap perfume and rotting garbage. These were the putrid and haunting stenches of her childhood, where she crawled and searched for scraps to eat hidden in the litter of her life. In the background she heard music playing, her earliest dancing to the sound tracks of Kurt Cobain and Merle Haggard, with John Denver always on repeat singing "Sunshine on My Shoulders."

Memory smothered her like a blanket and then hit her like a fist. Everything came rushing back and there was nothing she could do but scream and retch and scream and scream again. Then for a moment it all went black.

Lilly was still terrified when she came to her senses, again kicking and swinging, but wrapped inside strong arms. Anita and John had come to her aid, while Gerald watched from a corner of Lilly's sleeping room, a look of anxious helplessness written clearly across his face.

Slowly she calmed, the slamming of her heartbeat and gasps drowned out by the gentling repetition of "It's okay" and "We are here." An overwhelming taste of sour vinegar and blistering scent of bleach caused her to gag, and twice she vomited.

"Get her some warm tea," Anita commanded, sending Gerald scuttling off. "With milk and honey," she called after him, before returning her attention to Lilly.

"Take your time, dear one, and get your bearings." Anita's voice. "We are right here and won't leave you. You're safe."

Lilly began to cry. "Anita, I remember." Her voice was broken, rasping and hoarse. "Oh, Anita, I remember everything. I didn't want to . . ."

"Hush, child." Anita rocked the girl in her arms. Lilly could hear John quietly praying in the background, but all she wanted in this moment was to disappear, forever, inside this woman's arms. "No one will ask you to talk about anything that you don't want to or can't. It will be all right. Breathe in, breathe out."

Gerald soon returned with tea and then stood watch next to John. Occasionally Lilly shuddered and moaned as waves of realization washed through her. Exhaustion overtook her body.

Only when the turmoil had spent most of its energy did Anita hand her a warm washcloth to clean her face of snot and tears. Lilly took a small sip of tea. It spread throughout her body, sweet and warm and comforting. Only her poisoned arm remained cold and achy.

"Your naptime nightmare caused quite a ruckus. Poor Gerald hit the floor before he was standing and ran right into a closet. He got himself quite turned around, and if we had not been so distraught by your screaming, it might have been comical. Thankfully, he wasn't hurt."

Lilly barely had enough energy to smile, but she did.

"At first I was certain you were in the Vault," Gerald said, "but it turned out you were here in your room. Sound travels in odd ways through this place. Simon must be in the Study, the only place that is quite soundproof."

How Lilly wished in that moment that she could hide like Simon. What she had agreed to do was stupid. What had she been thinking? She hadn't thought at all—that was the problem. And if John ever found out, she would die of shame.

"Can I quit?" Lilly whispered. "I want this all to stop."

Anita patted her on the hand. "I know. I think that you are too old too soon, and I am quite outraged." Lilly could see fury behind her focused features. It felt good, that someone would be angry on her behalf, even if she wasn't worthy.

"Thank you! For watching out for me."

"Of course, my dear," Anita said. "Always! Now, you sleep until you wake. One of us will stay here."

Lilly wasn't about to argue and in any case didn't have the strength. The tea had made her feel drowsy. As she laid her head on her pillow and closed her eyes, she silently offered a plea that could have been a prayer: "Dear God, I don't want to deal with anything right now. Can I please just sleep?"

THE LIGHTING IN LILLY'S small room had changed from the wakeful yellow of artificial daylight to the calming blue of night-lights.

"How long have I been out?" She reached out and touched Anita's arm.

"Almost four hours." Anita smiled tenderly. "How are you feeling?"

"I don't know. Right now I don't feel anything at all. How do you wake up from a dream that is real? But see? I am pretty sure I'm awake." Lilly pinched the skin on her left arm until it hurt nearly as much as her poisoned arm did.

"Just making sure?" Anita asked, raising an eyebrow.

"Yeah. Everything's a question right now, everything." Lilly paused and then asked, "Anita, what did you mean when you said I was too old too soon?"

The Scholar thought before answering. "We are all children, regardless of our age, and although God designed us to grow in stature and in wisdom, They also intended we should remain children at heart. Sadly, evil forces many of us to abandon our childlike ways and we become too old too soon."

"How much do you know about my life?"

"Enough to see it deeply wounded you, and to know you are sorting through the rubble." Again anger edged her voice, heartbreak for Lilly. "That is not the judgment of a Scholar but the observation of a friend who loves you."

They held hands in the quiet for a time. "My mother sold me, Anita. My mother! She sold me to her boyfriend, and then he sold me to other men." As Lilly spoke, tears flowed down her face. Anita wept too. "How could a mother do that? She sold me for drugs. When she was high she called me Kris, 'cause that was her drug of choice, crystal meth. The men just called me Princess."

Anita squeezed her hand and let her talk. It wasn't a time for words from anyone else.

"You know the worst thing about rape? It's not the pain, it's what you're left with after. My mom would walk me down to the neighborhood church and leave me there. Maybe I was her attempt at confession, or maybe she wanted God to fix me just enough so she could break me again. I remember sitting in a class with other kids my age, I think I was five or six, and I would think, *What is wrong with these kids? How can they laugh with me sitting right here? Don't they know they could get my diseases?* They made fun of my 'holy' stockings, the same 'holy' stockings that men took off me before . . . before . . . you know . . ."

Lilly and Anita sighed heavily as one.

"Somebody called it soul rape. I think they're right. You're left with nobody and nothing 'cause that's all that you deserve. It's your fault if you're cute or pretty enough to be chosen. If someone else is picked, it's your fault because you aren't enough.

"I ran away again and again, but more men found me. They sold me and they sold me and they operated on me so that customers would think I was a virgin, and then they operated on me and took away the only thing that I had left. Anita, I know why I haven't had a period. It's because I can't. I can't ever have a baby. You see, I didn't come through a tragedy. I *am* the tragedy!"

Anita leaned over Lilly and encircled her in strong arms, lifting her shoulders off the bed and protecting her with the shield of love and shared grief.

"Anita, I can't have a baby, ever," she sobbed. "I always thought that no matter how bad I messed things up, one day I would do something right and have a baby, someone that I could love and who would love me and call me her momma, and now I can't, I can't . . ."

The woman held and rocked the girl. Lilly was so lost to her own sorrow that she didn't notice tears continuously rolling down the Scholar's face until they soaked through her hair.

When the emotions subsided and both women wiped their faces clean once more, they hugged tight and long. Lilly now felt embarrassed that she had spewed her life onto someone else. But there was no way to retract it.

"May I share something personal and precious with you, Lilly?" Anita asked.

"Sure."

"Gerald and I had a daughter, full-term but stillborn. It was the single worst day of my life. Her name is Nadja, which is Hope. We named her before we met her. She had the most delicate hands and feet, perfect and complete. She did have Gerald's ears, which would have posed a challenge that I'm sure she would have overcome. But since Nadja slipped into God's keeping, I have not been able to conceive a son or daughter, and not for lack of trying.

It seems that all the mechanics were there and functioning, but the timing was illusive. And now it is gone forever."

Anita paused and this time Lilly took her hand.

"Dear one, my story isn't the same as yours," the woman said. "Nothing was stolen from me, as it was from you. For me, though, it was slowly withdrawn. You and I share a certain loss in common. There is a grief that only a woman who cannot bear a child can apprehend. To make such a choice is one thing, but to have the wonder of it taken from you—that is a wound too deep to even bleed."

"I am so sorry, Anita. Your secret is safe with me," Lilly whispered back.

Anita whispered back, "I don't keep secrets, Lilly. True friends don't keep secrets, only surprises for another time."

Lilly smiled weakly. "Look at you, hardly objective."

"Clinical detachment is a myth, often a cover for cowardice. It is so much more arduous and risky to be authentic and present, and immeasurably more rewarding. Healers heal themselves while healing others."

Anita stood up and held out her hand, and Lilly took it.

"Lilly, Adam's turning crushed women, to be sure, but it was a disaster for men as well. Even so, some of them found the way out of Adam's shadow. Believe it or not, there are many men in the world who are not like the ones you've known. Shall we go find some good men and see if they have prepared something to eat? All this emotion makes me hungry."

Lilly laughed, and it was a relief of sorts. "Anita, you go ahead," she suggested. "I need to catch my breath, but I'll be there in a minute or two. Okay?"

"Of course, dear one." Anita smiled and hugged her one more time. "Thank you for letting me walk with you inside your holy ground."

"Thanks for not leaving me alone." Lilly held on to the woman's arm a moment. "Anita, you said something that reminded me of someone, a man. I remembered his face a few days ago, but nothing else until today. When they shipped me and the others in that container that washed up here, he was the man who tried to save us. We were used up, see? Sick, rejected—'No longer good for the domestic market,' someone said. This man's own daughter was missing and he thought she was taken in our group, so he joined the traffickers to try and find her. She wasn't there, but I think I reminded him of her. He's the one who put me in that compartment, but it happened so fast that I didn't get positioned right. When the other men broke in, I think they shot him first. I heard gunfire as I was passing out; it's the last thing I remember. His name was Abdul Baith. Somebody should know."

Anita patted her arm. "When we get back to the surface, I will make sure that we speak for him and celebrate him properly. One day you can thank him yourself. It's part of why we hope."

When she left, Lilly pulled out her diary.

I'm done with secrets. I had a really rough day. I found out or, more truly, finally remembered that . . . I am scared to even write it 'cause then it would be more real. I got fixed, like I was a dog or something, sterilized, and I don't even know who did it.

Anita told me she can't have kids either. I guess that's why I can write about it. I am SO SAD for her and for me, and I can't stop crying. I am so angry, but most of the time I don't feel anything, like I'm numb. I want to cut myself 'cause I don't feel anything. I don't do it but I want to feel and I get scared when I'm numb that I'm never going to feel anything again. I do feel my snakebit arm. It really hurts.

Maybe I need the ice under my feet to break so I can just fall through and disappear. Oh God, even if I am totally insane, would you come and find me? I think I really want to be found, by You, not just by the others.

I went back to the place where John stored all my belongings and that's when all my memories came back. Maybe not all, but lots, too many all at once. Then I spilled my guts to Anita.

But I think I know what I have to do now. It seems clear for the first time. Simon is right, I can change the world. But I can't do it as Lilly. Lilly was a little girl who died a long time ago, a weak and broken and powerless thing who deserves to be left in peace. It's time for me to make a new truth for myself, to give myself a new name and a new destiny. So, I choose Lilith, because Simon believes in her. The truth of who I am is that I am Lilith.

LILITH

Once she had made up her mind, everything, including the turmoil that had been raging in her heart, settled down. When she wheeled herself into the living area, John stood leaning against a wall and staring out into the ocean, its ebb and flow hypnotically moving the sea plants in a constant dance with tides and currents. Food was on the table, waiting.

Parking herself next to him, she broke the silence. "What are you thinking?" she asked.

"Hmm?" He didn't turn toward her. Some inner conversation played across his furrowed features. "You've experienced profound losses for someone so young," he began. "I'll probably never understand why the human soul has such an insatiable need to remember and revisit its tragedies."

"Anita told you?"

He raised one hand to stop her and slowly lowered it again when she fell quiet.

"For my part," he continued, his voice heavy with sadness, "some days, I feel my duty is to add more burden to your troubles, to poke at your pain. It wears me to the bone. I don't like it, and my dislike grows in direct proportion to my deepening affection for you."

Lilly reached up and touched his arm, a gesture she had never made. "You care about me?"

"Yes." He stated it matter-of-factly, still looking out at the flowing seaweed. "For me this has been completely unexpected. Apparently relationship has a life of its own and doesn't have regard for history or agenda or necessity. It's annoying. But it's also a gift, a joy even. A conundrum, as they say."

He took a deep breath and slowly let it out, a sigh of the soul. "So, yes, I care, and it clouds my judgment." He pursed his lips as if to keep them from spilling even more.

"Then stop," she offered, only partly sarcastically. "I'm not used to anyone caring about me. It feels weird. And like you said, it complicates everything."

"If only it were that easy. I've tried to stop, to convince myself you're just a mission I must manage. But it's no use."

She laughed so easily that it surprised her. "I can't believe it. You've been trying to like me less?"

He glanced at her and barely smiled. "It seemed the safer road."

"Believe me"—she laughed again—"roads are rarely what they appear to be and are not predictable. Maybe *safe* is about the company you keep and not about the road you take?"

He glanced again, surprised. "Now that is wisdom not earned easily," he acknowledged. "Thank you for that. We'd all do better to remember that."

Not sure how to respond, she announced with a sardonic tone, "Well, if it's any help, I do not particularly care for you. You're a curiosity, but I don't like you any more than I dislike you." She was not telling the truth and she suspected he knew.

"Hmm." He looked up and then, a minute later, back at her. "That's of no help whatsoever. Hasn't diminished one iota how deeply I feel about you."

She let go her touch as an unexpected fear ambushed her.

"You're not trying to tell me that you're in love with me, are you?"

"Heavens no!" he reacted. "In love? Like a romantic attraction where the knees go all buckley and you become a rather useless human being? That kind of in love? No, nothing like that."

"Good!" She sighed. "That would have weirded me out! Not that somebody couldn't be in love with you, but not you and me. You're old . . . ish, at least forty or fifty, right?" She gave him a grimace to emphasize her disgust.

"Whew." He laughed. "Glad we got that clarified," he teased, "and you are right. I am at least forty or fifty years old, and you just a baby."

"I'm not a baby!" she declared firmly. "I am a strong young woman!"

"And stubborn." He smiled again, but as he returned to looking out the window, his expression faded.

"Why so sad, John?"

"Because I already knew. I knew what they did to your body but didn't know how to tell you. The gift of bearing a child was taken from you long before the tragedy that brought you here, and even with all our skills we were unable to restore that. I am deeply, deeply sorry."

"Me too," she said. "Right now I just feel numb. Probably better that way."

"Perhaps," agreed John. "Grief is strange. Like joy it catches us by surprise, sideways and unexpected. Part of the rhythms of this life, part of being human."

"Is everybody broken, John? Is everybody grieving?"

"It's hard to be in this world long and not encounter loss. It's the thing we most have in common. Like your soul, the cosmos is broken into pieces. But listen." John faced her and squatted next to her chair. "Lilly, if you participate in your own healing, you open possibilities for creation to be restored as well."

"Me? My healing? Does everything depend on me?"

John seemed surprised and knelt next to her. "Everything depends on each of us, because each of us matters. We are all created in Adonai. In Him we are all connected one to the other, whether we acknowledge it or not."

Someone cleared his throat, and when Lilly looked, she saw Simon standing near the entryway. She wondered how long he had been there, how much he had heard. John stood and nodded a greeting.

"Excuse me," Simon said. "I was just coming to see how you were doing. I understand I missed some excitement earlier."

"I'm feeling better, thank you!" offered Lilly. And it was true. Although she was still aware of the fever and infection, she felt it might have slowed.

She expected Simon to be glad to hear the news, but instead

he looked perplexed. Lilly turned back to John, who was still lost in his own thoughts.

"John? I think I'm ready to go back to work, to witness what I'm here to see."

The man took a deep breath and smiled at her. She hated to deceive such kindness. The reminder of who she truly was, a lying manipulator, made her stomach turn. She let none of that show on her face.

"I don't think it's a good idea, Lilly," he began. "You do seem a little better, but you're exhausted. I think the cosmos can grant an extra day of rest. If it all explodes, then so be it. I care more for you than I do the destiny of our planet."

Completely fooled! This was her first thought. His words bounced off her like a pebble off a brass shield. *If he really knew the truth of me, he'd discard me in an instant.*

What could she do but acquiesce, to play the game of submitting to his guidance? "Are you going to eat anything?" she asked.

"Not today," he answered. "I may take a little water later. But you should. Then get some rest. I have a sense about tomorrow that I can't seem to shake, almost a foreboding. I am trying to get some clarity but that too might have to wait. Anita and Gerald have already taken their meals in their room." John leaned down and hugged Lilly longer than usual, almost as if to say good-bye. He kissed her on the forehead, then left toward his quarters.

Although it wasn't needed, Simon rolled her toward the table. "He's naïve and sentimental, or worse," he asserted, when John was out of earshot. "No one loves like that, unless they have a reason. Lilith, you're not falling for any of that, are you?"

215

"Of course not," she responded.

"It's sickening," Simon continued, "how they all are using you, each for their own purposes. John's the worst of all."

"How can you say that? He's given up everything for me—his home, his privacy, probably his money—"

"He hasn't given up a thing. This Refuge is his little kingdom, and you're the pawn who will solidify his power. You can't begin to imagine the authority he will possess when he owns the actual record of Beginnings. All of them stand to gain, can't you see? They'll be able to influence the whole world and craft mythology that suits them. Lilith, they are here to use you. You can't let them."

Lilly was surprised. "Do you really think he's using me for his own gain?"

"Isn't it obvious?" Simon sat down next to her and began choosing foods to pile onto her plate. "Haven't you noticed the hushed conversations he's always having with the others? They stop talking when I come near. They're plotting something, and I guarantee it is not in your best interests."

Lilly picked at the food, her appetite gone and inner turmoil returned. "And what is your agenda? Why are you here? Do you have my best interests at heart, Simon?"

The man stopped and looked at her, putting down his knife and fork before speaking. "No, Lilith, I do not have your best interests at heart. At least I admit it, not like the others, who are lying through their teeth."

Simon took her hand. His skin was unexpectedly cold and clammy but still felt good against her fever. "I do want good for you, but I confess I'm interested in you for my own reasons."

"What are those?"

"Lilith, if you really are the Witness who can change history, you may be able to bring my wife back to me."

"But, Simon, I thought you said she is dead!"

"Not to me, she's not. I said she is in a better place. She is in my every waking moment and in my dreams at night. She comes to me and I can't hold her or even touch her. She was my everything and I had lost my hope until I met you. You, Lilith, have given me the courage to live and hope again. Together, you and I, we'll change the world."

Lilly was stunned. Was Simon's affection for his wife true love or craziness? She couldn't quite decide. But the romance of it appealed to her, the thought that someone could one day love her like Simon loved his wife.

"How?" she asked, frustrated. "I wasn't able to stop Adam. He turned before I understood what was happening."

"I agree," said Simon. "But you can still stop her."

"Her? Who? You mean Eve? Stop her from what?"

Standing up, Simon began to pace around the room, clasping and unclasping his hands. "I've said too much. She has to make real choices for this to work, but if I say too much, then she may be coerced, and nothing will ever change." He wasn't even talking to her but rambling through thoughts as if they were calculations. "But perhaps if I say just enough, then the rest will fall into place. That's it!" He rushed back to her side and dropped into his chair.

"You must go back tonight!" he declared, putting his hand on her arm. She winced, recoiling deeper into her chair as if it might offer protection. His odd behavior had caught her off guard and she was afraid.

"Go where?"

"To the garden. You must witness, tonight."

"But—"

"Everyone is in their rooms. We can do this!"

"Do what? You haven't told—"

"Wait, there is something else that you must do first."

"What?" She was almost afraid to ask.

"You must look into the mirror again. It's the only way."

"I can't, Simon, don't make me do that, please."

"Lilith." He knelt before her chair and folded his hands on her knees. "Can't you see? This is the only way. Not only will the mirror reinforce the truth of who you are and why you are here, it will empower you to be substantial and present in the garden. It will give you the ability to participate, to *do* something! It's the mirror that empowers you to change things, to change history. You must trust it and what you see in it. Please!"

In a crazy sort of way, Simon was right. She had been more tangible in Eden after being stabbed by the mirror.

Wait—was it the mirror or the snakebite that had made this happen? Which had empowered her? She couldn't recall Simon's words exactly. Regardless, the mirror and snake seemed to be connected, so it probably didn't matter. More important, she had made the decision to take control of her destiny as Lilith, and Simon was presenting a way to do just that.

"Okay, the mirror is still in my room in the dresser. But I'm not putting my hand in there."

"I will get it for you."

As he wheeled her toward her room, another question occurred to her. "Simon, did you take the ring and key?"

"No! I have no need of either one. I hardly even saw them." He sounded certain and Lilly believed him.

Simon quickly found the mirror, still hidden in its covering, and handed it to Lilly. "How many times have you touched the stone?" he asked.

"Twice," she responded. "That was enough."

"Well tonight, you have to touch it three more times—not four, but not fewer than three."

"Three times!" she exclaimed, and Simon put his finger to his mouth to quiet her. "Three times?" she whispered. "This thing really hurts."

"Anything really worth doing is going to be painful," he asserted.

"Great!" she muttered. "If that's true, my whole life has been worth it."

"Three times. Four is too many."

"Simon, how do you know any of this? How do you know that I must look in the mirror to change history? How do you even know that four touches is too many?"

He hesitated. "My wife, Karyn, she touched it six times."

Lilly dropped the mirror into her lap. "This thing killed your wife? And you want me to touch it? Are you crazy?"

"No, no, you have it all wrong. The mirror didn't kill her, but it was with her the last time I saw her. When we found her, she was just a body with no one left inside. The real Karyn was gone, and she didn't come back. She had pushed the stone six times."

"And you expect me . . ."

"What happened to Karyn has nothing to do with you. I warned her. I warned her that the mirror was not for her. She wasn't a Witness. This mirror is for *you*! But now Karyn's sacrifice means something. But because of her I now have answers for you. You are the Witness who can change things."

Lilly slowly removed the mirror from its sheath and looked at it. As before, it was a swirling gray mass of shifting cloud, constantly moving but forming nothing.

"You said Karyn went to a better place."

"I don't know exactly where that is. When I see her in my dreams, she doesn't know me but seems happy."

Lilly held her right thumb above the red stone.

"Wait!" Simon commanded. Relieved, Lilly pulled back. "Remember three, not four. But if I understand how this works, three will be enough to give you authority to stay where you choose."

"So if I choose to stay in Eden?"

"Then you would stay as long as you want and not return. That is how you would be enfolded into history and change the world."

The sheer magnitude of what he had said took her breath away. Lilly didn't want this power. But Lilith did.

It was Lilly who spoke. "Shouldn't we tell John and the others?"

"We can't. They would never allow you to take this risk. They are here to get what they need from you. "

"And you, Simon, tell me again, what are you here for?"

"I am here to serve you, and if possible to find Karyn."

Without another thought Lilith pushed her thumb down on

the stone. Pain shot through her arm and into her shoulder, as if she had grabbed an ember from a fire. The stone absorbed her blood and the surface of the glass began to change. She thrust her thumb a second time, and the pain traveled farther, all the way down her other arm and descending toward her legs. Lilly gasped but controlled herself. A third time she pressed the stone, and this time the pain was so intense she felt as if she were coming apart at her seams. The fire was everywhere, in her feet and in her hair, every nerve and brain cell in agony, so intense she couldn't even scream.

Unable to resist, she looked into the glass. Looking back at her was the most hideous creature imaginable. Her face was rotting off, her eyes were yellow and oozing, her lips forming curses. She was looking at everything she feared most, a disgusting piece of damaged goods to be sold to the highest bidder. But behind the ugliness she could see the truth: she had never been deserving of real love; she was a mistake, an accident, a used-up piece of trash. Not good enough, not smart, not beautiful, and not even a woman. Strangely, that useless, shame-filled visage also gave her power.

She had nothing left to lose because she was nothing to begin with.

Placing the mirror in its sack, she handed it back to Simon, who quickly stashed it away.

"I am Lilith, and I'm ready," she announced. "I won't be coming back."

Sixteen

THE FALL

"Where are we?" Lilith whispered to Han-el, though no one else could hear them.

"Inside Eden, near the center. Look,"—the Singer pointed a short distance toward three figures moving through the grass—"the one who is now two approaches, and with them is the serpent."

"What's that snake doing here?" she asked, but realized the answer. "Adam's invitation?"

Han-el did not have to respond. As they approached, Lilith observed them closely, Eve especially. The young woman walked next to Adam confidently, slightly taller and darker than he, slim, fine-boned, and noble in her bearing. She too was naked except for the transparent light that was more like a glowing breeze billowing and cascading around her, attending every step and movement. The man looked hardly older, but his expression lacked presence. Even when he smiled, a hint of sadness tinged his eyes. Lilith had seen the same look in John's eyes too, but John was not Adam.

"Han-el, one day you will be a Guardian."

"That would be an honor beyond all imagining. I hope that it will be you I serve."

"It won't be me, but someone who is . . . worthy!" She surprised herself by referring to John that way, but in the moment it felt true, despite Simon's assertions.

Adam wasn't returning the attention of the young woman, who obviously adored him. Eve had asked a question but Adam either did not hear or was purposely ignoring her. She repeated it but could not engage him until she touched him on the shoulder.

The serpent seemed larger today. It glided across the ground as if not even touching. Suddenly it stopped and swift as lightning disappeared into the forest. A moment later it reappeared directly in front of Lilith.

Han-el stepped forward but she motioned him away and held her ground as it approached. It wore a crown she had not seen before, with settings for twelve jewels, but Lilith could see that three of them were missing.

"Your crown?" she asked. "It doesn't suit you."

"A gift from Adam, for serving his dominion."

Swaying back and forth, inches away, it scanned her top to bottom. The venom that burned within her responded to its presence, pulsating under her skin. Then it spoke.

"You don't belong here," it hissed.

"You don't either," she challenged.

"I am here by Adam's invitation and he is king of all creation, son of God. You are one of Adam's kind, the right place but wrong time. Who are you and why are you here?"

"My name is Lilith, but I am no one. No one is here to stop you."

"Riddles?" The serpent reared, then dropped toward her again. "Listen, little one, be careful where you step, and do not interfere."

"Is that a threat?" She moved even closer.

"Not to you. You matter not at all."

"I have nothing to lose," retorted Lilith. "What can you take from me that has not already been stolen?"

"That matters not to me. I have no need of anything from you. You are nothing and no one." With those words, the creature darted away, appearing once again behind Adam and Eve. The two had stopped at the edge of a meadow.

"Take me there," she said to Han-el. "I need to hear what they are saying."

Instantly she was standing feet away from the three, who were looking at a fig tree heavy with its fruit. The serpent looked straight at Lilith but spoke to Eve.

"Isha, did God speak directly to you and tell you, 'You shall not eat of every tree of the garden?' "

The question surprised Eve, and she glanced at Adam. Lilith knew from John's reading that the conversation with God had been not hers but Adam's. His gesture indicated she should answer.

"We may eat from the fruit of all the trees but this one standing in the middle of the garden." She tilted her head toward it. "Of this one God has said, 'You shall not eat from it, or touch it, or you will die.' "

Adam nodded his assent, saying nothing. She smiled too,

completely satisfied with her answer. After all, it was exactly as Adam had taught her.

"You surely will not die!" the snake declared.

Eve's eyes widened.

What a stunning thing to say, Lilith thought. This was not a covert insinuation made by this beast, but an overt and bold accusation against God's goodness. This thing had called God a liar?

Eve looked again to Adam, this time troubled and confused, as if expecting him to set this serpent straight. But he did not. Instead he stood in silence. Eve looked to the ground. In doing so, she missed the silent nod between Adam and the creature.

The serpent gave full voice to the darkness Adam had been hiding. "For God knows that in the day you eat from it, your eyes will be opened, and you will be like God, determining good and evil."

Was this true? Lilith was uncertain. This was not what she remembered in the Scriptures John had read. Perhaps she hadn't understood.

Again Adam stood silent and unmoving, waiting for Eve's response. She looked from one to the other and finally to the tree, bursting with its fruit.

Reaching out to stop Eve, Lilith felt Han-el's hand on her shoulder.

"You are here to witness," the Singer sang quietly in a minor key.

Lilith drew back confused, watching helplessly. Slowly walking toward the tree, Eve also faltered, as if grappling with an inner discordant clash of warning and desire, and Lilith could sense the war that raged within her.

Hadn't God made all the trees pleasing to the sight? Hadn't God declared them good to eat? Perhaps they had all misunderstood.

Adam followed Eve, and encouraged by this, she kept moving. The tree was lovely and alluring, offering the promise of sweet taste, but even more it seemed a shorter path to good longings and desires.

Lilith could feel it. How could the passion to be as God be anything but good? Was this not their destiny: to determine good and evil, to be powerful and wise? Here was an easy way to prove their worthiness, fulfill the purposes of God, and take their rightful dominion over *all* creation.

How beautiful, this heart's desire to be like God.

Eve hesitantly extended fingers until they barely skimmed the surface of the fruit, and then quickly pulled back. Nothing happened. The serpent had told the truth. There was no death in touching.

Again she reached, but this time grasped the fig tight and plucked it from its branch. Lilith smelled a potent sweetness as Eve broke open the lovely fruit in her hands. She offered it to Adam, but he declined, so she would taste it first. Slowly raising it to her mouth, she bit into it, chewed, and swallowed. She then held out the other half to Adam, who likewise bit and ate.

Eve grinned and laughed as the pulpy fruit dripped down his chin, but a moment later she placed a hand over her stomach. Her eyes were glazed with fear. Adam did the same and winced. What had been sweet in their mouths was bitter in their bellies.

They had eaten the forbidden fruit. Instead of trusting, they had transgressed, with death the consequence of choosing.

They seemed to know it too. The transparent light that had clothed them vanished and both were utterly exposed. Large tears rolled down Eve's face as she crumpled to the earth. Adam put a hand on her shoulder and she flinched. He leaned and begged, "Isha. Don't you see? It is done, and our dominion has begun. We have cut the cords that bound us to ignorance and dependence. How could we have dominion without knowing good and evil? We are now like God and this freedom is the good."

As Eve looked away, furious and ashamed, Lilith covered her mouth, the sense of grief unbearable. Everything was wrong and hopeless.

"It is not good to be uncovered and unprotected," Adam stated, leaving Eve groaning on the ground. He soon returned with his blade. When Lilith saw Machiara, she gasped and Eve recoiled, afraid. Adam ignored her as he began cutting down the lowest branches, handing them to her. Without a word Eve began stripping off and interlacing leaves. Her tears flowed as together they wove coverings to hide their shame.

"We may have been abandoned but we are no longer foolish," Adam finally spoke. Eve said nothing. For a time they sat against the tree, in silence, staring holes into the dirt. Adam turned his dagger over and over in his hands, frowning.

"Wait here," he said, standing. "I will be back." Then he crossed the clearing and disappeared into the woods. Eve did not watch him go.

When Lilith took a step to comfort the young woman, the serpent hissed a warning and Han-el moved to a place between them. The venom pulsing through her body reminded her of its potency, and she relented.

A long time later Adam returned and slumped down next to Eve. He was panting heavily, sweating, and was covered in what looked like blood.

Eve jumped up concerned. "What happened?"

"I tried to make it right, Isha." His chest and arms were lacerated, the knife still clutched in one hand and bloody to the hilt.

"You tried to make it right? Where did you go? Is this your blood?"

"No!" he exclaimed, still gasping. "This is not my blood. I went to destroy that little Tree of Life."

"Have you completely left yourself? Why would you do that?" She was outraged.

"Isha, it stands as a temptation. We don't need that weak and fragile tree for life, nor any fruit it produces. I tried to pull it out of the ground but couldn't!" He exploded, an edge of bitter resignation in his voice. "So I stripped it of its foliage and clustered fruit. I left it naked with two stunted branches, one on either side."

"What possessed you to do that? It is the Tree of Life! If there is any hope for us—"

"This"—he banged his head back against the trunk in frustration—"is our Tree of Life, our hope, too massive to destroy. Its fruit and seeds are planted deep within us."

Eve closed her eyes and gasped as if straining to breathe, her hand at her throat. She finally found the words, "Adam, what is this blood?"

"That worthless tree belongs to God, who is coming soon to kill us. I thought by offering the Tree of Life another's death to take our place, its blood might cover our transgression," Adam confessed.

"What have you done?" she screamed at him. "Whose blood is this?"

He clamped his hand over her mouth to silence her. "Hush!" he commanded, dismay in his eyes. "Listen!"

Lilith too could hear the sound approaching and it also filled her with a sense of dread.

Adonai and Elohim were walking toward them within the Ruach. What so recently had been a rushing wind of affection now sounded like a fiery raging tempest. Terrified, they climbed into the tree.

"They are hiding their disobedience, ashamed of being found." Han-el sang his grief to Lilith. "They are trying to disappear by blending into Good and Evil."

But it was not a terror who pursued them, it was a broken heart. And it was not fury and outrage in the Wind, but a plaintive melody. Standing at the clearing's edge, Elohim and Adonai called from inside the wind of Ruach, "Adam! Where are you?"

THE SHOUT CAME FROM the Vault, causing John to tumble from his bed. "Something is wrong with the Witness. Help!"

John quickly found his bearings and clothing and sprinted to the Vault, where he was stunned by the scene before him. Lilly lay thrashing in the Chamber of Witness, seizures racking her body. Her empty chair, reclined as a bed, was flush with the sofa as if she had rolled herself over. Turning her on her side, John used his finger to gently clear her airway of saliva and vomit. Gerald and Anita rushed in a moment later.

Simon paced. "I came to check something in the Study and heard noises, and this is where I found her. I didn't know what to do. I'm not trained to deal with anything like this."

"Hush, Simon," Anita told him. "Thank God you were close enough to hear. Another minute and . . . well, it wouldn't have been good."

"She is burning up," John muttered, as Simon withdrew to the perimeter of the room. Anger and fear tumbled inside John's chest. "What was she thinking coming down here by herself?"

"Do you think we should move her?" asked Anita, "She is going to need expert attention, someone you trust with access to the Vault."

"The quickest way to get help for her would be to transport her to the surface through the Map Room," he asserted. "We have to do something or Lilly is not going to survive this."

The decision was made, they lifted her back onto her bed and hurried to the Map Room. John barked orders to the others.

"Anita, Gerald, would you gather up our things before you return to the surface, including Lilly's, mine, and Simon's?"

"I can do that," offered Simon. "Being shifted to another place rather terrifies me—"

"No, I want you with me. I might need your youth and strength.

We understand the Refuge has been breached but we still have no idea what that means yet." The matter was settled, though Simon didn't look pleased.

"Gerald, you and Anita, when you are ready, hold our things and each take one of these triangles and touch this spot on the map. Don't worry about finding a receptacle, they will return here on their own after ten minutes. None of us will be back soon regardless."

They scuttled off, and John approached a console at the side of the map and began entering something onto the screen.

"What are you doing?" entreated Simon. "We don't have time and need to go now!"

"One moment and I am done. I'm notifying the Healers and changing entrance codes for the Vault. We can't be too careful, can we?"

Something about Simon's discovery of Lilly and his reluctance to leave had unsettled John, but he couldn't put his finger on it. "You first, Simon. We'll be right behind you."

Simon took a triangle. "Touch here," instructed John, and when he did, the Scholar vanished.

"I'd rather have sent you to another planet," John grunted, placing a triangle in Lilly's hand and touching his and hers to the map.

When he blinked, they were back to the surface, in the room where Lilly had spent so many months under repair. Letty was already there with Healers and Menders. There was nothing more for the men to do. Simon excused himself and John watched him go. Before John left, he prayed for Lilly. And he prayed for wisdom.

A CHILL RAN THROUGH Lilith's body as if from the inside out, but she ignored it.

"Adam, where are you?" It was a forlorn cry and invitation, but even Lilith knew it sounded like impending doom to the humiliated man and woman. The wind began to rustle through the branches of Adam's tree and then through the leaves that clothed him, and Lilith knew, as they did too, that no one could hide from this God.

Adam, climbing down, chose to take his stand next to the serpent, as if it offered him protection. Eve emerged, dropped to her knees, and bowed in broken glory as tears of confusion and grief continued to cascade.

Adam scrambled to distance himself from his choices, but even in his telling there was insinuation.

"I hid myself, because I heard the sound of You in the garden. I was naked and unprotected and afraid of Your presence, so I hid."

Eternal Man spoke, His question full of a parent's tender love. "Who told you that you are naked?" He reached out, but Adam backed away.

It was another invitation to turn again toward Love, but silence was Adam's shelter.

"Adam, have you eaten from the tree of which We told you not to eat?" Again, the voice was gentle and welcoming, an offer of relationship and reconciliation. But Adam reacted in defensive outrage.

He pointed his finger at Adonai's face. "The woman whom *You* put here with me, she gave me from the tree! I ate!"

The indictment hung thick in the air. Man had become the judge of God, had declared God evil in action and intention. But this blatant charge also finally unmasked the darkness of Adam's turning and uncovered his earlier expression through the serpent. His proud, self-justified rebellion was exposed.

And in his charge against God, the woman heard it too: the same voice of accusation as the serpent, the source of her confusion. Eve understood. She had been betrayed and now was being blamed by Adam for what he had conceived in his own heart.

Lilith was furious but frozen in the moment, helpless to do anything but listen and fume. How could Eve have been so naïve as to entrust her heart to Adam? And how could Adam turn against his greatest joy and make her take the fall?

God did not respond in kind. Adonai spoke no denunciation or condemnation. Instead He turned and offered His hands to Eve. "What is this you have done?" He asked without recrimination.

She looked at Adam, her face a flame of fury, as he stood with folded arms beside his guardian serpent. Turning her face to God, she stretched out her hands and accepted His, drew His palms to her face and, weeping, kissed them. Looking fully into Adonai's eyes, she told the wrenching truth: "The serpent deceived me. I ate!"

God kissed her forehead, acknowledging her confession, and then turned to confront the serpent. It withdrew. Its scales mirrored the Fire and Wind of God's presence, the nine stones of its crown also reflecting brilliant light.

Inches from the creature's head, Eternal Man made a declaration, not only to this creature, but to all the dark forces of Adam's turning that this serpent would ever embolden and empower.

"Because you have done this to the woman, I am snaring you, and binding you unlike any other beast in all creation. Your existence will be bowing on your belly as you feed from the dust of death, the dust of this man's turning."

The serpent visibly shrank and then fell, crashing to the earth. Its crown tumbled away until Adonai stopped it with his foot.

"And furthermore," Eternal Man avowed, "I will establish open hostility between you and the woman, between your seed and hers, and he, her offspring, will crush your head even as you bruise his heel."

Lilith sensed that a war had been declared, lines drawn and sides chosen. The woman took her stand with God against Adam and the serpent. Lilith had not yet chosen.

God turned Their face to the woman and gently spoke with words of sorrow. "This ambush and betrayal will increase your grief and sighing. With trepidation and a grieving spirit you will give birth to your children, and when your turning is to the man, he will rule over you."

Another chill ran through Lilith's body, this time deep in her core. She was shivering. What Adonai said was impossible, wasn't it? How could Eve go back to Adam after all that he had done? But also in that instant Lilith saw a possibility: finally a clear way for her to change history. Even though she hadn't been able to stop Adam from his turning, she could find a way to stop Eve from hers.

Adonai let His Word sink into the woman, and only then did He approach Adam. He drew near with hands extended toward His son as He had toward the woman. Gracious love and tender affection flowed in His words, just as tears ran from His eyes.

Adam turned his face away, his hands at his sides.

"My son, because you listened to the voice of the woman and not to Mine, and because you have eaten of the tree from which I told you not to eat, because of you I have ensnared and bound the earth. You have not only transgressed but hidden iniquity in your heart. With trepidation and a grieving spirit you will try to draw your bread of life from the very ground from which you were taken, but it will strain against you with thistles and with thorns. By the sweat of your downturned face you will leave my Rest to eat your work until the ground itself consumes you. From dust you were created; to dust you will return."

As God declared both the promise and the consequence, Lilith felt as if all creation groaned in grief and shifted.

Adam hesitantly approached Eve. Her eyes burned with rage and grief, and he couldn't hold her gaze. He petitioned her forgiveness with palms up. She refused to touch him.

"I acknowledge before creation," he finally said, his eyes fixed down, "that your name is not Isha. I am now dead, but you are Eve, because you are the Mother of the Living."

His humility didn't absorb the intensity of her wrath. It couldn't begin to bridge the rift that had opened up between them.

"These are for both of you." It was Adonai, holding out

garments of animal skin. "Better you are clothed in these than hiding in the covering that you believe this tree provides."

Hesitantly, Adam reached out and took what God was offering. "Where did these come from?" But he knew.

"Adam, these skins are from the animals you cursed and slaughtered and left impaled upon the Tree of Life. You are already stained in their blood, so let them cover you."

"I was afraid and ashamed," Adam tried to explain. "I didn't know what to do. I thought the shedding of blood would be life that could cover my death and appease you. Life for death?" His tone was hard, still tinged with accusation, but within his words there also was a plea.

"It is not We but you who need a sacrifice," responded Adonai, his voice as gentle as an evening breeze. "Adam, what you have begun, I will one day finish."

Then Adonai lifted his hand and spoke another declaration. "Behold, Adam has become like one of Us, knowing Good and Evil, but he must not stretch out his hand and eat of the Tree of Life, or he will merge light and dark, life and death, freedom and rebellion. And he will stay forever dead."

Again to Adam, God spoke kindly. "My son, you cannot dwell with joy in the presence of One you no longer love or trust. The darkness of your turning is at war with all things light. In order to return, you must leave, but I promise I will not leave you."

The Wind began to swirl around the great tree. Stepping away, Lilith watched in amazement as the gentle breeze of Ruach became a blasting tornado. With a roar She wrapped round the trunk and then tore it completely from the earth with every root and fruit and leaf. Like a weed it was extracted and carried away toward the garden's western boundary.

"Adam," Adonai explained, "in your dominion you chose that tree, so it belongs to you. The Tree of Life will grow forever within Eden, and it will be the tree for the healing of the nations."

Adam understood. "What will I do?" he asked.

"In anxious toil you will work the earth from which you were taken. You will look to it as if it were your life and source. You will require it to give you all that you can only find face-to-face with Us. And you and your kind will fight over ground until the day that you re-turn."

Adam, Eve, and God walked slowly together to Eden's western boundary, and Lilith followed, the serpent silent company. Again, Eternal Man reached out to take His son's hand, but once more Adam pulled away.

"You should have stopped me," he muttered. "Better that I had never lived than to continue to exist in death, alone."

"Not alone, my son. We will never leave you nor forsake you. But, Adam, the darkness of your turning will hide Our face from you."

Adam almost broke down, but he held his pride as they walked on. Finally Adam asked, "And this serpent?"

"The beast leaves with you. There is no place in Eden for accusers or dividers. By believing your own lies, you have unleashed and empowered a violent, lying terror. You have chosen it as companion and provider. It will build for you destructive beasts of devastating power. In exchange for its promise of security and control, you will give it your homage and obedience. Adam,

Our Love will not withhold from you the consequences of your choices. We honor and respect you, so We consent and submit to you. However, We also will reveal a living, loving purpose within your turning and the dust of death. One day We will redeem your disaster, and the serpent in you will be completely crushed."

Reaching the towering commotion of cascading light that roared like waterfalls, they passed easily through the boundary. But Eve and Lilith remained and watched within the dignity of Eden.

"Eve?" Adam called. Her name took the shape of grief. Now Lilith could see that he understood. The woman had been the Love of God in flesh and bone, but he had chosen instead to be alone. This Love, betrayed and dismantled by his independent turning, ranked large among his losses.

"You promised Eve's seed will crush the serpent's head," he said through tears. "How?"

"That, My son, is a mystery yet to be revealed."

Two mighty Cherubim appeared and, drawing swords, they touched the boundary. What seemed to have been water became a flaming furnace. They took their stands as sentries.

"From inside out one can pass as through water, but the return to Eden will be through fire," stated Adonai. "Adam, that is another promise. These Guardians keep the way back to the Tree of Life."

Eternal Man reached one more time to rest a hand on Adam's shoulder, and this time Their son did not flinch or pull away. But neither did he turn to face Them.

"Adam, from before your creation, We loved you. In time you

will forget, but all your choices will never make it any less true. We will love you now and always, and We will be the way to return you home."

When Adam reached up to touch the hand, it was gone. He sighed and slumped onto the dirt. The snake kept its distance.

Inside Eden, Adonai took the serpent's crown and one by one removed the nine stones from their settings. From within His light he brought forth one more stone, the tenth. Elohim produced another, and Ruach, riding as the Wind, presented Them with the twelfth. Then Adonai sang into the sky and twirled and spun until He was a blur. Twelve precious stones of colored brilliance exploded from within him, three in each direction of the compass. Colliding with Eden's boundaries, they penetrated deeply, then detonated in a rainbow of colored music and orchestrated brilliance.

Facing the fiery wall, Adam stood and began to scream, "Eve!" He called and called until his voice gave out. "If it is even possible," he whispered, "would you please forgive me?"

Eve and God, and nearby, Lilith, listened to Adam's wrenching cries.

Exhausted, Adam turned his back to Eden and faced his desolation.

Seventeen

REGRET

"Has anyone seen Simon?" Anita asked as she walked into the room where Lilly lay unconscious, surrounded inside an array of tubes and trays.

"He was here when I arrived with Lilly, but I haven't seen him since," asserted John, a hint of a grin on his face. Anita saw it.

"John, what have you done?"

"Nothing really, simple security precautions. All standard."

"Are you going to tell me?"

"I figured there would be no reason for any of us to attempt to return to the Vault, unless he or she were hiding something, so I may or may not have reset the return coordinates on Simon's triangle."

"You sent him away?"

"The triangles all disappeared as they are supposed to, and Simon seems to have gone missing as well. A mystery?" He shrugged.

"Are you saying he's behind this?" Anita looked at Lilly. "I've worried about his state of mind since the crisis over Karyn."

"I think he has been keeping secrets. And until I understand more, I'd like to be certain he's not going to interfere."

"A shrewd measure!" exclaimed Anita. "May I ask where Simon might be?"

"In a companion community hundreds of miles to the south. It will take him months to return. As soon as I can, I'll go back down to the Vault to see if I can uncover his true intentions."

Gerald entered the room. "How is Lilly?"

"Barely stable," answered John. "She is hovering . . . I think Lilly called it a coma. There's something in her system that we haven't identified yet, and I think she was infected in the Vault. Would you like to help me investigate? The good news is that the Caretaker has not come for Lilly yet, which means we have time."

Gerald nodded.

"I am staying with her," Anita announced. "I want one of us to be here if she awakens."

"I agree, and thank you! Gerald, let's gather some food and water for the journey down."

They left the room together.

"What are we looking for?" Gerald asked.

"We'll know when we find it."

FOR THREE DAYS, LILITH had felt her sense of presence in Eden growing, her ability to interact with her surroundings increasing as if she was gaining substance. She could eat fruit and drink water. She could sleep each night more restfully. Han-el was forever close, and his presence began to make her chafe. Mostly she stayed near Eve, who could not yet see her. Even if she had been able to, grief rendered her oblivious. But Lilith's anxiety was also growing; she needed to act, and soon.

Each day, when the afternoon sun began dipping into the horizon, Adam would emerge from the forest to stand as close to the wall as he dared and beg Eve to come to him. From Eden's side there was no impediment to seeing out. Lilly could clearly see him on his knees, pulling at his hair and screaming his anguish. He couldn't see in, which only added salt to his wound.

The third day, Eve, her hands against the misty veil, watched Adam descend down a path toward a nearby pond. Lilith was close enough to watch and listen, as Eve buried her face in Adonai's shoulder and began to wail and beat on Him. He held her in His strong arms until she calmed.

"I hate him!" she formed the words, "I hate him!"

"You hate what he has become," said Adonai. "He is not what he has become. The very Good will always be deeper than the turning."

"Do You still love him too?"

"That has never been a question for Us, as it is for you. We always knew and yet We love him still."

"If You knew, then why would You allow it?"

"True love requires open hands. Without the power to say no, love never will be real, just illusion."

"And you created anyway?"

"You are a marvelous wonder, Eve, made in Our own image.

This creation is the best, and Man, the wonder of all wonders. We created to share with you the Love and Life that We have always known. But We always knew that for our yes, you would declare a no."

"But why even create at all, if You knew?"

Adonai hugged her tight. "One day, Eve, you will be a mother and will better understand. True love is not about the other's choices, but who you know as they are. But as you see, relationship is indelibly affected by the choices of the other."

"Am I betraying myself? I did this to him. I could have stopped it. I could have asked You but I didn't. Instead, I wanted to be more than I already was, for him, for You. I wanted to be like You."

She touched the boundary again and knew that if she chose, she could walk right through it. "Adam," she whispered. Lilith knew he couldn't hear. "Please forgive me too.

"God, I am so angry! He raised me, cared for me, and then betrayed me. I am breaking into pieces." And then the next emotions arose in her words. "But I can't endure that he is there, alone, and without me."

"He is without you," Adonai agreed, "but he will never be alone. He is not that powerful."

Eve smiled weakly. "That is a comfort to me but not to him. What is he going to do?"

"Adam will work with his hands and by the sweat of his brow to extend Eden without Our presence or Our word. He will turn to the ground for security and worth, identity and meaning, though it cannot give what it does not have."

"But you said that I would have a seed, a man-child. How could that be possible if . . ." She looked at the barrier between her and Adam.

God smiled. "With that you must trust Me. I fashioned you from Adam's side and him from the dust of creation. My promise and My word are one. It will surprise you."

"You said that one day I would turn to him. I don't think I can or will. Should I?"

"In turning to the man, as Adam has to the ground, and in demanding of him what he cannot give, you would trap him in his shame. Not knowing who he is, he will either run away or exercise dominion over you. If you turn, this will be the consequence of your choosing."

"Why would I ever again choose such a devastating path?"

"You would have your reasons. You have the freedom to trust and the freedom to turn. This is the profound and sometimes painful mystery of community and love."

"Will I always have this terrifying freedom?"

"Always! This is Love."

In that moment Lilith loved Eve and felt more compassion for her than she'd ever felt for anyone else. She had to save her from Adam's fate. Eve must not leave Eden. If Lilith could change Eve's path, then she could change history, including her own story. She could save Simon's wife and countless other girls. Perhaps it was possible to be something besides worthless. It was time.

"Stay here!" she ordered Han-el. "Don't come with me." The Angel bowed and held his place. She slipped easily through and out of Eden's wall. Lilith knew she never would return here either.

"WE FOUND IT!" GERALD exclaimed excitedly. "What Simon was hiding. We found it!" They startled Anita in the middle of a bite of supper. Recovering, she looked at both men, confused, as John had a fist upraised as if to show her. But he was holding . . . nothing.

"Congratulations!" She rolled her eyes and wiped her mouth. "I send men to find something and they come back excited about nothing."

"My dearest heart," Gerald entreated, "it's a blender's bag. It absorbs the light to become virtually invisible: that's why we didn't see it before. But this time when we went through Lilly's room, it was sitting hidden on her journal."

Anita put down her spoon, the expression on her face shifting from annoyance to amazement. "Well, what's in it? Did you find the ring and key?"

"No," added Gerald. "Something sinister, an ancient blood-stone mirror."

John drew it out of its sheath carefully, with two fingers by the handle until it was totally exposed. He laid it on table. The three gathered around it.

"I've studied these," said Gerald. "They are very rare, a dark arts favorite—mirrors that lie to you."

Anita chuckled. "Personally, I have found this true of almost every mirror."

"Not like this one," continued Gerald. "Do you see how there is no image on the surface, just a swirling gray, and right here"—he pointed, keeping his finger at a distance—"is the blood stone, in this case a diamond. This you mustn't touch, for it will draw your blood. If you look closer you can see dried blood here and here. Lilly's, I suspect. We'll test it. The stone is said to absorb your life and then reflect your deepest truth of being, who you are at the very core of your soul."

"It can do that?" asked Anita, astonished.

"Of course not," reassured Gerald. "That is all hocus-pocus. The intention is to draw your attention to the blood, but that's only misdirection. What it really does is inject you with a poison, whatever that might be, a drug or neurotoxin or combination to make the person highly suggestible. It plays on their worst fears and self-loathings."

"I will get this to the Scientists right away," said John, returning the mirror to its cover and putting them both into a box. "We can't ascertain what Lilly saw, but I am certain it was not good."

LILITH DIDN'T HAVE TO go looking for the serpent. It found her soon after she had left Eden's sanctuary.

"State your purpose," it demanded, and Lilith smiled. The snake was barely able to raise its head above the ground, and she towered over it.

"A win-win plan," she stated. Lilith had intended to go directly to Adam, but alliance with the beast could be helpful if Adam needed to be persuaded.

"I am listening," the creature replied.

"I heard Adonai's promise to Eve, that her child would one day crush your head."

"I have had better days. What do you propose?"

"As long as Eve remains in Eden, she can't bear a child. Could one who has the power to crush your head be born apart from Adam? If they remain apart, won't you rule in safety?"

The serpent was silent for a long time before speaking. Finally it said, "Adam is inconsolable. He seeks any means to bring her here."

"He turned his face from God and from his counterpart. He is alone, but I can ease his loneliness."

The beast understood. "You? You would offer yourself to him? Why?"

"To keep Mother Eve safe, and many others."

"Ah, you are Eve's daughter. But that makes you all the more dangerous, to Adam and to me. Adonai said her seed would crush my head, but could not that seed be you?"

Lilith was ready. "No! Eve said it would be a man-child. I was prepared for such a choice as this. I cannot bear a child and will never be a threat. I can serve a purpose both to Adam and to Eve."

"And why would Adam want a miserable nothing nobody like you, who willingly would sell herself for this purpose?"

The serpent spoke the truth about her. She stopped walking and scowled down at it. "You think I am a whore? Does it matter if I am? No. What matters is that we will all get exactly what we want."

The snake coiled itself as if to strike, then rested its head upon the ground. "Adam's darkness is maturing, but it can't compare with yours. You either have no idea who you are, or you no longer care. I will find Adam."

The serpent slithered out of sight, leaving Lilith shivering in the early evening cool. She sat on a rock, looking down at dirty hands and legs, her dress torn ragged by thistles and thorns. A brook and pond sang their innocent song, and Lilith washed her hands and face. A lingering sun reflected off its mirrored surface, and she beheld a young girl's face that was strong and full of promise. Running her hand through the image, it rippled out and away. It only told the lie, not the truth beneath it.

Soon she heard Adam's approach in heated conversation, but when he saw her, he stopped and stared, until Lilith became uncomfortable.

"Who sent you here?"

"Eve. She loves you and is sad that you are lonely." It wasn't an outright lie but was probably as far as truth could be bent without completely breaking. "Adam, I will be your companion. Leave Eve with God in Eden. She's better off there. With me you won't feel alone. I can satisfy you. Leave her with God, I beg you."

Adam raised a hand to silence her and think.

"You are right," he finally said. "I have been thinking only of myself and the things that I have lost. I understand clearly. I will no longer go each day and beg for her to leave and come to me. She is in the better place, where toil is not her existence and she is embraced by God's Love."

He sat down on the ground and repeatedly threw dirt up on his head, moaning, "I miss her to my bones. Each day I feel less reason to be living."

Lilith took a spot next to him on the ground, close but not touching. Adam's tears mixed with the dirt, and mud became his shroud. Without looking he reached out and took her hand.

"The serpent tells me you are Eve's daughter? Truly?"

"I am."

"And you would do this for your mother? Become my wife?"

"Yes, by my own choice."

"Can you promise me a son?"

And in that question Lilith was trapped. Did Adam know? Had the serpent told him? If she lied and he knew it, that could be the end of her plans. If she told the truth, that could also be the end.

"Some things take time and—"

"Lilith." Adam squeezed her hand. "Can you promise me a son?"

Despair descended and gripped her heart, the words barely able to form. "No, Adam, I cannot."

"Look at me," he said tenderly. As difficult as it was, she raised her head and looked into his dark and gold-flecked eyes, his face a mess of dirt and tears, a tired smile embedded there.

"Even if you could promise me a son, I would have said no. Eve is my beloved and I will learn to live without her. I will not betray her a second time. Lilith, Eve has no substitute and neither do you. This deceptive darkness I perceive in you, that would cause you to sell yourself for less than love, I know I am its source. One day, perhaps, you will find a place within your heart to forgive me too, for I must be your father."

Lilith came undone. She had been rejected. Her fury toward the men who had made her this damaged property now fueled her own self-loathing. She wrenched herself away from Adam and stood.

"I hate you!" she snarled, and turning, ran into the darkness of the forest. Adam let her go. The only thing left for her was to find a place to die.

JOHN RUSHED INTO THE room where Gerald and Anita were poring over books.

"Lilly has taken a turn for the worse," he announced.

"Who is watching her?" snapped Anita like a brooding mother hen.

"Letty is with her," replied John.

"I was afraid of this," moaned Gerald, slamming the tome he had been reading down on the table. He picked it up and slammed it down again. "I can't find what it is that is catalyzing the poison. We know its chemical breakdown, we know the plants from which it is derived, we have given her every variation of antidote and antitoxin and anti-everything, but she is dying and I feel completely helpless. And I've been praying too, in case you are wondering. Haven't stopped praying."

"Me too, Gerald, me too!" Anita whispered.

She wrapped her arms around her husband and he let her hold him, the sobs of his pent-up frustration finding some release.

"Maybe there isn't a cure," John suggested.

"What do you mean?" asked Anita. "There has to be one."

"Not if the poison is not biological or chemical or neurological. What if what Lilly saw in that mirror took away her hope? Or her sense of meaning?"

"Or significance or love," added Anita. "That makes sense. Without hope, even an otherwise healthy person can die. And

Lilly had barely begun to heal physically, much less emotionally."

"If this is true," Gerald said, "what do we do?"

"Gerald, you've already said it," John said. "We do the only thing we know to do and leave the rest to God. We will pray and sing and talk to her, and anoint her with oil. Are we not elders?"

Letty poked her head into the room. "Pardon my intrusion, but I have news. Don't look at me that way, Anita. Lilly is never left alone. The Caretaker is arriving tomorrow, but we don't know for whom he's coming. Possibly Lilly."

It was an unexpected blow and John recovered first. "Then we had better get busy praying and anointing, shouldn't we? I know prayer is never magic or any other kind of manipulation, but right now, I am prepared to bargain with my life."

LILITH'S LAST HOPE WAS that death would find her quickly and painlessly. She curled up in a little ball under a massive, ancient tree. The irony of trying to stay warm while trying to die didn't escape her. Sometimes natural survival mechanisms were a nuisance.

She could feel her soul slowly leaking out her life, fractured and full of holes that even lies could no longer seal. Her last words screamed at Adam were the ultimate proof of a wasted life. In this moment she was brutally honest: she hated everything. "Damn you, Adam! Damn you, God! Damn me! Damn us all!" she shouted. But who was she to make such withering pronouncements? She was nothing and no one.

It was as if someone had captured her entire life in a series of photographs. Lying there dying, she was forced to look at every one. Each picture of a memory was one more accusation. There was no Good in her.

Whether dreaming or delusional, she danced in ragged clothes, surrounded by broken toys and the clicks of locking doors. And in the mix of harsh colors, and as the music slowly faded away, she thought she glimpsed Adonai's presence but then turned away. Peace washed over her. She was glad to die. Finally she would find the rest that would sweep her cares away. Heaven was no option, but hell could not be worse than the life she'd known.

There He was again, offering a smile, a kind look, a brief touch as she tried again to turn away.

The leafy branches she had gathered for a last bed now seemed a living cushion, the weight of her life lifted and held in tender mercy. Her last thought as the darkness of unconsciousness descended was, "If dying is this easy, I should have done it sooner."

Eighteen

FACE-TO-FACE

They were not soft branches that held her but the strong and tender arms of Adonai. He sat under the ancient tree and sang to her an ancient song of stars and of Beginnings, of joy and hope and all things Love where nothing was unkind. It was the sweet song of healing and rest. It called to deepest longings and welcomed her like home was always meant to.

Taking a deep breath, Lilly slowly opened her eyes. At another place and time she would have denied His presence, but here and now it felt as though nothing else had ever been as real. She was done with all her running, had fallen and hit the ground, then finally found a place on which to rest. So she did what any child would do. Turning, she buried her face into His chest, sobbing, tears cascading as He wrapped His peace and love around her.

She had been waiting her entire life for this. She was knowing and being known beyond understanding, grasping the deepest mystery of why music invades, ignites, and then dwells in the

255

soul, finding a forever habitation. There was nothing she wanted other than to be completely found inside this Eternal Man, to be heard and seen and celebrated.

"Lilly, it is you I love," came the voice like healing waters. The words themselves were living and dismantling. She felt that she would never have to hear another sound or syllable. This was sufficient, and in this firm and everlasting embrace, all that had been broken or stolen could be found, restored, and celebrated.

"Lilly, do you trust Me?" It was a question not about belief but about person, character, and relationship, and only asked for this solitary moment suspended in the fabric of the time's cosmos. It needed no justification, reason, or defense. It was simple and clean, and so too was her immediate response, delivered in a mixture of snot and tears.

"I do." And she meant it but even as she said it she felt herself resisting.

Internally Lilly stepped back a bit. "I mean, I really want to."

The hug squeezed a bit tighter and Adonai spoke. "Lilly, you have always been worthy of being loved and I have always loved you. That has always been true, but you didn't know."

If there was anything deeper to undo, any lies, insinuations, or accusations that were closer to the bedrock of her self-awareness, she couldn't have imagined it. She let the waves engulf her and sweep her back together, the fiery flame of His affection disintegrating everything that was not Love. For a moment it felt as if nothing would remain, but that thought itself ignited and burned away and she no longer cared, because in this single moment she trusted.

When the tumult and tides all settled down, Lilly realized that she was still curled up on Adonai's lap as He leaned against the tree.

"Lilly,"—Eternal Man's voice was gentle—"trust is about relationship, not power. When two dance, each is always respectfully attuned to the other. There is a timing to relationship, and that is Ruach's playground."

"And You trust the Holy Spirit?"

"I do," Adonai laughed. "I mean, I really want to."

Now Lilly laughed, recognizing her own words. "Trust has never been an easy thing," she said with a sigh.

"It is not a thing at all, Lilly. It is the giving of your very self to another, to be weak and naked and unashamed. You have history and experience that tells you trust is a mountain impossible to climb. But you can and will."

"Will I, Adonai? Will I ever climb that mountain?"

"Yes, dear one, you already are climbing, one step at a time, and not alone."

She leaned back against his chest and closed her eyes, letting the sun caress her face and the sounds of insect activity capture her attention.

"How did You find me? I was sure I was going to die. It seemed easier for everyone, especially me."

"You have never been lost to Me. Lost to yourself, but not to Me."

That made Lilly smile, comforted and assured. "Now what? Can we stay here like this forever?"

"Come," He said, and standing up, He lifted her to her feet. "Lilly, do you trust Me?"

"I do!" And together they walked holding hands until they rounded the bend of a creek and she saw the fire of Eden's boundary.

"What are we doing here?" she asked, perplexed and anxious.

"I am here to take you back inside. Lilly, do you trust me?"

"I can't go through there," she gasped. "I don't belong there."

"You are partly right. Lilith can't go through the fire, but Lilly can, and it is Lilly who has always belonged here."

Another choice, another crossroad. To dare to enter through that wall would mean that lies would be burned away. Could she let Lilith go? She felt an intense war within, as if Lilith were pleading.

"Lilly," Adonai said, "look up and into My face. I am here and will never leave you. In any dance you sometimes lead, but always both submit. So now, dear Lilly, you must choose, and I submit to you."

Holding out both hands, Eternal Man now backed into the fire. As he did, His eyes turned into flames, His robe cascading brilliant light, His feet like burnished brass.

Three times He had asked her to trust, and for the third time she made her choice. Reaching up, she took His hands, and He slowly led her inward until they were engulfed in a mass of blazing fire. The pain of holy judgment poured through her like a torrent raging and she gave herself to it, allowing it to rend from her the lies that had inhabited her spirit, soul, and body.

And when it seemed that all was undone and nothing remained, Almighty Voice of furious Love made an ultimate declaration.

"Whatever is alive will never die, and what is dead will be completely burned away."

Lilly stepped through and opened up her eyes.

"LETTY?" SHE RASPED. "WHAT are you doing here?"

"I'm knitting. Can't you see? Knitting!" As if nothing had happened, the tiny woman returned to her familiar and welcome humming and her knitting.

"Where are we?"

"You are back in your room in the Refuge. The others have gone to catch some sleep. You have kept them up long hours, but your fever finally broke awhile ago and already you are rapidly improving, praise be to God. We thought you were a goner."

Lilly laughed, her voice hoarse. "A goner? Really? So you drew night duty? Shortest straw?"

"I volunteered. I don't need sleep like the others." Letty allowed her needles to rest in her lap a moment, and she leaned in close to Lilly's face. "What happened, Lilly? What brought you back? We thought you had lost all hope and we didn't know how to reach you."

"Adonai!" Lilly cleared her throat. "Adonai made the difference. He came and found me and healed me inside fire."

"Ah, yes!" Letty smiled. "Everyone goes through fire, dear one, but the flame of His affection is *for* not *against* you. It purifies anything that is not Love."

"Is it permanent?"

That made Letty laugh. "Hah, dear one, the truth is always permanent, but you will still have to work out your new life with trepidation and trembling, being as you are so fragile and naked."

"We were created to be that way, weren't we? Naked and unashamed?"

"Indeed." The little woman nodded, concentrating on her needlework once again.

"Letty, what are you making?" Lilly asked, curious. "It doesn't seem like knitting is anyone's *thing* around here."

"I actually have no idea, but it helps me think and pray. I have dozens of these . . . these *things* that have no rhyme or reason. One day I will gather them all up and see if together they make any sense."

"You are the best," Lilly said with a giggle, letting the quiet of the night enfold them. Finally, Letty put down her tools and spoke, in a different tone entirely.

"Lilly, I have a confession to make."

"You did something wrong?"

"Oh no, not that kind of confession. This is more like saying out loud something that you have been keeping to yourself."

"Great, more secrets. I'm done with secrets."

"No, not a secret either. A good surprise that has been waiting for the right time."

"So is this the right time?"

"It is. Lilly, I am not exactly, well, I don't really know how to say this, but I am not human."

"Really?" Lilly laughed as if it were a shock. "That's your

surprise? Letty, I was never sure what you were, but human wasn't one of my guesses. So, if not human, then what are you?"

"Well?" She let out a little laugh. She was enjoying this. But the chuckle then led to a giggle, and that to a snort, which got them both laughing.

"Just tell me already," Lilly insisted between her chuckles.

When Letty had finally settled down enough, she leaned forward, the clicking of her needles resuming again. "You know that Han-el is John's Guardian, right?" Lilly nodded. The woman waited a moment. "Well, I am yours."

"Mine?" Lilly was completely surprised. "Like my Angel Guardian?"

"Didn't see that coming, did you?"

Lilly lay back in the bed, flabbergasted. "But aren't you the town mayor or something, on the council and who knows what else?"

"I multitask."

"Have you always been my Guardian?"

"Yes, always."

"But I thought Guardians, you know . . . guarded."

Letty stopped her knitting. "Did someone tell you I was good at this?" She laughed her shrill giggle. "Lilly, what we do would be simpler if humans weren't so complicated. Most of you have such a low opinion of yourselves, you don't begin to realize how powerful your choices and dominion are. Even human choices that are born of shadow-sickness must be treated with respect, because it is human beings who make them. So we watch and attend and then interfere when allowed, which is my favorite part. It's one of the reasons your prayers are so powerful. It lets us mess with things."

They could hear John coming down the hall, whistling his usual melancholy tune.

"Does he know?" asked Lilly.

"No." She grinned. "He just thinks I'm old and odd. A Curmudgeon is what I think he calls me."

John entered, glanced at Lilly, and looked so relieved that she thought he might cry.

"Lilly!" he exclaimed, and gave her a hug, which she returned. Something had changed inside her and she felt none of her usual hesitation or caution. "To see you awake and looking so well is the best gift I can imagine. You two have been catching up, I see."

"Some," acknowledged Lilly. "But I still have lots of questions. I take it you know about Simon and the mirror?" It felt good to not have secrets to hide anymore, and Lilly was determined to keep it that way.

"Yes, we know," John said. "Simon has been shadow-sick from the first day he arrived here with Anita and Gerald."

"You knew and didn't tell me?" Lilly was shocked.

"Would you have believed us?"

"Probably not," she acquiesced. "Why didn't you stop him?"

"We needed time to determine what he was after. To tell you without proof would have driven you deeper into the dark that you were fighting."

"Well, he said some pretty terrible things about you and the others."

"In the nicest sort of way, I imagine," grunted John. "You have to give him an A for effort."

"So where is he? Simon?" Lilly wondered, and again the other two exchanged glances.

"I set a trap, which he voluntarily sprung. As we speak, he is miles to the south being companioned, like Karyn is to the north. They need to discover they are not alone before they can really be together."

"Karyn. His wife? But I thought she was—"

"Karyn was the Scholar who became shadow-sick before they even got here. That mirror of hers probably had a lot to do with it. Terrible device. Anyway, our hope is that after their individual healing they will be reunited, embarrassed but better."

"So why did he want me to use the mirror?"

"When I confronted him, he said he truly believed that you could use the mirror to change history and return his wife to him."

"Where's the mirror now?"

"Locked away deep in the Refuge. Scholars will try and mine its secrets. A preventive measure." John clapped his hands as if to end the discussion. "So, Lilly of last questions, anything else come to your mind before we take you to the kitchen and feed you? Oh, and by the way, I came just now to see if the Healers were right. They said you have made remarkable progress. *Unprecedented*, I think was their term, an ambitious term for experts. They told me that you could even try and walk, if you are up for that. But very slowly and with a lot of help."

Lilly was thrilled. First, John helped her sit at the edge of the bed, which they then lowered until her feet touched the floor.

Carefully, she stood for the first time since her arrival. It was liberating, such a small success, but the effort left her light-headed, and after only a couple of wavering steps, she returned to the bed now converted into her chair.

"Amazing," John declared, and Letty smiled ear to ear. "We will work on that and more. What do you think sparked such an *unprecedented* recovery?"

"Adonai," Lilly replied.

"Of course," affirmed John. "Adonai, and timing. Something I will never quite understand, but for which I am grateful!" He spoke it into the air as though talking to Someone invisible.

Letty led the way as John wheeled Lilly out. To Lilly, everything felt different, almost new, her senses heightened. She was thankful too and silently whispered such to Whoever might be listening.

Gerald and Anita, upon arriving in the dining area, rushed to give her hugs, which again she returned easily and openly.

They had barely sat when Lilly blurted out, "My thankful heart today is my best offering." The others looked at her, bemused. "Well, I figured if I was ever going to learn to pray, this was as good a start as any."

Over a comforting meal of soft eggs and buttered bread that tasted better than anything Lilly had ever put into her mouth, each person told their version of the past few days, with many laughs and occasionally a tear or two.

"Was I awful to you?" asked Lilly. "I was, wasn't I? I am so sorry."

"Not to worry, dear," offered Anita. "We all were aware that there was much more going on behind the curtain than we could see."

"Oh!" exclaimed Lilly. "It was a lot worse than you could have imagined. Simon and the mirror convinced me I was Lilith."

"Lilith? Really?" Gerald blurted, obviously irritated by the mere suggestion. "Sheer fabrication! Mythology that has no truth in history."

"I remembered how you feel about her, but it didn't matter. That mirror and its poison reflected back the lies I already believed about myself. That I was a worthless, ugly girl, who might redeem herself by doing one good thing—save the world by stopping Mother Eve from turning."

"Wow!" stated John, surprised. "And how were you supposed to do that?"

"I'm embarrassed to say," stated Lilly slowly. "I thought if I gave myself to Adam as a substitute for Eve, he would stop trying to get her to leave the garden and join him, and then the world would be changed."

"I didn't know about this," admitted Anita, "but I don't think anything has changed." She looked back at Lilly. "Has it?"

"I don't think so," Lilly replied, now herself a little uncertain.

"What happened?" asked John.

"Adam rejected me, or rather, Lilith. He chose Eve. That's when I thought I was going to die, and Adonai came and found me."

"So if nothing has changed," surmised Gerald, "then at some point Eve must have left the garden."

"I don't know," stated Lilly sadly. "But that seems to make sense. And Adonai seemed to think she would. Why would she do that?"

No one had an explanation that aligned well with what Lilly knew about Eve.

As the conversation continued, Lilly became aware that Anita and Gerald seemed to be hesitant about finishing their meal, as if they were keeping something from her. Finally she asked, "What is going on, you two?"

Anita clenched her jaw and couldn't speak, so Gerald attempted, but a cascade of tears flowed with his words.

"We have received a summons, a request and invitation to another time and place, and we have accepted. We didn't know how to tell you. I guess it seemed that if we kept talking, we would not have to say good-bye. I know that is silly, but it's how I . . . we feel."

"You're leaving?" Lilly felt a rush of emotions. "When?"

"Soon," Anita said sadly. "In a couple of hours. It was very sudden, but we both agree it warranted a quick response. I'm so sorry, Lilly. If there were another way . . ."

"No, it's okay, really. I just didn't expect it. You two have become . . . special to me, and I . . ." Lilly didn't know how to find the words to say how much the couple mattered to her.

"We love you too," said Gerald.

"And, Lilly," continued Anita. "I have learned over a lifetime to trust God with everything that becomes precious to me, as you, dear one, have become to us. This is only the beginning of our story. If we didn't have that sense, we would not be leaving."

Lilly was quiet and then said, "I need to go and get something I would like to give you. Please don't go without saying good-bye, okay?"

"Of course. At any rate, we also heard the Caretaker was coming for a visit later this afternoon, and we decided that if he wants either of us, he will have to put a little more effort into it."

"I don't understand! Who is this Caretaker person?"

"I'll explain that to you later, Lilly," said John. "But right now Gerald and Anita need to prepare for their next journey. Let's all meet back here in an hour or so to say our farewells."

"Letty, would you take me to my room?" asked Lilly, and without a word the Guardian pushed her out and down the hall.

"Thank you." Lilly sighed. "I didn't know what to say about all that I am feeling. It's like . . . I mean, it's as if I've finally found a family, and just as quickly they all get taken away."

"Nothing stays the same, dear one. Trust is not a once-in-a-lifetime decision, but a choice made within each moment as the river runs. We are thankful for the gifts that surround us, and then we let them go, trusting that nothing will be lost, even if we lose it for a time."

"I am really trying to understand, I am. You probably think I'm just a mess."

"I think you're a teenager." Letty laughed. "The words often go together."

That made Lilly laugh and she felt better.

When everyone gathered again in the living area to say their good-byes, Lilly handed her journal to Anita, who looked surprised.

"Your journal? Lilly, what is this?"

"It is my gift to you, the one *thing* that is most important to me, and I want you and Gerald to have it. You two mean more to me than anything I have, even something that is most precious."

Anita and Gerald were both stunned. John looked on like a beaming father.

"Thank you," said Gerald. "Truly, one of the greatest gifts we have ever received."

"John made me this book, and it's actually a recorder, like the ones down in the Vault. I've recorded everything I've witnessed, the good and the not so good, because I want you to have that too. I've done my part, and now I think it's time for some Scholars to figure out what it all means."

John showed Lilly how to add the Scholars' hand-signatures so they too could access its contents. "I assume," he told them, "that you will find another Vault in the place where you are going. There you can store and play it back for study."

"We will see you soon enough, Lilly. It's just a matter of time." Without more fanfare everyone exchanged hugs with forehead touches, and then the Scholars left without looking back, for reasons that Lilly understood.

She parked her chair a few feet from the filament window and tentatively stood. John moved close but didn't assist as she made a few weak, tottering steps to look down onto the beaches below. "I did it," she proudly exclaimed, and John clapped in agreement.

Gingerly and carefully, she made her way back and sat, exhausted but elated. "John, will you wheel me to the Castle Patio so I can feel the wind and sun?"

For a second he hesitated before he spoke: "I would like that very much." They soon made their way up the ramp and were about to go through the door and out into the sunshine, when Han-el unexpectedly appeared in front of them.

The Guardian smiled. "John," the Singer sang, "I will be attending."

John lowered his head for a moment and thought before nodding. "Thank you!"

"Attending what?" Lilly asked, a sick feeling creeping into her stomach.

Without answering, John pushed her past the Angel and into the open sun. Instead of feeling warmth, Lilly's heart was gripped by a chill. She took a sharp, surprised breath. Looking out over the water was a stranger in a three-piece suit, his head topped by a black bowler hat that accentuated his pasty and anemic skin. The man's eyes were hollowed and dark. In contrast to the blacks and whites he wore was an accessory completely out of place: a bow tie of bright scarlet.

"You're the Caretaker?" she uttered, still trying to curb her fear.

The stranger didn't turn but answered, his voice smooth and cold. "I have been looking for a friend, a particular one for a long, long time. A Collector. I think you know him, do you not? Is he close by?"

"I'm right here, Caretaker. As if you didn't know," John stated flatly.

One could almost say he smiled, this solemn man, but if that is what his expression was, it didn't last for more than a fleeting moment.

269

There was something eerie about both his demeanor and authority, and Lilly edged her chair away. She instinctively didn't want to be near him, not so much because he might be an imminent threat, but more because he stirred up profound trepidation and uncertainty in her heart. It was hard for her to imagine this man close to anyone, especially John the Collector.

"He might be your friend," she whispered. "But he gives me the creeps!"

"A matter of one's perspective, I suppose," John laughed.

"He makes me think of a mortician," she noted. "Except for that bow tie."

"The tie?" He laughed again. "That has never made any sense to me."

Now John spoke directly to the stranger. "So you have come for me?" The question caught Lilly by surprise.

"Wait—you knew he would be here? Why didn't you say no when I asked to come up here?" she sputtered.

"Lilly, not once have I told you what to do or not, so why should I start now?" And leaning down, he kissed her on the forehead.

The Caretaker turned and for the first time acknowledged the Collector and nodded to Han-el.

"Hello, old friend," he said to John. "You have been a wily one, difficult to trace."

"I had help." He tipped his head toward Han-el, who stood with arms folded.

"True, but now your passport is full. It's time for you to go."

"John," Lilly hissed, "what is he talking about? Go where?" She was afraid to hear the answer.

"Go where?" John asked the visitor on her behalf. "Another island in between worlds somewhere, or in between dimensions?"

"No, not this time, John. Today, you go home."

As if things were not strange enough, at these words John burst into tears.

"Home? You've come to take me home?" he sobbed, his legs giving way. He slumped to the ground next to Lilly's chair. She put an arm protectively around him, but she was devastated. Twice in one day, it now seemed, she would be losing someone.

"I know why you came up here." She breathed the words through gritted teeth. "John, you're going to die, aren't you?"

John, gathering himself, stood. But he was smiling through his tears. "May I have a moment to say good-bye?"

"I will wait only long enough for that before I dance you home."

Ignoring the Caretaker, John knelt to speak to Lilly, face-to-face. "Lilly, I didn't know for sure. I had my suspicions but was uncertain. I am sorry it is so sudden."

"I hate this!"

"I know and understand," he reassured her. "Lilly, listen to me. Because of Adonai, what looks to you like death will be for me more living."

"I don't understand!"

"You will, dear Lilly, you will."

"But aren't you sad? I'm so sad, I think I am going to fall apart."

"It is always sad to leave one place and time and enter another, especially when you leave something, someone who is precious. When you get to be my age, you know when a new beginning is close—it's a premonition maybe? Letting go is also a returning."

"John, you have helped put my heart back together. Do you know that you are the first man I've ever trusted, ever loved?"

"My honor and my privilege," he whispered. "Lilly, God is such a magnificent artist that no one is ever healed alone. One day you will see how much healing you've brought me."

"Me?"

"Lilly, I am not asking you to trust me for a lifetime, just for now, today and in this moment. Will you trust me?"

It took her minutes to catch her breath as he wiped away her tears. Finally, she said, "Yes! I will trust you, in this moment."

"Then tell me good-bye."

And she did. She hugged him and kissed his cheeks and cried and cried some more. And then she whispered, "Good-bye, John. I will see you soon."

"You will!" he declared, and taking a deep breath, stood.

"Wait! I have one last question."

John laughed, clean and clear. "Of course you do, what is it?"

"In Eden there are so many names for God. What do you call Him?"

"That is an easy one. My favorite name for God is Cousin!"

"Cousin?"

"Yes! I have always loved to tell anyone who asked that God is my cousin!" John beamed, as if he were growing younger. "Adonai, Jeshua, Jesus, the second Adam—my cousin, you will see!"

As he turned to face the Caretaker, Han-el appeared walking next to him and took him by the hand.

"I love you too, Lilly Fields!" John yelled back at her, his childlike joy radiant.

And reaching up above the rail, the Caretaker opened what appeared to be a door materializing in the air. He took John's other hand and with a single agile step the three disappeared right through it. Lilly sat, her mouth open, as the portal shimmered and then evaporated like an image on the water disturbed by a splashing stone.

"Such a show-off," stated Letty, standing next to her. "Come on, Lilly, we still have work to do! Good thing I don't need stairs and ramps. Let's get out of here!"

Nineteen

THE THREE

When the mist cleared away, Lilly found herself sitting beside Letty in front of the Vault's door.

"Told you!" said Letty. "So much faster than walking with John."

Lilly laughed in spite of all the emptiness she felt. "What are we doing here?"

"You have an appointment," the Guardian announced with a wry little smile.

"I'm meeting someone in the Vault?"

"Nope, better than that." She paused dramatically and then swept her hand across the surface of the door. "Through here!"

"The door?" Lilly took a closer look. Beside her, Letty hummed happily. The door was still inscribed with the images she had seen: Adam on his knees scooping dirt, Eve reaching out toward him, the infinity snake swallowing its own tail, the One Mountain topped by an all-seeing eye. It seemed almost a lifetime ago since she had been here, though it had only been a few days.

"I thought the Scholars said that if I go through the door, no one will be able to get me back."

"That's why I'm here!" Letty clapped her hands together. "I know all about such doors, and I can get you in and out. One of my specialties."

"Of course it is. So what do I do?"

"You take my hand and touch wherever you would like to go," instructed Letty.

"I want to see Eve."

"As I thought you might." Letty's smile was as bright as Lilly had ever seen it. Without another word, the girl stood up from her chair, reached out, and grabbed the Angel's tiny wrinkled hand, soft as baby skin, then touched the rendering of Eve. A jolting blast went through her, and everything shifted.

When Lilly opened her eyes, she was standing on a mesa overlooking a series of valleys that fell away into the distance. She could make out jagged lines of green haphazardly following creeks and rivers through an otherwise barren wilderness. An arid wind gusted, blowing her skirts around her and carrying the scents of farmed soil and livestock.

To the west, smoke drew Lilly's attention.

"They fight over grazing land," Letty explained.

The hand holding hers felt different, and when Lilly glanced down, it was not Letty's. Turning, she was shocked. Gone was the teeny woman, and in her stead stood an imposing, magnificent blue light-being, shimmering between opaque substance and transparent energy-wave. It instantly reminded Lilly of the blue sentinels standing at the fringes of Adam's birthday celebration.

The vibrations of Letty's being resounded from her center, cascading out and stirring up the frequencies of everything in the area. This, then, was the source of the humming.

"Wow!" Lilly gasped. "Letty? Is that you?"

"What! You thought that tiny old thing was how I looked in real life?" The sense of humor was definitely Letty's, but the voice was younger and full of vitality. "There are many more places you can go without creating waves if you are not impressive." Letty's laughter danced around the girl like a happy child.

"I don't know," Lilly answered with a chuckle, "I was always pretty impressed by that grumpy little thing."

The air was warm and dry, the sun pleasant on Lilly's skin.

"We are headed that way," Letty directed, pointing behind Lilly. She turned and looked. A short distance away, a stone escarpment rose a thousand feet and blocked her view of the sky. Nestled into its base, near a waterfall, were dozens of tents that billowed and danced in the breeze. Intermittent gusts tugged on their ropes as if teasing them to fly free. Even from a distance, the flapping of the hides was distinct and sharp.

"Is she in the tents?" Lilly asked.

"Yes! Would you like to walk or just be there?"

Lilly giggled. "Let's walk. No snakes, right?"

"I'm here, so no snakes within a hundred miles." Lilly believed it.

Letty led the way. The radiance of the Angel was like a mirage spilling over the ground. In the Guardian's wake, plants emerged and formed a pathway, buds opening up like miniature umbrellas to reveal flowery goodness, which had been dormant in the sands.

"I do that," Letty announced. "Make deserts bloom. Easier than knitting."

"Letty, you are full of surprises."

"That's why I get along so well with children," the Angel said. "They're all about surprises."

As they approached the dwellings, Lilly realized that another similar green and flowered path ran toward theirs from the opposite end of the mesa. It ended where they were heading, directly in front of the largest of the tents.

"Another Guardian," Letty declared, offering no other explanation.

Around and behind the gathered tents, Lilly could see a small valley dipping down toward the rock wall, which offered shade. It was full of plants and small trees, shrubs blooming in every color, fruits and vegetables laid out in creative arrangements.

Near the waterfall, the valley narrowed and then opened into a pasture where grazing sheep were feeding. The air itself was fragrant, the rocky cliffs standing like protectors of this idyllic place, the sounds of falling waters welcoming and joyous.

By the time they arrived, a woman had emerged from the tent. Lilly recognized her immediately. It was Mother Eve, older than she had been in Eden but not as elderly as when she had visited the Refuge. Lilly ran the short distance that remained, and Eve swept her up into an embrace. If ever there was home inside someone's arms, other than Adonai's, this was it.

"I've waited a long time to finally meet you," Eve said, and hugged her tightly again.

"What do you mean?" Lilly inquired. "We have met many times, although you were older."

"Well"—the woman laughed—"this might not be the first for you, but it is for me!"

Turning to the Angel, Eve bowed slightly. "Leticia, it has been a while. I'm so honored by your presence."

"It is my joy, Mother Eve, to be witness to this day. What a momentous occasion."

"Indeed." Eve raised her hands. "Now, please come inside and rest awhile. Lilly, for you, we have food and surprises waiting."

Lilly followed her through a series of flaps and into an ornately decorated and open living area. Several women occupied the space. Most were seated on mats, preparing food and crushing aromatic herbs. One played with several children; another sat at a loom, weaving.

"These are my daughters," Eve said, smiling. "Adonai's promise, my joy. And this young woman," Eve announced to the others, as she took Lilly's hand, "is also my daughter."

In spite of the activity in the closed space, air moved easily and freely, the temperature a cool relief against the heat of the day. Baked breads and sweets, fruits and nuts, and an array of dried meats and other delicacies abounded. Eve motioned for Lilly to sit within an arrangement of soft rugs and cushions.

"Let me look at you," Eve stated, and she did. Lilly returned her gaze. Eve swallowed as the tears filled her eyes. "I can't believe it's you!" she finally said. "Since the Beginning I was promised that there would always be three, but did not think that in my lifetime I would meet the other two."

"I'm sorry, Mother Eve," Lilly confided, "but I don't understand what you mean."

"It's true, she doesn't know," Letty said. She stood near the flap where they had entered.

Eve put her hands over her mouth and then began to laugh. "She doesn't know? That is the greatest gift of all. She doesn't know!" Before Lilly could grow uncomfortable, Eve said, "My dear one, Lilly. I am overwhelmed and filled with joy that I will get to tell you."

"Tell me what?" Lilly asked, curious and interested.

"First," Eve continued, "you must tell me why you have come."

"I came to talk to you! I have so many questions, but it seems a little strange now that I realize that you don't know me."

"Oh, Lilly," exclaimed Eve. "I know you, though we may have never met, at least not in my memory."

One of Eve's daughters brought Lilly a cup of warm and frothy goat's milk. Lilly accepted gratefully and sipped.

"So where are we?" she asked Eve.

"We are outside Eden's gate, a little to the west, but not far."

"And when is this?"

Eve lifted her eyes to the tent's apex. "How would I tell you? Lilly, I mark time by the seasons, and four seasons mark a year. For me time began the day of my own turning, the day I chose to leave the garden to find Adam."

This confirmation of Gerald's theory broke Lilly's heart. "How many years ago was that?"

"Almost four hundred, since . . ."

"Why?" Lilly blurted out her question. "Why did you turn and walk out of Eden's rest? Why didn't you stay inside the care of God?" It came out stronger than intended, but Eve didn't seem offended.

Eve drew in a long deep breath and then sighed. Lilly could see that the question pained her. The answer was written already into the lines on her otherwise youthful face, her hair beginning to show the gray that Lilly so remembered.

"I couldn't trust," she said. "Lilly, I couldn't trust that Adonai would meet all my longings, that all my desires would find fulfillment apart from Adam. I couldn't trust that God would create a way to bring about Their promise. I began to believe that it was up to me to make it happen. Adam turned to the place from which he was drawn—the ground—and looked to it and the works of his hands for meaning, identity, security, and love. I behaved much the same. I turned to the place from which I was drawn. I looked to Adam."

"What happened?" Lilly felt disappointment in Eve . . . and herself.

"The ground cannot give to man what only God can grant, and only face-to-face. So the earth reacted with thorn and thistle. Adam toils against creation with a grieving spirit. Our male children war against one another for land because they deceive themselves and think it can produce what they believe they truly need."

Lilly set her cup of milk aside. "And you, Mother Eve, what happened to you?"

"When I turned to Adam to give me what only God can grant, and only face-to-face, Adam and his sons reacted with power and dominion. Now I, with a grieving spirit, toil against these men to bring my children into this world." Eve lowered her voice and glanced at the gathered women. "My daughters compete and war one against another for men and family, as if these could produce what we had hoped and now are demanding."

The weight of this truth crushed Lilly. So much of the devastation on the earth came back to this: we turned away from God.

"Why did you leave the garden?"

"Every day Adam would come to Eden's boundary, and every day I would sit and listen to his appeal. As furious as I was with him for all his betrayal, I didn't want him to believe that I had abandoned him. Perhaps this desire to reach out to the other, to make amends and repair loss, to build a bridge and heal, is a part of God's maternal being that is in all of us. Womb-love, mercy!

"But then he stopped coming. Adam disappeared, and day after day I came to the boundary and waited. Every day I would ask God what I must do and every day God would ask me again to trust, and I would until the next day. But the days came and went, and Adam did not return. I began thinking about the promise God had made me, that I would have a seed that would crush the serpent's head. The more I thought about it, the more alone I felt, the less I would seek the face of God, and slowly I turned my face away. I didn't want to trust, I wanted answers."

"Why didn't God give you answers?" Lilly asked.

"God asks for trust," Eve declared. "I was wrong to turn."

"But why didn't God stop you? Why did God let you turn your face away?"

"Lilly, I have learned that God has more respect for me than I do for myself, that God submits to the choices I make, that my ability to say no and turn my face away is essential for Love to be Love. Adonai has never hidden His face from me, nor has He kept from me the consequences of my choosing. That is why many of my sons and my daughters curse the face and name of God. But God refuses to be like what we have become and take power and dominion. He has the audacity to consent and even submit to all our choosing. Then He joins us in the darkness we create because of all our turning."

Lilly burst into tears. "It's all my fault!" she wailed.

Eve was immediately with her, arms around and rocking, as any mother should. Another woman brought bread, hot and scented with olive oil, as if it might help. "Your fault, my dear? Whatever are you saying?"

"I'm the reason Adam stopped coming to the wall of Eden."

"Hush now, Lilly, I told you, I know who you are."

"You do?" Lilly asked between her sobs. "How would you know me?"

"Adam told me."

Lilly looked up at the woman, who offered a cloth. "Adam told you?" She blew her nose.

"Of course he told me." She smiled. "He thought your name was Lilith, but in a dream, Adonai told me the truth of your being."

"Adam told you what I did?" Hot shame washed over her skin.

"Yes, every detail, but Adonai told me why and who you really were. You never were this Lilith. She was a lie from the beginning."

Finally, Lilly was relieved of her burden. She started laughing and then crying and then laughing some more, and so too did Eve. A wide-eyed child brought Lilly a white desert flower as a comfort, and Lilly accepted it happily. She took the little girl on her lap. Eve ran her elegant hand over the child's coarse hair, smiling.

When she calmed again, Lilly asked, "I still don't understand why you left the garden. Was it because you felt bad for Adam?"

"Ah, if only I were that noble. The truth is much more twisted. As I have looked back over time, I realize I did it for myself. I was trying to fill the void I created by my own turning, to counter the fear that all my longings would go unmet. I did not admit that at the time. I justified my actions in the most beautiful and God-pleasing ways.

"I kept wondering how I could produce a promised seed apart from Adam. It wasn't long before I thought that God was putting me to a test, to see if I would mature and make my own decision. Instead of trusting God to do what I considered impossible, I believed that leaving Eden and joining Adam would accomplish the promise. I didn't need a serpent to deceive me; I lied to myself and then believed it. I believed that leaving Eden was an act of godliness, a participation in God's purpose."

"Oh my goodness," Lilly declared. "I did the exact same thing when I left Eden and offered myself to Adam."

"Well, you and I are probably not the only ones to try to satisfy our own longings. Adam was devastated to see me, but after we found a way back to each other, we conceived. Months later we had our first child."

"The one God promised?"

"I again convinced myself he was the promised seed, to justify my choices. When he was born, I cried out, 'I have delivered a man-child, Adonai.' For years after Cain's birth I blindly held on to this hope, until I began to see the turning in him too. When his brother was born, I named him Abel, which means 'sighing,' because my hope was fading away.

"Even though Adonai warned him of his own turning, Cain killed Abel. Adonai again reached out to Cain, but he spurned the mark and covering that God offered. Instead he separated himself from us and entered the land of wandering and restlessness. He built the first city there, and named it Enoch, which means new beginnings, after my grandson. He no longer speaks of Adonai, but only of the one God, Elohim. To him Ruach is only the ghost of a memory. My descendants through Cain are full of darkness, murder, and deceit."

For a time silence cradled the women's grief and regret.

Lilly said, "Is there any hope for us?"

Eve sighed and smiled. "Yes, Adonai is our certain hope, and that is why you are here!"

"I still don't understand what any of this has to do with me."

"Lilly, I told you there were three."

"Three what?" Lilly shook her head.

"Three women who would frame human history. The one to whom the promise of the seed was given—that would be me. The one through whom the promise was delivered. And that would be . . ." She turned around and indicated a smaller woman seated close by, patting dough into loaves. At first glance the woman appeared not much older than Lilly, her bright dark eyes set wonderfully inside a smooth complexion, noticeably lighter than the others.

"That would be me!" she stated, an impish grin upon her face.

"You see, Lilly, you were not the first to arrive here today," said Eve.

The woman stood and brushed flour from her hands before approaching Lilly. "Just like Eve, I have waited my entire life to meet you." The child on Lilly's lap ran off to play with others as Lilly rose and greeted her.

"It has been a challenge to hold my tongue!" the woman said, embracing her cheerfully.

For the first time Lilly noticed another spirit being standing near Letty. They were similar in form, though their vibrating shades and hues differed.

"Who are you?" Lilly asked, pulling back.

"I am Mary, the mother of the promised seed, the second Adam, Jesus."

All the pieces came together in Lilly's mind. "No way! You are Mary, the mother of Jesus? John tried to explain about the second Adam to me, and I didn't understand."

"John sends his greetings, Lilly, even though you have barely been apart. He already misses you," Mary said.

"John? He changed the world for me."

"John is like that. As a Witness, he's done that before."

Without drawing attention, Lilly pinched herself to make sure she wasn't dreaming.

"So who is the third?"

Eve and Mary spoke in unison. "You!"

Lilly blinked. "Me?"

"You! Lilly, you are the Bride, the one to whom the promised seed will forever be united."

"Me?" Fresh tears began to rise from an even deeper well, from a sacred place in the depths of the soul where only God has access. "No one would want me. I'm too broken."

"My son wants you," stated Mary. "And to show His love and relentless affection, He has sent along a gift. Leticia?"

From within her shifting robes of light, Letty produced the ring Gerald had given Lilly.

Lilly laughed out loud. "You took my ring?"

"Better than leave it for a snake," Letty replied.

"It was always meant for you, dear one." Mary took the ring and held it out to her. "It is a Betrothal ring, a promise of a wedding."

"Adonai wants to marry me? Why?"

"Lilly, in you dwell we all. You embody both our breaking and our healing," said Eve, as she and Mary surrounded the girl. "You are the one!"

"But I can't have any children!"

"That's what I once believed about myself," admitted Eve. "I didn't trust, but Mary did. See? When I got caught between the promise and impossibility, I chose to turn away. Mary kept her face toward Elohim, and by trust participated. God did the impossible, and the promise was soon born."

Eve gently took Lilly's hand in hers. "My daughter, have you learned nothing from my turning? God wants you to abide face-to-face with Him. Dwelling in and with Him is the greatest Good."

"How did you do it? How did you trust when it was impossible?" Lilly asked of Mary.

"I had a lot of help," Mary said. She looked at the Angel standing next to Letty. "Right, Gabriel?"

"A little," came a distinct and powerful voice.

"Always humble," groused Letty, but her voice was also full of affection.

"Is this like an arranged marriage?" Lilly asked, still overwhelmed.

"Are there other kinds?" asked Mary, and they all laughed.

"I have one last question," Lilly declared.

"Ah, John warned me about this," Mary said.

"What do I do now?"

"You wait," declared Mary. "For the appointed time. And while you wait, your work each day is to trust Him in whatever lies before you. When time is full, my Son will come for you and take you to the grandest wedding celebration, the one creation is longing for."

"Do you accept this invitation?" asked Eve. "To daily trust and wait?"

It was that simple. "I do," she said, and put the ring on her finger. Mary and Eve placed their hands on hers, and Mary touched her forehead to Lilly's. "Child, God keeps Their promises."

Lilly closed her eyes. "Today, I trust Them."

Twenty

BEGINNINGS OF THE END

Lilly opened her eyes and found herself standing once again in front of the Vault's door. Letty, having resumed her teeny form, was beside her, still holding one of her hands.

"Did that happen?" she asked.

"Too beautiful for words!" Letty said in the shrill, high-pitched voice that Lilly now adored.

"So what now?"

"You already know," answered the Guardian. "Now the real work begins! But you are going to need this."

Lilly saw what Letty held out to her, and she laughed. Anita's silver key. "I should have suspected when you gave me the ring! You took the key too?"

Letty shrugged. "I knew more than the givers did about why it would be needed."

The girl looked down at the key, flipping it over in her hands. "I think I know what this is for, but I'm scared."

"To fear is to be human. But remember, you are loved."

"No one will ever believe what has happened to me here. Will I remember?"

"God will give you wisdom about what to say to others, and yes, this you never will forget."

"Thank you, Leticia." Lilly grinned.

"Letty will do, little one."

"Letty, one day you will have to tell me all the times you saved me."

"Teenagers!" Letty laughed. "We Guardians sometimes refer to you as job security."

Lilly felt stronger and took a step away from her Guardian. Her injured foot wobbled underneath her.

"That thing is going to take time to get used to," Letty said, tapping her cane on Lilly's leg. Its response was hollow and metallic.

"What?" Lilly pulled up her skirt to look at her metal leg. "What happened to my freckles?"

"Prosthesis!" Letty grumped. "It's the best your world and time can offer right now. It will have to do."

Lilly stooped and pulled the woman close. Letty returned the hug.

"Don't leave me, okay?"

"Lilly, I will always be close. But Adonai will never leave you nor forsake you. As Mary said, They always keep Their promises."

"Okay, then let's do this."

Lilly slowly turned away and hobbled her way down the hall. She didn't have to go a great distance, but she was short of breath by the time she got to the locked door that John had warned her about, the one she had tried to open her first day in the Vault.

She turned the knob. Still locked.

For a minute she stood staring at the door, knowing that if she went through it, nothing would be the same. But then, nothing was the same anyway. What she once thought was true about herself and others had been turned on its head; what she once tried to control had been surrendered to Adonai. Certainty had been revealed an imposter and control empty imagination. What did she have to lose? There was no reason to stay at the Refuge. If God would never leave her and Letty remained close at hand, if the work was simply to trust Adonai one day at a time, she could do that. At least for today.

Lilly inserted the key into the lock and turned it. Then she opened the door.

THE SPACE WAS WARM and inviting, a living room with chairs and a sofa, a desk, and cabinets full of books. Lilly recognized it. She had been here many times before. It was a safe place, where healing was encouraged as far as Lilly would allow it.

"Well, good morning, young lady! Please, come on in." The woman who spoke sat behind a laptop computer at the desk, but she closed it and took off her glasses, set them on the desk, and rose to extend a hand.

She was tall and slim and black, dressed in a colorful skirt and blouse. The woman was almost regal, with a demeanor informed by the dignity of wisdom and kindness.

"Please, sit. Anything I can get you?"

"No, I'm fine, thank you," replied Lilly, choosing a chair that looked comfortable. The woman drew up another alongside Lilly, close enough to comfort but not invade.

"I don't know if you remember me, but I'm the doctor helping you to process the tragedies you've experienced, your losses, and your recovery. My name is Evelyn."

She smiled. "And mine is Lilly Fields."

The doctor looked surprised. "That's good, Lilly. Since you've been here, you've sometimes coped by taking on other personas, which is entirely understandable given the intensity of your experiences."

"Personas?"

"Yes. There is Kris, and there is the Princess."

"Oh, that makes sense," admitted Lilly, recalling the names given to her by her broken mother and the men who had used her. "But I don't think I need them anymore. If I'm going to do the work of getting well, I probably need to figure out how to be one person."

Evelyn's lips parted for a moment before she spoke, as if Lilly had startled her again. "Excellent. Sometimes it takes a person years to get to this point."

"How long have I been here?"

"About a year, but much of that was in the medical wing. Some of the most brilliant people in the country have been working hard to restore you physically. I don't know how much you remember, but you almost died before they found you."

"I remember," Lilly stated. "Shipping container. Trafficked. I remember."

Evelyn's eyes registered shock, but her smile radiated warmth and hope. "Good, that is where we will work from." She reached for the folder on her desk and took out one piece of paper. "Lilly, we have received a request from your biological mother. It took a lot of time to find her. She is in a halfway house, in recovery from addiction. She has requested permission to see you. When you are willing."

The request was unexpected, and a wave of anger and resentment took her breath away. *Trust*, she thought, and the room came back into focus. She focused on the light slanting in through the windows. "Do I have to decide now? I don't think I'm ready for that yet."

"No, not at all. I wanted you to know. I am not one who likes secrets. I would rather have—"

"Good surprises for another time, right?" said Lilly, and the woman laughed.

"Exactly! Like you read my mind. Also, two other therapists will be joining us. They're a husband-and-wife team, specialists who are new to us. Today they're going through orientation, so you'll meet them tomorrow. From everything I've heard, I think that you and I will get along well with them."

"And John?" she asked before she could stop herself.

Evelyn sat back, as if trying to make a decision. "John? The volunteer caregiver?"

"Right," said Lilly.

"Lilly, John was elderly and passed away a couple of days ago. He simply fell asleep and didn't wake up. I'm sorry that no one told you."

"It's okay," Lilly said, but some tears found their way into her eyes and down her cheeks. She didn't hide or wipe them away. "John would come and visit me. I liked him. He was kind when I wasn't, and funny, and he went out of his way for me. I am going to miss him, that's all."

The doctor nodded. "To grieve the things we've lost, and the people who have slipped out of our lives, is human and important."

"What about Letty?"

"Letty? Oh, I think you mean Leticia, the night custodian? It seems like she's always around. That woman! Keeps giving me these things she knits and I don't have the heart to tell her that I don't even know what they are." Evelyn's laugh held affection. "Like this one," and reaching over to a shelf, she pulled out a knitted something. "Gave it to me just yesterday."

"I'll take it!" offered Lilly, reaching out her hand. "Whatever you don't want, just pass them off to me. I collect them."

"You're a collector, are you? Then it's a deal," Evelyn exclaimed, handing it to her. In doing so she looked at Lilly's hand. "That's an unusual ring. I don't remember having seen that before."

Lilly turned it on her finger. "It's a special ring. From one of the few trustworthy men I've ever known. It's a promise that I have always been worth loving."

"Lilly, if you know that profound truth, there is nothing we together can't find our way through."

Lilly smiled. "I know!"

Evelyn picked up a pad of paper. "So, Lilly, are you ready to do the hard work? It won't be easy, but it will be worth it."

"I'm ready. Where do we begin?"

Lilly's Poem

There is a
True, above,
between,
beyond the
One or Two.
Both One and
Two, They
are the Three
within Whose
Love They sing
you into being
and becoming.
It is there I
rest from
death's
demands,
from works
that turn my
face away,

and in this
ease I breathe
in life and,
re-turning,
hear the Voice
I trust, and
I am known,
am freed,
to now and
evermore
participate
in seeing.

Author's Letter

Dear Reader,

The book you hold in your hands bears a cover image that grabbed me from the first moment I saw it—and even more so when it prompted vigorous discussion internally at Simon & Schuster. "I love your book," early readers said. "But why does the cover feature an apple when you have Eve and Adam eating a fig in the book?"

"Aha," I replied. "This is a terrific question."

I love good questions. In fact, that's the reason I write. I want to explore the feelings and assumptions we make when approaching the biggest questions. And what symbol is more loaded with assumptions than the apple? While the apple, figured here on *Eve*'s cover, is truly iconic, it is not mentioned in the Genesis story and the association possibly originates with medieval monks who were playing with words: "apple" being *malus* and "evil" being *malum*.

For centuries in the rabbinic Midrash storytelling tradition, various fruits and nuts were suggested as the fruit forbidden in the Garden of Eden, but there is one fruit that is in the Genesis story itself and also in the Midrash—not the apple we've all imagined, but a fig. The fig symbolizes brokenness in the scriptural stories.

297

Consider, for instance, the New Testament references to Jesus cursing the fig tree or that Adam and Eve sewed fig leaves as covering. There's richness to that tradition, isn't there?

When you eat an apple, you don't eat the seed. You don't ingest its core life. But when you eat a fig, you can't avoid eating the seed. When you do, the fruit—the symbolic "brokenness"—becomes part of you. That strikes me as profoundly true.

What's more, the iconic apple on the cover is whole, with no bite yet taken, thus it's a perfect and complete image of the old view of the biblical story—the view Lilly has at the beginning of *Eve*. It represents my own assumptions growing up and possibly the ones you may have had when you picked up the book. My hope is that I've been able to challenge some of the existing assumptions and upset the applecart by the story's end, restoring Lilly and maybe even the reader to a wholehearted and deeper reunion with God. This is an invitation to live in face-to-face union with the Divine and a declaration that each of us is a unique work of art, not to be constrained by cultural law or limitation.

Thus this small thing—the conversation this evoked—is part of what I hope happens with *Eve* in a larger sense. May it break our assumptions—and our hearts—open in a way that allows something profound to happen within each of us as individuals and together in community.

With great affection,

Acknowledgments

Eve has been the single most arduous creative work that I have ever engaged, a forty-year process of questions, study, and living life. One does not accomplish such a task alone. I am surrounded by a host of family and friends, in-laws and outlaws, a myriad of scholars and thinkers, dreamers, schemers, and artists; each who have contributed in unique and significant ways to this work.

At the center of it all is Kim, who gives me the gift of staying grounded; she believes in me but is not easily impressed. Our children, their spouses, our grandchildren, and the joy that each one brings, makes the work worth the sweat, tears, and prayer. As the ripples move outward, we are surrounded by the incredible friendships of those who continue to cover us with affection and prayers. To name them all would take another book, but these include: Closner, Weston, Foster, the Ninjas and the Posse, Scanlon, Linda Yoder, Graves, Troy Brumell, Miller, the other Miller, Garratt, the Toronto and Vancouver Minions, Huff, TCK family, Larson, Wards, Sand, Jordan, the NE Portland family, Gillis, my Canadian family (Young and Bruneski), including Mom and Dad, Debbie, Tim and their families, the Warren Clan, especially "The Force," Goff, Marin, Gifford, Henderson, and MacMurray.

Special thanks to C. Baxter Kruger, who talked me off the ledge a couple times when the creative process took me there and has been a consistent and encouraging sounding board as I struggled to weave essential elements of coherent scholarship inside an accessible story. Also to Howard Books and Simon & Schuster, a publisher that has consistently been encouraging, with a special hug to Jonathan Merkh and Carolyn Reidy, who have unequivocally supported this project from the outset.

I have always said that a good editor is worth their weight in gold, so thank you Ami McConnell, Becky Nesbitt, Amanda Rooker, and especially Erin Healy (Erin you were a godsend, truly).

Thank you to the myriad of voices being raised worldwide that will make this century the Century of the Woman, like Jimmy Carter, Stephen Lewis, and Emma Watson (your UN speech was profound); for organizations such as Opportunity International, Stop Demand; and a host of religious, political, business, and philanthropic organizations that are chipping away at the massive inequities in our world, especially those centered on women's rights and issues.

I drew from many scholars, ranging in expertise from linguistics and antiquities to philosophy, psychology, theology, and science. Again, it would take another book to list them all, but I will highlight only a few. Thank you, Jacques Ellul, who now sits in the great cloud of witnesses, along with Katherine Bushnell. William Law, Keith Barth, and George MacDonald. Thank you too, to Fuz Rana, Hugh Ross, and the folks at Reasons to Believe, who helped me craft the days of creation in a way respectful to both the text and to science.

Another list, too long, would be the music that is the backdrop and sound track of my work, the constant companionship of bards and tune and lyric. My thanks to them is represented in my thanks to Bruce Cockburn, a poet of life's journey. If I could have gotten the requisite permissions in time, I would have printed the lyrics of his "Creation Dream" and "Broken Wheel" at the back of this novel.

Thank you, Biliske Meiers (Spokane area) and Jay and Jeni Weston (Mt. Hood area) for space and time to concentrate and work. Such gifts are a great kindness.

Framing this project were two men and their families, without whom this project would have never gotten off the ground. Thank you, Dan Polk and Wes Yoder, who oversaw and hammered out each detail, men of integrity and compassion. No one represents my heart better than you two.

Thank you, readers and listeners. I hope this story finds a space inside your world that puts an arm around you and whispers that you have always been worthy of being loved and always will be. Thank you to all our international publishers and readers, we are in this together! I pray this story will bring a little more freedom to us all—women and men.

Finally, at the true center, is the self-giving other-centered love of Father, Son, and Holy Spirit, displayed so perfectly and extravagantly to us in the person of Jesus. We are learning how to re-turn and trust you, and slowly learning to trust one another as well. Thank you!

Contact the Author

Is it possible to craft a space for community and conversation free of the divisiveness of politics or religion or ideology . . . a space to explore life, God, the world, and what it is to be fully human, alongside a growing group of friends?

I would love to try. If that sounds like something you're interested in, join the ever unfolding conversation about God, life, and the world at:

WmPaulYoung.com

Or write to me at:

PO Box 2107
Oregon City, OR 97045
USA

For management inquiries, please contact:
Dan Polk of Baxter/Stinson/Polk LLC at www.bspequity.com.

To schedule speaking engagements, please contact:
Ambassador Speakers Bureau at Info@AmbassadorSpeakers.com.